DECEPTION

911

MASS EFFECT™

DECEPTION

WILLIAM C. DIETZ

Orbit
An imprint of
Little, Brown Book Group
100 Victoria Embankment
London EC4Y 0DY

An Hachette UK Company
www.hachette.co.uk

www.orbitbooks.net

ORBIT

First published in the United States in 2012 by Del Rey Books,
an imprint of the Random House Publishing Group
First published in Great Britain in 2012 by Orbit

A CIP catalogue record for this book
is available from the British Library.

ISBN 978-1-84149-985-7

Printed and bound by CPI Group (UK) Ltd, Croydon, CR0 4YY

Papers used by Orbit are from well-managed forests
and other responsible sources.

For my dearest Marjorie

ACKNOWLEDGMENTS

First a salute to Drew Karpyshyn for the excellent novels that preceded this one and made *Mass Effect: Deception* possible.

Plus many thanks to Casey Hudson, Mac Walters, and Tricia Pasternak for their advice and guidance.

PROLOGUE

On the planet Khar'shan

Many weeks of effort had been required to track the object from the point where it had been stolen to the batarian homeworld and the ancient city of Thondu. There were lots of things Kai Leng didn't like about the place, including the crowded streets, the asymmetrical architecture, and the food. But most of all he didn't like the batarians themselves. Not because so many of them were pirates, slavers, but because they were aliens and therefore a threat to the human race. That made him an extremist, not to mention a racist, and that was fine with Leng.

The auction house was located off one of Thondu's serpentine streets. A flight of stairs led up to the front door. Because of an injury sustained during a recent and especially difficult mission, Leng was using a cane as he mounted the steps one at a time. Having passed through a pair of open doors he entered a generously proportioned lobby where he was confronted by a security checkpoint and two batarians. Each alien had four eyes, all eight of which stared at the human with open suspicion.

Leng offered the invitation to the guard on the right who passed it in front of a scanner. The electronic document was real, having been purchased from a local businessman at considerable expense, and the batarian nodded respectfully. "You can enter, but the handgun stays here. And leave the cane too."

"No problem," Leng replied, as he gave both items to the second guard. "Take good care of them."

"You can pick 'em up on your way out," the other guard growled, as he placed both the pistol and the cane on a table loaded with weapons collected from other guests.

At that point Leng was ordered to empty his pockets onto a tray. The effort produced three coins, a pill box, and a stylus. The first guard eyed the collection, uttered a grunt, and motioned toward a metal frame. "Please step through the metal detector."

Not having set off any flashing lights or buzzers, Leng was allowed to recover his belongings and proceed to the room beyond. It wasn't that large, and didn't need to be, since only a limited number of people were wealthy enough to buy the type of merchandise the auction house specialized in. With nothing else to look at all eyes were on Leng as he made his way to the front of the room and took a seat next to an elderly turian.

It would have been nice if he'd been able to intercept the object *before* it was offered for sale, but having failed to do so, Leng was prepared to do it the hard way.

Time seemed to drag as two additional guests arrived, took their seats, and waited for the auction to begin. Finally a well-dressed volus appeared and took his place behind the podium. "Good afternoon gentle beings. My name is Dos Tasser and I will serve as your auctioneer today.

"All of you have had access to the catalog and are therefore familiar with the items that will be offered today. Bids will be submitted in increments of a thousand or a million credits and all sales are final. Are there any questions? No? Then the auction will begin.

"The first item in the catalog is a Prothean Egg, which, when activated, opens to reveal a holographic star map. And because the map is not consistent with any part of known space, experts assume that the system depicted lies somewhere beyond our galaxy, and must have been important to the protheans.

"If so, and if the purchaser is able to figure out where these planets are, they might be able to claim a technological treasure trove so valuable that the cost of the egg will be negligible by comparison. Bidding will start at ten million credits. Do I hear eleven?"

There was a bid at eleven, followed by many more, and a final offer of fifty-two million, which was sufficient to secure the elaborately decorated egg for a beautifully dressed asari whose face was hidden by a carefully draped veil. Did she intend to find the star system projected by the egg? Or to place it on a shelf where it would serve as a conversation piece? Leng didn't know and didn't care.

The next object was a vial of tears that had been shed by a turian saint. Or that's what Tasser claimed, even though there was no proof of such a thing, and the liquid in the container could have been tap water. However, that didn't stop the turian seated next to

Leng from paying five thousand for the relic. And, judging from his demeanor, he was happy to do so.

With that out of the way it was time for Tasser to take bids on the object that Leng was after. "And here it is," the volus said, as he raised what looked like a crystal gemstone for the audience to inspect. Light reflected off the device and made a pattern on the walls.

"Here, sealed inside a protective matrix, is the design for a DNA-specific bioweapon. The seller, who prefers to remain anonymous, claims that if released among the human population this disease would target a person known as the Illusive Man. An individual said to be the founder of Cerberus.

"We, of course, cannot attest to the truth of that— nor be held responsible for the results should such a disease be released. So, ladies and gentlemen . . . bidding will open at five million. Do I hear six?"

Leng not only knew about Cerberus, he worked for the organization, and had for more than ten years. And because of that he understood the threat. Not just to the Illusive Man, but to tens of thousands of people who were distantly related to him, all of whom would be equally vulnerable.

And that was why Leng threw the coins. They struck the floor all around Tasser, producing a series of loud bangs and a cloud of dense smoke. Leng was already on his feet by then. A few swift steps carried him to the front of the room where the volus was just starting to turn away. Leng grabbed a wrist, took the matrix, and let go. A well-aimed kick put the auctioneer down.

But Leng wasn't the only person in the room who wanted the object, or was willing to commit violence in order to obtain it. Like Leng, the man who attacked him was unarmed, but he was strong, as became evident when he wrapped an arm around Leng's throat.

Leng grabbed on to the attacker's arm with both hands and pulled down while simultaneously pressing his chin against his chest. That allowed him to take a precious breath while he bent both knees and lowered his center of gravity. Then he pulled, straightened, and felt the man flip up and over. He continued to hold on to the man's arm, which caused the assailant to land on his back. Leng stomped his face, felt something give, and knew that part of the fight was over.

Then, having turned toward the back of the room, Leng pressed the button on his stylus. His pistol, or what looked like a pistol, produced a loud *BOOM* as it exploded, hurling shrapnel in every direction. When he entered the lobby both of the batarian guards were down and one was clearly dead. "Don't bother to get up," Leng said, as he bent over to pick up his cane. "I'll find the door on my own." Then, having completed his mission, Leng limped away. His right leg was on fire. But the matrix was safe, the Illusive Man would be pleased, and he could leave Khar'shan. Life was good.

ONE

THE CITADEL

"I don't want to go," Nick said stubbornly. "Why can't I stay here?"

David Anderson didn't have any children of his own, and had the matter been left to him, the ex-navy officer would have ordered the teenager out of the apartment with possibly unpleasant results. Fortunately, the woman he loved knew how to deal with such situations. Kahlee was in good shape for a woman in her forties, or thirties for that matter. As she smiled tiny creases appeared around her eyes. "You can't stay here because David and I may want you to tell the Council what happened on the day Grayson invaded the Grissom Academy. It's important to make sure that nothing like that ever happens again."

Nick had been shot in the stomach during the attack and sent to the Citadel for advanced medical treatment. So he knew about Grayson firsthand. Nick, with shoulder-length black hair and a relatively small frame for a boy his age, looked hopeful. "Can I go to The Cube on the way back?"

"Sure," Kahlee replied. "But only for an hour. Come on—let's go."

A crisis had been averted, and Anderson was grateful. As they left the apartment the door locked behind them. An elevator took them down to the first floor and out into the hectic crush of the lower wards. A monorail loomed overhead, the pedways were crowded with individuals of every species, and the streets were jammed with ground vehicles. All of which was normal for the huge star-shaped space station that served as the cultural, financial, and political hub of the galaxy.

Anderson had been an admiral, and the Alliance's representative to the Citadel Council, so he had spent a lot of time aboard the habitat. Everything was organized around a central ring. It was ten kilometers across, and the Citadel's forty-kilometer-long "fingers" pointed from it to the stars beyond. The total population of the station was said to be in excess of thirteen million sentients, none of whom had played a role in creating the complex structure.

The asari had discovered the station 2,700 years earlier while exploring the vast network of mass relays put in place by a space-faring species known as the protheans. Having established a base on the Citadel, the asari learned how to create mass effect fields, and made use of them to explore the galaxy.

When the salarians found the space station a few decades later the two races agreed to form the Citadel Council for the purpose of settling disputes. And as more species began to travel the stars, they had little choice but to follow the dictates of the technologically advanced Council races. Humans were relative newcomers and had only recently been granted a seat on the Citadel Council.

For many years it had been assumed that the protheans were responsible for creating the Citadel. But more recently it had been learned that the *real* architects were a mysterious race of sentient starships called the Reapers who conceived of the space station as a trap, and were responsible for annihilating *all* organic sentients every fifty thousand years or so. And, even though Reapers were trapped in dark space, there was evidence that they could reach out and control their servants from light-years away. And that, Anderson believed, was a continuing threat. One the Council should deal with immediately.

The problem being that day-to-day interspecies rivalries often got in the way of the big picture. That was just one of the reasons why it had been so difficult for Anderson and Kahlee to get the Council to look beyond historical grievances to the greater threat represented by the Reapers. Anderson and Kahlee were certain that the Reapers had been in at least partial control of Grayson when he invaded the Grissom Academy, but they were still struggling to convince certain members of the Council. And that had everything to do with the presentation they planned to give. Hopefully, if they were successful, the Council would agree to unify behind an effort to counter the danger that threatened them all. Otherwise the Reapers would do what they had done before—wipe the galaxy clean of sentient life.

As Anderson led the others aboard a public shuttle he was reminded of the fact that the Reapers had created the Citadel as bait for a high-tech trap. One that had been sprung so successfully that now, two years later, some of the damage the sentient machines had caused was still being repaired.

The vehicle came to life as Anderson settled himself behind the controls. The contragravity speeder was powered by a mass effect field and would carry them from the lower wards to the vicinity of the Presidium where the Council's offices were located. Kahlee was sitting next to him and Nick was in the back, fiddling with his omni-tool. The device consisted of an orange hologram that was superimposed over the teenager's right arm. It could be used for hacking computers, repairing electronic devices, and playing games. And that's what Nick was doing as Anderson guided the shuttle through a maze of streets, under graceful ped-ways, and into the flow of traffic that ran like a river between a pair of high-rise cliffs.

Ten minutes later the shuttle pulled into a rapid-transit platform where they disembarked. A short, tubby volus pushed his way forward to claim the speed-ster for himself. He was dressed in an environment suit and most of his face was hidden by a breathing mask. "Make way Earth people—I don't have all day."

They were accustomed to the often rude manner in which the Citadel's citizens interacted with each other and weren't surprised by the stranger's contentious tone. The volus were closely allied with the raptorlike turians—many of whom still felt a degree of animos-ity toward humans resulting from the First Contact War. And that was just one of the problems which prevented the races from trusting each other.

As Anderson, Kahlee, and Nick walked toward a bank of elevators they passed a pair of beautiful asari.

The species were asexual, but to Anderson's eye they looked like human females, even if their skin had a bluish tint. Rather than hair, waves of sculpted skin could be seen on the backs of their heads and they were very shapely. "You can put your eyeballs back in your head now," Kahlee commented as they entered the elevator. "No wonder the asari get along without men. Maybe I could too."

Anderson grinned. "Just looking, that's all. I'm partial to blondes."

Kahlee made a face as the elevator started upward and the salarian standing in front of them lost his briefcase. It had been tucked under his arm but suddenly slipped out and landed on the floor. Like all of his kind the salarian's head was narrow and crowned with two hornlike appendages. As he bent to retrieve the object it scooted away from him.

"Nick!" Kahlee said crossly. "Stop that . . . Give him the case and apologize."

The teen looked as if he might object, saw the expression on Kahlee's face, and apparently thought better of it. Having removed the folder from the floor, he gave it back to its owner and mumbled, "Sorry."

The salarian had seen biotic pranks before and wasn't amused. "You have a talent," he snapped. "Use it wisely."

Nick was one of the rare individuals who could manipulate the gravity-like force found in all of the otherwise empty spaces in the universe. The boy had been working to refine his biotic skills of late and the subtle combination of energies required to dislodge the briefcase and then move it around was quite impressive. It was also annoying and made Anderson frown. Fortunately for Nick, Kahlee was more patient. Maybe *too* patient.

The elevator doors opened smoothly and the passengers spilled out into a lobby that opened onto the Presidium. In marked contrast to the densely packed wards it was almost entirely open. There were artificial clouds in the blue sky, sunlight streamed down from above, and, as Anderson accompanied the others out onto a curving walkway, he could feel a light breeze touch his neck. The parklike area was home to a lake, clusters of trees, and a large expanse of well-manicured grass. People representing various races were constantly coming and going. Some appeared to be in a hurry while others strolled along or sat on benches.

Anderson's pace was more purposeful as he led the others toward the Citadel Tower, located at the very center of the massive space station. It was difficult to appreciate the structure by looking straight up at it, but Anderson knew it could be seen from many kilometers away, and was the most important landmark on the Citadel.

The Council Chambers were positioned toward the top of the spire and it wouldn't pay to be late, so Anderson set a brisk pace. The Council's agenda typically remained in flux right up until the beginning of each meeting. So Anderson had no way to know if their presentation would be first, last, or somewhere in between.

But before the threesome could enter the tower it was necessary to check in with the Citadel Security Services (C-Sec) kiosk located outside the main entrance. The person in charge was turian. Bright eyes stared at Anderson from bony sockets that were surrounded by a tracery of scarlet tattoos. A flat, thin-slitted nose was flanked by hard facial plates. The officer's mouth formed an inverted V and wasn't designed to smile. "Yes, sir . . . What can I do for you?"

"My names is Anderson. Admiral David Anderson. This is Kahlee Sanders and Nick Donahue. We were invited to appear before the Council today."

The turian said, "One moment please," as he scrolled the list of names on the monitor in front of him. "Yes, here you are. Now, if you would be so kind as to look at the scanner we'll confirm your identity."

The device was built into the kiosk. And as Anderson looked into it he knew that it was scanning his retinas. From there the data would be sent to the Citadel's central computer where it could be checked and confirmed. All in a couple of seconds. The turian nodded. "You can proceed to the elevator, Admiral . . . Welcome to the Citadel Tower. Miss Sanders? Please look into the scanner."

Once all three of them had been cleared it was time to enter the transparent elevator that would carry them up the outside of the tower to the Council Chamber. They were alone and, as the platform shot upward, a broad swath of the Presidium appeared. A view so remarkable that it earned a "Wow!" from the normally taciturn Nick.

The view was no accident, of course. It was meant to impress visitors and did. Way off in the distance Anderson could see all of the space station's wide-spread arms. They were frosted with lights that glittered and faded into the hazy distance.

Then the trip was over as the elevator slowed and stopped. Doors parted and Anderson followed Kahlee and Nick out into a hallway. A broad staircase could be seen at the far end. As the threesome approached it they passed between eight honor guards, four to each side of the marble-lined corridor. There were two turians, two salarians, two asari, and two humans. The latter having been added once humans were granted a seat on the Council.

An asari in a beautifully draped floor-length gown was waiting for them at the foot of the stairs. "Good morning. My name is Jai M'Lani. The meeting is about to begin. You are fourth on the agenda. Please go up the stairs and follow the pathway to the right. It will take you to a waiting room where you can watch the proceedings. Refreshments are available. Approximately ten minutes prior to your presentation I will come to get you."

Having thanked M'Lani, Anderson followed Kahlee up the stairs and off to the right. The waiting room was a luxurious affair equipped with two dozen seats, all facing a large screen. About half were filled. As the humans entered the other petitioners turned to stare at them. The group included turians, salarians, and a human female. After satisfying their curiosity they turned back to the screen.

The threesome found three chairs and sat down. Nick consulted the glowing omni-tool attached to his left arm as Kahlee leaned in to whisper in Anderson's ear. "They put us halfway down the agenda. Not a good sign."

Anderson knew what she meant. The Council had a well-known tendency to tackle the items they believed to be most important first. And their number one priority quickly became clear as the huge wall

screen came to life and a wide shot of the Council
Chamber appeared. Viewed from the back of the huge
amphitheater one could see that all of the spectator
seats were filled, signaling that something of interest
to a significant number of people was up for discussion.

There was a raised platform off to the left where
the Council members were seated. The Petitioner's
Stage was located directly across from them with a
male quarian ready to speak. The quarians were a
nomadic race who were typically a bit smaller than
the average human. As was typical for his kind, the
petitioner was dressed in a motley collection of clothing, held together by a variety of straps and metal
fasteners. His face was obscured by a reflective visor
and breathing apparatus. The essence of the quarian's
request became evident once he was given permission
to speak. "My name is Fothar Vas Maynar. I appear
before you as a duly authorized representative of the
quarian fleet."

"Duly authorized scum is more like it," one of the
turians seated in the waiting room growled. And Anderson knew why. It was the quarians who had created the artificial intelligences known as the geth
three hundred years earlier. Later, in the wake of the
hard-fought geth rebellion, the quarians had been
forced to take refuge on a collection of starships
called the Migrant Fleet. And because of that history
other races looked down on the nomads.

The audience seated in the Council Chamber uttered a chorus of boos which garnered a stern warning
from the human master-at-arms. Her voice boomed

over the PA system. "There will be order! My soldiers will clear this room if necessary."

The noise died away and the asari Council member spoke. She was in the matriarch stage of a very long life and known for her reasonable nature. Her bluish skin seemed to glow as if lit from within. "Please accept our apologies, Representative Maynar. You may proceed."

The quarian delivered a half bow. "Thank you. The matter I wish to put before you is simple. While it's true that my race unintentionally loosed the geth menace on the galaxy, it's also true that we have paid for that mistake and continue to do so.

"The Council may recall that many years ago, in the wake of the geth rebellion, we were ordered to close our office in the Presidium. And we understand why. But a great deal has changed since then and we believe the time has come for a *new* relationship. That is why I come before the Council seeking permission to reopen a quarian embassy on the Citadel. After all, even the batarians have such an office in the Presidium, so why should the Migrant Fleet be excluded?"

That brought a roar of opposition from the crowd and, true to her word, the master-at-arms sent troops in to clear the amphitheater. That took ten minutes and the quarian had to stand and wait until the process was completed. Then the debate began in earnest and it soon became clear that the Council was split. The salarian and human members were in favor of the proposal while the others were opposed.

After fifteen minutes of give-and-take it was the asari who offered a compromise. "I oppose the concept of reopening a quarian embassy, because it implies the existence of a cohesive government. And Representative Maynar has yet to prove that such an organization actually exists.

"However, that being said, he has a point. I believe that the creation of formal linkage through which the quarian fleet can communicate to the Council would be a positive development. So rather than an embassy I suggest that we authorize a quarian consulate. Then, when and if conditions warrant, that presence can be elevated to the status of a full-scale embassy."

Both the salarian and the human agreed to the suggestion, leaving the turian to scowl powerlessly as Maynar expressed his thanks. There would be no embassy, but a step had been taken, and the fleet would be pleased.

The next hour passed slowly for Anderson, Kahlee, and Nick. But finally, after three additional presentations, the asari named M'Lani came to fetch them. As Anderson stood Kahlee took the opportunity to admonish Nick. "Wait here . . . And be ready in case we need you."

Nick was playing a game on his omni-tool. The puzzle was designed for biotics so there were no physical controls. Just receptors through which dark energy could be channeled. "Yeah, yeah," he said without looking up. "Then we're going to The Cube. Right?"

"Right," Kahlee agreed, as she got up to leave. "Wish us luck."

Having returned to the main staircase Anderson and Kahlee followed it up to the Petitioner's Stage. It was one thing to see it on-screen and another to actually stand on the platform and look across fifty meters of empty space to where the Council members were seated. The asari was on the far left. The salarian came next, followed by the turian and human. A five-meter tall holographic likeness of each person could be seen over the Council members' heads, making it possible for petitioners to see their facial expressions.

Though not in uniform, Anderson stood as if he was, with his back ramrod straight and his arms at his sides. He had black hair, a rounded face, and olive-colored skin.

Kahlee had served in the military many years earlier but had spent even more time as a civilian. Nevertheless she understood that appearances were important and was careful to maintain eye contact with the Council members. The asari was the first to speak. "Greetings Admiral Anderson and Miss Sanders. First, before you make your report, let me say how much we appreciate the work you've been doing. Who will speak first?"

"I guess I will," Anderson replied. "As you know, Miss Sanders and I agreed to follow up behind the investigation of what took place at the Grissom Academy and, after considerable study, we believe that the Reapers were involved."

"The Reapers?" the human Council member inquired cynically. "Or Cerberus? Frankly, I feel the Reaper angle to be a bit far-fetched."

Knowing the man as he did Anderson had attempted to lobby the Council member in advance of the meeting, but with no success. So, being unable to rely on support from that quarter, Anderson chose his words with care. "Both, actually," he replied. "There is evidence that Paul Grayson, the man who invaded the academy and murdered a number of staff members, was a Cerberus operative at one time. Then, for reasons we aren't sure of, the Illusive Man turned on him. At that point he was imprisoned on a space station and subjected to a series of experiments that placed him under Reaper control. We know because we saw the lab with our own eyes. It's difficult to say exactly how much influence the Reapers had over Grayson, but we think it was extensive."

"Oh you do, do you?" the turian Council member inquired. "Based on *what*? I've read the reports. And the man was a red sand addict. You admit that he was employed by Cerberus. Why concoct elaborate theories regarding the Reapers when his motivations are so obvious?"

"What you're saying is true," Kahlee admitted. "Grayson *was* an addict. But he was also the parent of one of my students. A very talented biotic named Gillian. And Grayson doted on his daughter. So to attack the place where she went to school ran contrary to his interests. But he did it anyway. And where did he go? To our research lab. The place where all of the data pertaining to our students was stored. Then, after killing three staff members, he entered the OSD library, where every readout and every test result were stored. Moments later he began to send the data out."

"You have evidence of that?" the human demanded. "Calls that went out over the extranet? You can *prove* that Grayson sent information to the Reapers?"

"No," Anderson admitted. "We can't prove it. But Grayson's body had been extensively modified and we believe he had the capacity to transfer information without using conventional communications technologies."

"Even so," the asari said reasonably. "Isn't it more reasonable to assume that Grayson was acting on behalf of Cerberus? And that the data was sent to *them*? No offense Admiral, but the person in question worked for Cerberus. A pro-human organization that's willing to do just about anything to advance its cause. And *you* are human. Therefore it would be understandable if you sought to shift the blame away from your own kind. Not consciously, I know that you're too professional for that, but unconsciously.

"As for Miss Sanders," the asari continued, "there is evidence to suggest that Grayson liked and trusted her. And perhaps that was enough to influence her judgments."

Anderson felt a rising sense of resentment. It took all of the discipline acquired during a career in the navy to keep from snapping at her. "Cerberus is a threat," he said tightly. "But if you read all of the material that Miss Sanders and I submitted prior to this presentation you know that Grayson's body was examined by three independent scientists, and they agreed that his implants were of unknown origin. Plus, to the extent that they could be tested, the mechanisms installed in his body are far too exotic to have been created by Cerberus. But seeing is believing. So with your permission I would like to call for Exhibit A."

The human Council member produced a look of pained exasperation before leaning back in his chair. "If you must you must. The sooner this farce is over the better."

A spotlight came on and a gentle *hiss* was heard as a glistening metal column extruded from the floor below. It rose until the display positioned on top of the piston was located halfway between the Council members and the Petitioner's Stage. And that was when the Council members saw the thing that had been Grayson. The body was enclosed in a transparent stasis field. It sparkled as dust motes came into contact with it.

Grayson's body was naked and his skin had a grayish tint. There were two blue-edged projectile holes near the center of his forehead and his eyes were disturbingly open, as if looking up at the person who had pulled the trigger. Considerable damage had been done to Grayson's torso as well. The implants that had been installed in his limbs were dead now, bereft of the energy that once animated them, but could still be seen running snakelike under the thin semitranslucent covering of his flesh. It was as if his entire body had been systematically repurposed.

"My God," the asari Council member said feelingly. "I had no idea. The poor man."

"The poor man indeed," her human counterpart agreed soberly. "One can only imagine his suffering. But, much as it pains me to say it, there are no observable limits to man's inhumanity to man. I can't explain where Grayson's implants came from, or what their purpose was, but Cerberus is known for its cruelty. And I still don't see a credible connection to the Reapers."

"I agree," the salarian put in. "But I don't think we can afford to simply dismiss the possibility of Reaper involvement. I suggest that Admiral Anderson and

Miss Sanders be encouraged to continue their investigation. Assuming they're willing, that is."

Anderson looked at Kahlee and saw her nod. His eyes flicked back to salarian. "We're willing."

"Good," the asari said, as if glad to dispose of the matter. "Please remove the body. We've seen enough."

Even though the public had been forced to leave the amphitheater dozens of the Citadel's employees were still present. As the spotlight was extinguished, and Grayson's body rode the gleaming shaft down into the staging area located beneath the main floor, one of the uniformed functionaries took a look around. He had *two* employers. And the second had an unquenchable thirst for information. He slipped away.

Kahlee entered the waiting room and scanned the seats. Nick was nowhere to be seen. Most of the other petitioners had left by then, but a salarian was present and still waiting his turn. "Excuse me," Kahlee said. "We left a teenage boy here . . . Do you know where he went?"

The salarian looked up from his omni-tool. "He left about fifteen minutes ago. I haven't seen him since."

Kahlee thanked him, activated her omni-tool, and spoke Nick's name. What she got was a recording. "This is Nick. Leave a message. I'll call you back."

"No answer?" Anderson inquired.

"Just voice mail." Kahlee was worried and it was visible on her face. "I told him to stay here."

"You know Nick," Anderson replied. "Chances

are he got bored and took off for The Cube. He's been talking about the place all morning."

"You're probably right," Kahlee agreed. "But let's make sure. The Cube is on the way home."

Anderson thought Kahlee was a bit too attentive where Nick was concerned. The boy was eighteen for god's sake. But she'd been responsible for Nick's well-being at the academy and agreed to serve as the boy's guardian during his stay on the Citadel. A responsibility she took very seriously.

They took the glassed-in elevator down to the ground floor and left through the main entrance. The same turian was on duty so Kahlee paused to speak with him. "We passed through security earlier with a teenager named Nick Donahue. Have you seen him?"

The police officer nodded. "He left fifteen or twenty minutes ago."

Kahlee frowned. "And you let him go?"

The turian was clearly annoyed. "My job is to keep people out—not in. And if you lost the boy whose fault is that?"

Anderson chose to intervene before Kahlee could reply. "We understand. Was he alone? Or with someone?"

"He was alone."

Anderson looked at Kahlee. "That's good. Come on."

It took a short shuttle ride and the better part of fifteen minutes to reach the workout facility called The Cube. It had been built by biotics for biotics as a place where they could compete with each other and sharpen their skills. In order to join a person had to have a proven ability to throw, pin, or block objects.

Or to use spatial distortion to destroy targets with rapidly shifting mass fields.

The asari were natural biotics although some were more skilled than others. But for other races, including the krogan, turians, salarians, and humans, biotic abilities were the result of exposure to element zero, or eezo. And most if not all biotics were equipped with implants called Bio-amps that served to amplify and synchronize their talents. Such individuals were classified as Level 1, Level 2, or Level 3, according to their strength and stability. Nick was an Level 2 and had been working out at The Cube in hopes of qualifying as an Level 3.

The gym, if that was the right word, was located on a dimly lit commercial thoroughfare and identified with a glowing sign. A reptilian krogan was stationed outside the front door to keep the merely curious away. He was about two meters tall and weighed upwards of one hundred and fifty kilograms. Like all of his kind the doorkeeper had a slightly hunchbacked appearance as a result of the shell-like layers of flesh and bone that rode his powerful shoulders. His face was flat, brutish, and notable for the absence of any discernible ears or nose. A pair of small, wide-set eyes regarded Anderson with a brooding hostility. His voice sounded like a gravel crusher in low gear. "Members only."

"Our son is a member," Kahlee lied. "We'd like to watch him work out."

"Name?"

"Nick Donahue."

The krogan eyed his terminal, located what he was looking for, and uttered a grunt. "You can enter."

The door gave access to a cramped lobby from which members could access the locker room and the area beyond. A narrow flight of stairs led up to a small balcony where spectators could view the action below. "Come on," Kahlee said. "We'll watch him throw people around."

"And then we'll chew him out," Anderson said sotto voce, as he followed her up.

The viewing area was empty. So they followed a ramp down to the front row where they had a good view of the cube-shaped space for which the gym was named. The walls were padded and divided into softly glowing squares so that when a salarian was "thrown" across the room he was able to bounce off and land uninjured. One of the boxes lit up, a tone was heard, and a computer-generated voice delivered the score. "Five, three, advantage Atilus."

But the match was far from over as became apparent when the salarian's turian opponent was "lifted" off the cushioned floor and brought back down with considerable force. "Five, four," the voice proclaimed. "Advantage Atilus."

"I don't see Nick," Kahlee said, as she peered over the edge. At least a dozen biotics were down on the main floor sitting or standing along the walls. Some of them clapped as the point was scored, but were forced to scatter when the turian took his revenge, and the salarian came flying their way. "I think the office is in the basement," Kahlee added. "Let's see if he checked in."

Having made their way down to the main floor, and from there to the basement, the pair found themselves in a dimly lit office. A roly-poly volus was ensconced behind a messy desk. "Earth-clan biotics are welcome here. One membership or two?"

"None," Kahlee answered. "We're trying to locate our son, Nick Donahue. Has he been here today?"

The volus turned to his terminal, entered the name, and turned back. "No, he hasn't. You could extend his membership though. Two hundred and fifty credits for six months."

"Thanks, but no thanks," Anderson said firmly. "Tell me something . . . Does our son have friends here? People he tends to hang out with?"

The volus shrugged. "I don't have time to track personal relationships. But I have seen your son with Ocosta Lem and Arrius Sallus. They work out together."

"Who are they?" Kahlee wanted to know.

"Lem is a salarian, and Sallus is a turian. Both are listed as Level Threes."

"Have they been in today?"

The volus consulted the terminal. "No."

"Where do they live?" Anderson inquired. "We'd like to speak with them."

The volus hesitated as if reluctant to part with the information, but when Anderson placed both fists on the desk and frowned, the volus complied. Three minutes later the humans were back on the street. Kahlee eyed the slip of paper. "Lem and Sallus share the same address."

Anderson didn't like that. Not one little bit. But he decided to keep his concerns to himself as they dropped two levels down and made their way through increasingly claustrophobic streets lined with bars, strip joints, and sim clubs. Some of the people who swirled around them watched the couple the way predators eye their prey. But appearances were everything. And thanks to the fact that Anderson and Kahlee looked like they knew what they were doing they were allowed to pass unimpeded.

"Here it is," Kahlee said as they arrived in front of a seedy-looking structure. The sign out front read SUNSU ELECTRONICS. A commercial building seemed like an unlikely place for the biotics to live.

Anderson opened the door and they went inside. A middle-aged woman was seated behind the front desk. She smiled. "Can I help you?"

"Yes," Kahlee replied. "We're looking for Ocosta Lem and Arrius Sallus. We were told they live here."

The receptionist frowned. "There must be some mistake. Nobody lives here. Other than the duct rats that is . . . and they don't have names."

"You're sure?"

The woman nodded. "I'm sure. There are three employees and we all go home at night."

They thanked her and left. The moment Kahlee was outside she made another call and got the same result. Nick was missing.

TWO

SOMEWHERE IN THE CRESCENT NEBULA

The Illusive Man was seated in front of an oval portal that looked out onto the frozen wastes of a planet in the Crescent Nebula. He could see the ruins of an abandoned mining operation in the foreground and a line of jagged peaks in the distance. It was a miserable place, but one that would help ensure his privacy, which was very important to him. A tone sounded and a female voice said, "Kai Leng is here to see you."

The Illusive Man turned toward the door. "Send him in."

The hatch hissed open and Kai Leng appeared. The operative had proved himself many times and was a very important part of the Cerberus operation. He had black hair and brown eyes that harkened back to his Chinese ancestry. But the shape of his face and the color of his skin hinted at what might have been some Slavic DNA as well. The guest chair sighed as he sat down. "You sent for me?"

"Yes," the Illusive Man said, as he removed a silver cigarette case from the surface of the metal desk. "We need to talk." The head of Cerberus selected a cigarette, set fire to it, and took a deep drag. He liked the process, the taste, and the feel of nicotine entering his bloodstream. Words mingled with smoke. "A call came in a few minutes ago. From an operative on the Citadel. It seems that Paul Grayson has been testifying against us."

Leng's eyebrows rose. "I find that hard to believe. I put two projectiles in his head."

"Yes, you did," the Illusive Man agreed, as he flicked ash into a tray made of black oynx. "But you may recall that we were forced to leave Grayson's body behind as we fled the space station. That allowed David Anderson and Kahlee Sanders to preserve the corpse and use it as part of a presentation to the Citadel Council. And in spite of Anderson and Sanders's efforts to warn the Council members about the Reapers, they blame Cerberus for what took place. I don't like that. Our credibility is at stake."

Another operative might have said something unnecessary at that point. But not Leng. He just sat there, his face empty of expression, waiting. The Illusive Man liked that. He took another drag and let the smoke emerge with the words. "And there's something else too. The Council gave Anderson and Sanders permission to continue their investigation. So I want you to go to the Citadel, keep an eye on them, and retrieve Grayson's body."

Leng stood. "Is that all?"

"Yes."

The Illusive Man waited until Leng had left before touching a button. A beautiful brunette arrived one minute later. She was wearing a nicely cut jacket, miniskirt, and knee-high boots. A bottle of Jim Beam

Black and a single glass were sitting on the tray, which she placed on his desk. Then, having poured three fingers of the amber liquid into a glass, she left.

The Illusive Man watched her go before picking up the glass and turning toward the portal. The icescape was like the universe itself. Cold and inimical to human life. *But the race will survive,* the Illusive Man thought to himself, *no matter the cost.*

ABOARD THE SLAVE SHIP *GLORY OF KHAR'SHAN*

The *Glory of Khar'shan* was more than a hundred years old and not especially pretty to look at. But her hull was sound, her drives were practically new, and she was well-armed. That was important in a galaxy where slavery was frowned on and ships like the *Khar'shan* were targeted by governments and pirates alike. But the *Khar'shan*'s virtues were lost on Hal McCann and the other one hundred and thirty-two beings crammed into her stinking hold.

It was a gloomy place; what little light there was emanated from a row of disks that ran the length of the compartment. Curved supports gave the impression of ribs, so that from McCann's position it looked like he was imprisoned inside an enormous beast. The way condensation oozed down rust-stained walls, and the unrelenting stench of unwashed bodies, added to that impression, as did the intermittent rumbling noises which the plumbing produced just prior to a "wet down." The wet down consisted of a monsoon-like rainstorm that was supposed to cleanse the slaves and flush their waste materials into the ship's recycling system. So, as one of his fellow slaves put it, "We can drink our own piss."

But what was—was. All McCann could do was try to carry out a regimen of isometric exercise, fantasize about regaining his freedom, and doze. And that's what he was doing when a batarian backhanded him across the face. "Wake up, Cerberus scum! Or would you like to lose your feet?"

McCann swore and brought his head back around. The batarian was humanoid, if it was possible to refer to something with four eyes, eight nostrils, and bulging cheeks as "human." "Screw you, four eyes," McCann said, "and your motherless caste."

That earned McCann another blow as machinery whined and a formfitting cage was lowered over each slave—all of whom had to sit up straight and pull their feet back to avoid injury. The restraint system was designed to allow the slave masters to isolate and control troublesome individuals, and to protect them if the ship was forced to execute high-gee maneuvers. So McCann knew the batarians were preparing for one of those possibilities. But which one?

The answer came as a tone sounded and a voice was heard over the intercom. "This is the captain. Secure the ship for battle. All crew members will report to their battle stations. Primary weapons are armed. Secondary weapons are armed. Tertiary weapons are armed. Estimated time to contact forty-seven minutes. That will be all."

Now the slaves knew more. But some critical pieces of information were still missing. Were the batarians about to be attacked? Or about to attack someone else? And if so, what were they after? There was no way to know. A woman started to pray, a turian told her to shut up, and McCann found himself in the strange position of hoping that his captors would win the upcoming battle. Because if they lost, and the *Khar'shan* was destroyed, his life would be over.

ΛBOΛRD THE QUΛRIΛN SHIP *IDENNA*

Gillian Grayson was on duty when the alarms went off. Drills were a common occurrence aboard the *Idenna*, so she assumed that Captain Ysin'Mal Vas Idenna was putting the crew through yet another simulated emergency, until he spoke over the intercom. "This is *not* a drill. I repeat . . . This is not a drill. What may be a pirate or a slaver is closing with us and, based on our preliminary sensor readings, will make contact in about forty-two minutes. All adult personnel will report to their battle stations—and all minors will enter the Creche. Keelah se'lai." (As our ancestors will it.)

At eighteen Gillian qualified as an adult, although her status as one of only two humans on board put her in a slightly different class, as did the fact that she was a Level 3 biotic. Which was to say the *only* Level 3 on the *Idenna*. And that was why she'd been assigned to the ship's boarding party along with her tutor and guardian Hendel Mitra, who had been both an Alliance soldier and security chief for the Ascension Project. It was an important assignment because the boarding party would play a critical role in defending the ship should they make hull-to-hull contact with their attackers.

And that was the thing about both pirates and

slavers. In order to profit they had to board and take over. There was no profit to be made by destroying their prey. Only geth raiders would do something like that. So Gillian rushed to don the human-style kinetic armor that the quarians had given her. It was orange, and included a sleek almost quarian-like helmet and visor combination, plus a tight-fitting torso protector. After donning a sculpted air pack Gillian was ready to fight in a vacuum if need be. Just like the quarians who swarmed all around her. They were accustomed to the human by then. So much so that they had given her the name Gillian Nar Idenna—Gillian, Child of the Ship *Idenna*.

With the armor in place it was time to remove the human-manufactured Hahne-Kedar pistol and holster rig from her locker and buckle it on. Hendel had arrived by then and stood head and shoulders above the quarians around him. His armor was white with black markings, and his personal arsenal consisted of a Sokolov shotgun and Hahne-Kedar pistol. He smiled grimly. "What were you thinking? Orange isn't your color."

"I think they wanted to see me coming."

Hendel laughed. The sound was muffled as he pulled the helmet over his head. It was, Gillian reflected, a very different type of conversation from the adult-child interactions so typical back at the Grissom Academy. She had been a very unstable twelve-year-old when they first met. Now, some six years later and thousands of light-years away, the relationship had matured. It had been difficult for Hendel, but bit by bit he'd been able to evolve away from stern authority figure to something more akin to a wise uncle. And she had grown as well, both as a person and a biotic, although she still had a tendency to lose her temper. But so did he.

A male named Ugho was in charge of the boarding party. He completed a quick head count, said "Follow me" and led the team out into the main corridor. From there it was necessary to pass through the equivalent of what would have been the crew deck on an Alliance warship. But rather than the usual galley, sleep pods, and medical bay the space had been divided into cubicles. They were arranged in groups of six, separated by half-walls, and accessed through openings that were normally sealed off with colorful curtains. The fabric partitions had been pulled to one side and secured lest they slow the ship's damage control parties.

Then the group dropped to what the quarians referred to as the "trading deck." It was lined with lockers, one for each member of the crew, where they could store items they weren't using but were willing to share with others. A "take what you need" system that served to put goods in the hands of those who needed them and was consistent with the limited amount of space on a ship like the *Idenna*. Like the living spaces located higher up, the trading deck was clear and the lockers were closed.

"Okay," Ugho said, as the boarding party came to a stop in front of the main hatch. "You know the drill. If the ancestorless scum try to take control of the ship it will be through this lock. The rest are too small for more than two people at a time to pass through. Our juveniles could handle that. So get to work on those barriers. They won't move themselves. Gillian, we need to chat."

The barriers were a little over one meter tall, about two meters long, and ninety centimeters thick. They were mounted on rollers so they could be moved easily and were equipped with hooks that slotted into the decking. Once in place they would channel the boarders and provide the defenders with much needed cover. There was a loud rumbling noise as the barriers were moved onto the outlines already spray-painted onto the deck.

Ugho wasn't known for his sociability, so Gillian knew that rather than a "chat" she was about to receive some orders. It was impossible to see Ugho's face through the reflective visor, and Gillian was equipped with one as well, so there was no such thing as eye contact. His voice was flat and matter-of-fact. "The captain will try to destroy the enemy before they can close with us. That's our advantage. We can use our primary armament and they can't if they want to capture the ship intact.

"But if they manage to come alongside, and blow the lock, we'll have to hold them off until reinforcements arrive. You humans are the only biotics we have and your skills could make a critical difference. Especially if we can take them by surprise. So stay back, conserve your energy, and wait for my order. Got it?"

Gillian could tell that Ugho was worried and felt the weight of some very adult responsibilities settle onto her shoulders. Could she do it? Was she good enough to make a difference? There was a hollow place where her stomach should have been. She nodded. "Got it."

"Good. Let's get to work."

Aboard the slave ship
Glory of Khar'shan

Captain Adar Adroni sat at the center of the *Khar'shan*'s U-shaped control center with his first officer to the left of his thronelike command chair and the navigator on the right. A curved screen was situated in front of them. On it they could see a computer-generated display that included images for all of the local planets, an icon that represented the ship they were pursuing, and lines of data that scrolled down both sides of the monitor.

The *Khar'shan* had been on its way to deliver a load of slaves to a mining operation when a host of alarms sounded. The whole thing was a matter of luck really. *Good* luck for Adroni and bad luck for the gas-sucking quarians.

So thanks to his good fortune Adroni was about to pick up a substantial bonus. Quarian slaves were especially sought after due to their sophisticated tech skills, and their ship had value as well. Adroni's thoughts were interrupted as the first officer spoke in his ear. "Two disruptor torpedoes are coming our way, Captain. ETA one minute and twenty-two seconds."

Adroni nodded. "Fire four interceptors. Two apiece. That should take care of it."

And he was correct. Both of the incoming missiles were destroyed in a pair of overlapping explosions. Then, as the range began to close even more, the quarian vessel turned on the batarians and opened fire with two magnetic accelerator cannons. They were very dangerous weapons, especially at close range, and the devastating projectiles they put out couldn't be intercepted by a missile. So all the batarians could do was take the punishment as the distance between the combatants continued to close.

But Adroni's ship was equipped to deal with such situations. The *Khar'shan* was powered by a standard Tantalus Drive Core *and* equipped with H-fuel cells that could deliver the extra power required to stop the hail of incoming projectiles.

Still the onslaught put the batarian barriers to the test as a shield went down exposing the ablative armor beneath. The incoming shells were busy chewing their way through that layer of protection when Adroni gave the order the weapons officer had been waiting for. "Fire the drive killers."

Drive killers were very specialized weapons designed to shut down but not destroy a ship's propulsion system. In order to make good use of such weapons it was necessary to get in close lest those in the other ship have time to intercept and destroy the small missiles. But that requirement had already been satisfied and Adroni uttered a grunt of satisfaction as one of two drive killers made it through the incoming fire and hit the other ship's hull. Not just anywhere, but at a location intended to sever the connection between the engine's drive core, and the rest of the ship. The damage could be repaired but it would take time—and the gas suckers would have to rely on backup power until then. "Close with them," Adroni ordered, as the fugitive ship lost power. "And send the boarding party. There is work to be done."

Aboard the quarian ship *Idenna*

There was a resounding *BOOM* as the spaceships made hull-to-hull contact, and Gillian was knocked off her feet. "Here they come!" Ugho said over the comm as she picked herself up, and a muffled explosion was heard. The outer hatch had been blown and the batarians were in the airlock. Seconds later the metal around the control panel on the inner door began to glow. Then a jet of plasma punched its way through and began to trace a red hot line around the box. There was a loud *hiss*, followed by a *clang*, as one of the slavers gave the control panel a kick and it fell in onto the *Idenna*'s deck.

Atmosphere was already rushing out, taking anything that wasn't secured with it, but the suction grew even more intense when the batarians pushed the hatch open. Then, as both sides opened fire, pressures were equalized and the flow of air stopped.

Because of the vacuum there was no sound other than what came over the comm. So Gillian couldn't hear the gunfire that lashed back and forth. But there was an almost nonstop flow of orders and commentary from Ugho as a phalanx of heavily armored batarians pushed their way into the *Idenna*.

The weight of their armor slowed the slavers down but enabled them to take a lot of punishment as the quarians opened fire on them. "Hit them hard!" Ugho urged. "Chew through their armor. We have to stop them before they can reach the barriers."

From her position toward the rear, where she was mostly concealed behind the last barrier, Gillian could see the wisdom of Ugho's words. The weapons being used by combatants on both sides fired particle-sized rounds at relativistic speeds. That meant a single magazine could hold a lot of rounds. The downside being a steady increase in heat. Failure to eject an old heat sink and replace it with a new one could disable a weapon and leave its owner vulnerable to attack. Just one of the many things Gillian had to remember.

A batarian fell as a steady stream of quarian projectiles burrowed through multiple layers of protection to find flesh and bone. The result was a horrible-looking geyser as the slaver's bodily fluids were sucked out through the hole in his ruptured suit. The sight was enough to make Gillian feel sick to her stomach as she pointed her pistol at one of the invaders and pulled the trigger. Sparks could be seen as the rounds struck, but the projectiles made no appreciable difference as the batarian lumbered forward.

Then an already difficult situation took a turn for the worse as a krogan mercenary entered the fray. Gillian knew very little about krogan firearms but didn't need to see how powerful the newcomer's assault weapon was as he cut two of her fellow crew members down and Ugho rose to throw a grenade. There was a flash of light as it went off but the effects were minimal.

The krogan fired at Ugho and the quarian began to backpedal in a futile attempt to stay vertical. Then it was over as the heavy slugs beat the quarian's kinetic armor down and tunneled through. The resulting hole was so large that the quarian's suit ruptured. As Gillian looked on in horror the vacuum sucked most of Ugho's organs out of his chest cavity and dumped them onto the deck.

Gillian felt the emotion boil up from deep inside of her. There had been a time when the combination of anger and grief would have been her undoing. But she had grown since then and learned to use hate as fuel for her talent. So as the quarians were forced to back away from the barriers and the steadily advancing krogan, the teenager emerged from hiding. Hendel shouted, "No!" over the comm, but Gillian Nar Idenna wasn't listening. The *Idenna* was *her* ship, Ugho was one of *her* people, and it was Gillian's duty to protect them.

Having returned the pistol to its holster Gillian raised her hands. Then, having gathered energy until she couldn't contain it anymore, there was no choice but to let go. The krogan was stomping a wounded quarian to death as the bolt hit him. In spite of his size the monster was plucked off the deck and thrown into a steel bulkhead. He fell, hit the deck hard, and was struggling to rise when Hendel took command. "Now! Kill the bastard."

Gillian was already in the process of collecting *more* energy by then. And as Hendel and the others shot at the krogan she targeted a batarian who was about to circle around the barriers and attack the defenders from behind. The first step was to lift the slaver twenty feet up off the deck. Then, as the terrified batarian sought to walk on air, Gillian let him go.

The *Idenna*'s mass effect generators were still on, so the invader came down hard. A leg gave way, he collapsed, and Gillian fired into the batarian's faceplate. It caved in.

Even though it seemed longer, only ten minutes had passed since the battle had begun. Enough time for quarians from other parts of the *Idenna* to grab weapons and rush to the trading deck. And their timing couldn't have been better. As Gillian paused to insert a fresh heat sink clip, quarians flooded into the space and charged the lock.

Having lost the krogan, plus some of their own, the batarians were forced to turn and run. Hendel was quick to see the opportunity and seize it. "This is our chance! Follow me."

And follow him they did, through the batarian lock, and into the *Khar'shan*'s hull. The lock opened onto the slave deck and Gillian saw at least a hundred slaves seated with their backs to the bulkheads, all locked into place by formfitting steel cages. But there was very little time to analyze her surroundings as a handful of batarians turned to fire on their pursuers. Some of the rounds went wide, and a couple of slaves were hit as Hendel shouted, "Kill the bastards! We need to take the control room before they can break loose."

Gillian had been giddy with excitement as she followed the rest of the quarians onto the batarian ship. But now she realized how much danger they were in. If the slavers managed to break contact with the *Idenna* the quarians would be trapped.

That possibility caused Gillian to push her way forward. Having caught up with Hendel she followed him to the emergency access shaft at the forward end of the compartment. "We can't use the lift," he explained. "They might shut it down and trap us inside. Be careful, Gillian—you were lucky back on the *Idenna*."

Gillian knew he was right as she swarmed up the ladder to the control deck. It was heavily defended and this became apparent when projectiles struck Gillian's armor, pushed her back, and forced her to take cover in the shaft. "Freeze 'em," Hendel advised from a few rungs below. "But let us squeeze past first."

Some biotics could create a moment of stasis, meaning a mass effect field that could lock an opponent inside, rendering them momentarily invulnerable to attack. And while that ability wasn't as natural to Gillian as propelling an object through the air, she'd been working on it. But would it be effective on targets she couldn't actually *see*? There was no way to be sure.

As Hendel led the others upward Gillian sought to gather as much energy around her as possible. Having done so she shaped it into a sphere and "saw" it freeze some imaginary batarians in place. Then came the struggle to sustain the stasis field for as long as she could. Three seconds later Gillian felt the bubble "pop" and lunged upward.

She stepped out of the shaft with pistol in hand. Half a dozen bodies were scattered around the center of the U-shaped control area and three batarians stood with hands on top of their heads. "You did it," Hendel said proudly. "You froze two of them *and* Ibin Vas Idenna. He's pissed, but he'll get over it."

Gillian felt an enormous sense of relief followed by a sudden emptiness as the aftereffects caught up with her. "Catch her," Hendel said, and everything went black.

Aboard the quarian ship *Idenna*

Six hours had passed since the end of the battle and Hal McCann felt disappointed. Rather than being freed he and all the rest of the slaves had been placed under guard and led onto the quarian ship. It was a sensible precaution. He knew that. The quarians wanted to find out who the slaves were before turning them loose.

So as the ships remained locked together, and the quarians worked to bring their command and control systems back online, teams of interrogators were interviewing the slaves. Some were freed, but some weren't, and McCann felt a sense of apprehension as a couple of them were led away in handcuffs.

The line snaked across the bloodstained trading deck to a table where a couple of quarians were seated. Finally, having waited through the queue, it was McCann's turn to answer questions. The interrogators were invisible behind their reflective visors, and like many people in the galaxy McCann had a poor opinion of them. "Name?"

"Hal McCann. There were humans among the boarding party. Two of them. I respectfully request that they be present during my interview."

There was a moment of silence as the quarians looked at each other then back to him. Had they been communicating via a comm? It seemed that way when one of them pointed to a spot off to one side. "Wait there. Next."

McCann did as he was told. His legs were free, but his wrists were cuffed, and a heavily armed guard was stationed three meters away. He didn't have a watch, but what seemed like an hour passed before the humans appeared. McCann was sitting cross-legged on the deck by that time, so he pushed himself up into a standing position as the newcomers went over to speak with the quarian interrogators.

When they came his way McCann saw that the man was over six feet tall with a closely cropped mustache and goatee. He had rusty brown hair, dark-colored skin, and an air of confidence about him.

The girl was shorter, but not by much, and thin. Her hair was black and pulled back away from a long narrow face. Her wide-set eyes seemed especially intense somehow, as if the mind behind them was hard at work. "Hal McCann?" the man inquired. "I'm Hendel Mitra. This is Gillian Grayson."

McCann felt a sense of shock so profound that his mouth opened and closed like a newly landed fish. "*Gillian* Grayson? Paul Grayson's daughter?"

Gillian's face brightened. "You know my father?"

"Well, yes," McCann admitted. "We were on a Cerberus space station at the same time."

Gillian's coal black eyes seemed to drill holes in him. " 'Were'? What happened?"

McCann could tell that the girl wasn't aware of her father's death—and knew he would have to be very careful in order to win his freedom. "The turians attacked. We fought back but were outgunned. I took a hit right here."

So saying McCann pulled his long unkempt hair aside so that the other two could see the patch of white scar tissue. "It knocked me out. When I came to a body was lying on top of me. The turians were searching them—taking whatever they wanted. So I played dead, and given all the blood on my face, they bought it.

"Eventually they carried all of the bodies including mine off the station and onto a shuttle. Based on what I overheard the dead were supposed to be transported to a ship. But I knew better than to go along with that. So as soon as the shuttle got under way I fought my way free of the bodies, took one of the weapons that the turians had captured from us, and went forward. There was a pilot and a copilot. I shot both in the back of the head."

"But what about my father?" Gillian wanted to know. "What happened to *him*?"

"I didn't know at that point," McCann answered honestly. "The shuttle had a basic FTL drive. All I could do was point the shuttle at the nearest mass effect relay and head for Omega. I figured that was the best place to go since I had no way to know if the Illusive Man was still alive. Plus I was at the controls of a stolen shuttle. So where else *could* I go?

"That part of my escape went well," McCann continued. "I sold the shuttle at a steep discount, but still walked away with a hefty chunk of change."

"Then what?" Hendel demanded skeptically.

McCann looked down at his filth encrusted boots. "I figured I'd take the money and double or even triple it playing Star Cluster. So I went to a batarian-owned club called Fortune's Den."

"Don't tell me," Hendel said disgustedly. "You lost all your money."

"Yes, I did," McCann admitted shamefacedly. "But I lost more than that. I bet my freedom and lost that as well."

"My father," Gillian insisted. "Tell me about my father."

"That's where I heard about him," McCann said, as his eyes came back up. "Aria T'Loak had people combing all the bars on Omega looking for him. So when they entered Fortune's Den, and said they were looking for a human, the batarians brought me up out of the basement. Money changed hands and I wound up in front of T'Loak. But the whole thing was over by then. According to T'Loak your father was killed on a space station in orbit around Elysium."

Gillian's eyes grew wider. "The Grissom Academy. That's where I went to school. You're sure? My father's dead?"

McCann shrugged. "No, how could I be sure? But Aria had no reason to lie. Not to someone she sold to a batarian slaver two days later."

The first emotion Gillian experienced was a deep and abiding sorrow. She was forever cut off from the only person who hadn't been paid to care about her. Paul Grayson had been less than perfect. That was why she and Hendel had been forced to hide aboard the *Idenna*. To escape her father and whatever was controlling him.

But she believed that he loved her, to the extent that such a flawed being could love another person, and she loved him in return. In spite of all the things that he had done. She fingered the jewel that hung at her throat as tears trickled down her cheeks. "*Who* killed him? And why?"

McCann had been there. Had *seen* the horrible things the Illusive Man and those working for him had done to Grayson. More than that, he'd been part of the team.

And there was no way the Illusive Man would want people to find out what Cerberus had been up to. So if Grayson had been able to escape, somebody had been sent to kill him. Kai Leng perhaps? Quite possibly. But it wouldn't be very smart to tell Gillian Grayson about his role in her father's captivity and he didn't. "I don't know," McCann lied. "But one thing I *can* tell you is that your father talked about you all the time."

Gillian's sorrow began to morph into anger as she thought about what had been taken from her. The only person other than Hendel that she could count on. She wiped at the tears with the back of a wrist. "I'm going to find out who killed my father. And when I do they're going to die."

McCann nodded sagely. "I don't blame you. Chances are the information you need is on the Citadel." There was no basis for that, at least not that McCann was aware of, but that was where *he* wanted to go. Omega was out of the question. "I'll help you," he promised. "We'll figure out who did it."

"That's ridiculous," Hendel put in. "There's no way to know where the killer or killers went. Besides, how would we get there?"

"The slave ship," Gillian proclaimed tightly. "We'll take the slave ship."

Hendel frowned. "The slave ship? Why would the crew of the *Idenna* give you that? It's theirs to recondition or sell."

Gillian's mouth was a horizontal line. "They'll give it to me because I saved every single person on the *Idenna* from slavery. Ask them. You'll see." And, much to Hendel's amazement, she was right.

THREE

ON THE CITADEL

The electronic concierge was waiting to greet Anderson and Kahlee as they entered their apartment. "Welcome home. All systems are functioning properly. Five voice mails, twenty-three text messages, and two holos are waiting."

"Nick isn't here," Anderson said after taking a quick look at the guest room. "And his belongings are gone."

"Let's check those messages," Kahlee said. "Maybe he left one of them."

"I'll tackle the voice mails," Anderson said. He was deleting a message from the retired officers' association when Kahlee called him over.

"Here it is, David. Come look."

Anderson turned to see a holo shiver, back up, and start again. Nick was seated on a chair in a pool of light. He was dressed in the same clothes he'd been wearing earlier in the day. That suggested that the message had been recorded after he left the Citadel Tower. There was a guilty expression on his face. "I'm sorry about taking off from the tower," Nick said, "but there's no need to worry because I'm with friends."

Anderson and Kahlee looked at each other. Were the so-called friends the mysterious biotics named Ocosta Lem and Arrius Sallus? Both feared that was the case.

"There's something I have to do," Nick said importantly, "and that's to make things better. That's what you're doing, right? Only I have skills that most people don't. So it makes sense to use them. Not by myself, but as part of something larger, a group called the Biotic Underground."

What followed had a formal singsong quality. As if the words had been memorized. "We believe that because biotics are special, they have a special responsibility to help others. And the best way to do that is to bring *all* of the races together. The creation of the Council was a good first step. But thousands of years have passed and the various members are *still* bickering with each other. So now it's time to take a significant leap forward by forming a single government. An organization that will be run by biotics representing all of the various races."

Anderson ordered the holo to pause before turning to Kahlee. "It sounds like these people are biotic supremacists."

Kahlee nodded soberly. "Nick's very idealistic. They're taking advantage of him."

Anderson said, "Play holo," and the three-dimensional image jerked into motion. "But that will take time," Nick continued. "So you won't see me for a while. Please tell my parents not to worry. I'll be in touch from time to time but only if I'm left alone.

Otherwise it will be necessary to cut off all communications."

At that point Nick looked to his right as if seeking approval from someone before turning back. "I guess that's all. Thanks for being so nice to me." The holo imploded at that point. Motes of light sparkled and disappeared.

"Damn him," Anderson said.

And rather than object the way she might have otherwise Kahlee nodded. "He knows better. Or should have. What will we tell his parents?"

"The truth," Anderson said grimly.

"And C-Sec?"

"We'll contact them immediately after we talk to Nick's parents."

Kahlee sighed. "They live on Anhur. I met them at the academy. I'll work on a call."

"Use my priority—it could take days otherwise."

The call didn't go well. Nick's father was furious. He blamed Anderson and Kahlee for his son's disappearance, calling them "careless" and "negligent."

Nick's mother was a little more understanding, but not much, and broke into tears when she saw the holo. Both parents wanted to board a ship for the Citadel to join the hunt for their son but lacked the money required to do so. Anderson assured them that C-Sec would be notified immediately—and that both he and Kahlee would participate in the search.

Nick's mother was concerned about the possibility that Nick would break off all communications the way he had threatened to, but eventually surrendered to arguments put forward by the others, and left her husband to complete the call. By the time it was over both Anderson and Kahlee felt even worse than they had before.

It was getting late by then, but they knew it was important to start the search as quickly as possible, so Anderson called a C-Sec officer named Amy Varma. She'd been one of Anderson's aides before he retired from the navy and was currently working as a shift supervisor in C-Sec's Customs Division. That meant she could help them file a missing person report—and ensure that the Citadel's customs personnel were watching for Nick. Otherwise the shadowy biotics who had befriended the boy might try to take him off the space station. Varma promised to warn her people immediately.

It had been a long and exhausting day. So Anderson and Kahlee ate a simple dinner and went to bed hoping C-Sec would find Nick during the artificial night and the whole episode would be over before morning. But it wasn't to be. At the point when the alarm went off and they rolled out of bed, the only call waiting in their inbox was from a volus-run travel agency trying to interest Kahlee in a trip to Earth.

So they showered, ate a quick breakfast, and went to meet with Varma. The officer had short black hair, bangs that fell halfway down her forehead, and brown eyes. They were bright with intelligence and Kahlee took an immediate liking to the young woman as she came out of her glassed-in office to meet them. The Customs Division was headquartered in one of the towers that circled the station's inner ring. "Admiral Anderson. It's good to see you again, sir. And Miss Sanders is ex-military as well, I believe."

The last was said with a smile and Kahlee responded in kind as they shook hands. "It's been awhile, but yes. Have you been reading my file?"

"Of course," Varma said unapologetically. "With a case like this there's no way to know what kind of information will turn out to be important."

"So, no luck?" Anderson inquired.

"Nothing actionable I'm afraid. But all of our people are on high alert, so who knows? We could get lucky. In the meantime Central Command has been hard at work. So we have some images to review. Please follow me."

Anderson and Kahlee followed Varma down a sterile-looking hallway. "CENTCOM terminals are located at various places on the Citadel," Varma explained. "And all of them are restricted. So we'll have to pause for a scan."

Once cleared through the security checkpoint Anderson and Kahlee found themselves in a chilly room. The dome-shaped space was lined with what Kahlee thought were colorful tiles until the salarian seated at the center of the room pointed a wand at one of them. It blossomed into a large three-dimensional holo of a batarian holding his hands up. A pair of uniformed officers entered the shot moments later with their weapons drawn.

"As you know there are hundreds of thousands of security cameras on the Citadel," Varma said, as the holo was drawn back into the video mosaic covering the walls and ceiling. "And by monitoring them we're able to respond to violent crimes within a matter of minutes. Fraud, confidence games, and the like are harder to detect as they take place. But later we can go back and search CENTCOM for relevant evidence. And that's what we did in this case.

"The photo you provided was uploaded to CENTCOM along with a command to scan all images of Nick Donahue captured since the moment you discovered he was missing. And here's what it came up with. Officer Urbo? Roll the video for case number 482.976 please."

Urbo was seated on a raised platform behind a curved semitransparent control panel. His fingers seemed to flicker as he entered the number into a ghostly looking keyboard. Moments later another six-meter-tall holo appeared. It quickly became apparent that snippets of video from many different cameras had been edited together to create a jerky but nevertheless telling record of Nick's movements after he left the Citadel Tower.

Anderson and Kahlee watched via a number of camera angles as their charge passed through the Presidium, took public transportation home, and disappeared into their apartment building. The next shot was a time lapse that showed Nick leaving twelve minutes later. And there, waiting outside, were two individuals. Ocosta Lem and Arrius Sallus. Varma ordered Urbo to freeze the holo. "Here they are," she said. "The biotics you told us about.

"And, as it turns out, they had come to our attention before. Both have been involved in political demonstrations on behalf of an organization called the Biotic Underground. A couple of the gatherings turned ugly when some antibiotic pure breeders turned up and our friends began to throw people around. Officer Urbo has one of the scuffles cued up for you to take a look at. Watch the people in the background."

The holo jerked into motion. The image had been captured in an area where thousands of menial workers lived. Lem could be seen in the foreground "lifting" an irate turian off the ground. As that took place an illuminated circle appeared off to the right. It wobbled for a moment before settling over a very familiar face. Nick was not only there, but judging from the expression on his face, entranced by what was taking place. "So," Varma said, "it looks like Lem and Sallus found what they were looking for. A new supporter."

"Nick's more than that," Kahlee observed. "He's a Level Two biotic with the potential to become a three. So they could use him in all sorts of ways."

"Good point," Varma agreed. "And all the more reason to keep looking."

"So where did they go from the apartment?" Anderson wanted to know.

"They disappeared," Varma said simply. "They knew about the cameras, everyone does, and were last seen in the red ward entering a restaurant with Nick. I sent an officer down to check the place out. A back door opens onto a narrow pedway. All three cameras in that area had been disabled by a local street gang."

"And the gang was paid off by the biotics," Anderson said sourly.

"That's the way it looks," Varma agreed.

"But then what?" Kahlee inquired. "Surely you were able to pick them up somewhere else."

Varma shook her head. "Not so far. But we'll keep looking."

"What about Nick's omni-tool?" Anderson wanted to know. "Can you track it?"

"We have it," Varma countered. "The signal led us to a bin under a public disposal chute. There's another possibility though . . . One I hate to bring up. A place we haven't checked."

Kahlee frowned. "Where's that?"

"The morgue."

ABOARD THE LINER *PARSUS II*

There were times when Kai Leng was required to deal with various forms of hardship. This wasn't one of them. After receiving his orders from the Illusive Man, Leng traveled to Illium where he booked a passage on the *Parsus II,* which was bound for the Citadel. And, in keeping with the identity he had chosen, Leng was traveling first class. That meant he could watch the arrival process from the comfort of his suite rather than one of the public areas where lesser passengers were gathered.

During Faster Than Light travel it was impossible to see anything, so the floor-to-ceiling viewport that occupied the outside wall of his cabin was filled with beautiful starscapes provided by the ship's NAV-COMP. But after entering normal space Leng could see the incredible space station that functioned as the political, economic, and cultural center of the galaxy. The Citadel resembled a piece of fantastic jewelry surrounded by luminous particles that were actually stars.

But before the *Parsus* or any other ship could dock with the Citadel it was necessary to get rid of the powerful charge that had accumulated in the ship's drive core during FTL flight. That was accomplished by pausing at one of the free-floating space stations designed for that purpose. It was a tiresome business, but absolutely necessary for safety reasons, and gave Leng the opportunity to enjoy the space-going equivalent of a fireworks show as the *Parsus* came alongside a discharge station and fingers of coruscating blue light strobed the inky blackness. Then, having been cleared, the liner was free to proceed.

The better part of three hours passed before the *Parsus* was allowed to dock with the Citadel. Being a first-class passenger had its advantages and Leng was among those allowed to leave the ship first. The Cerberus operative was equipped with a pair of self-propelled suitcases that trundled along behind him as he left the ship. It wasn't that he needed everything stored in them, but the luggage served to support his cover story and provided more things for the customs officers to inspect. Because the more material they had to look at the less time would be spent on each individual item, thereby increasing the likelihood that agents would miss the fact that his cane could be converted into a rifle barrel—that the ornate carving set acquired on Illium included a razor-sharp knife that could be used for slicing just about anything.

So Leng felt a not altogether unpleasant sense of tension as he led his suitcases across a causeway and into customs. A turian with white facial tattoos was seated behind a waist-high counter. "Good afternoon, sir. Passport please."

The folder that Leng handed over was nothing more than a frame for a chip on which information regarding his false identity had been painstakingly recorded by one of the first-class forgers that worked for Cerberus. The idea was to protect his *real* identity for as long as possible. A tone sounded as the turian slid the passport into a reader and CENTCOM acknowledged that the chip was properly formatted. "Thank you, Mr. Forbes," the customs officer said, as he eyed the screen. "Look at the scanner, please."

Leng knew the moment of truth was at hand. Would the colored contacts he was wearing spoof the retinal scanner the way they were supposed to? Or set off an alarm and bring a quick response team down on him? His heart beat a little bit faster as he took a step forward and turned right. A tone sounded and the turian removed the passport from the reader. "Welcome to the Citadel, Mr. Forbes. Please proceed to station two."

Leng smiled. The specially designed contacts were a success. "Thank you."

Flashing arrows led Leng and his suitcases to station two, where a robot was waiting to lift his luggage up onto a stainless-steel table. A uniformed officer greeted him, asked Leng to open both cases, and gave the contents a cursory examination. The cane, which he continued to lean on, went uninspected. "Welcome to the Citadel," the officer said, as he motioned to the robot. "Please follow the floor lights out to the arrival area."

Leng ordered the suitcases to close themselves, waited for the robot to place them on the floor, and made his way out into a large room where a crowd of about a hundred people was waiting to greet friends or relatives who had arrived on the *Parsus*. From there it was a short walk to the Presidium. Leng was on the Citadel—the Illusive Man would be pleased.

Thousands of people died on the Citadel each day. Most of them were identified within a few minutes or hours at most. Then, in accordance with the directives they had left behind, or in keeping with instructions from the next of kin, their bodies were shipped to whatever planet they called home, or disposed of on the Citadel itself.

But there were some, a few hundred each day, that went unidentified. So on the chance that Nick had been murdered, Anderson and Kahlee had agreed to take the grisly stroll through the section of the space station's morgue dedicated to bodies waiting to be identified. They could be seen inside gas-filled capsules, each standing as if still alive, eyes closed.

Only twenty-two percent of them were human. That made the process a bit easier. But it was still hard to take and Kahlee was grateful as they followed Varma out of the morgue and into a brightly lit hallway. "I'm glad that's over. Thank god Nick wasn't there."

Varma nodded. "I'm sorry you had to go through it, but now we know. That's all we can do for the moment. I'll let you know if any new leads come in."

"So what now?" Kahlee inquired, as they followed the flow of foot traffic to the elevator that would take them up to the Presidium level. "Any ideas?"

"Yes," Anderson replied. "First we need to have dinner. A good one. Then we'll go home and get ready for tomorrow. I'm going to become a shady businessman—and you'll play the part of my girl-friend."

"I *am* your girlfriend."

Anderson smiled. "Yes, you are. That makes you perfect for the role."

Kahlee laughed. Anderson liked the sound of it. Their relationship had begun when they joined forces to battle the Spectre named Saren, been interrupted by the requirements of two different careers, and re-kindled when the threat represented by Cerberus brought them together again. "So," Kahlee said, "why are we going to play dress-up?"

"Because as we used to say in the navy, there's the way we're *supposed* to do things, and there's the way we actually do things."

"Which means?"

"Which means that while C-Sec continues to do things by the book we're going to break the rules."

Kahlee smiled as they strolled out into the artificial sunlight. "A naughty admiral. I like it. Come on," she said. "I'm in the mood for an asari stir-fry tonight."

He grinned. "And for dessert?"

"*That,*" Kahlee said, "is for me to know and for you to find out."

They rose early the next morning and ate at a local restaurant before beginning the journey into one of the Citadel's more dangerous neighborhoods. Ander-son was dressed in an expensive business suit of the sort that was way too flashy for an actual business-man. A stylish wraparound visor concealed his eyes and part of his face. And Kahlee was attired the way his companion should be, in a formfitting emerald green pantsuit with lots of gold jewelry.

But the most impressive part of the disguise was a krogan bodyguard Anderson had hired through a security firm. His name was Tark, he was dressed in light body armor, and he was armed with a stunner and baton. Both of which were properly licensed. The idea was to make Anderson and Kahlee look like bona fide members of the Citadel's underworld.

So as they dropped two levels down, and gradually entered what was both literally and figuratively the underworld, Tark led the way. Just the sight of him was sufficient to keep beggars, street thugs, and pickpockets at bay. Of course, the hulking bodyguard drew attention as well—and that made Kahlee feel uncomfortable. "Where are we headed again?"

"We're going to visit a batarian named Nodi Banca. He runs a company called Camala Exports. And, according to my old friend Barla Von, he's an expert at getting things off the Citadel. That means cheap manufactured goods for the most part. But Von says that Banca has been known to smuggle people too."

Kahlee had met Von and knew the volus to be a financial whiz who had helped Anderson before. "Which means that the Biotic Alliance could have hired Camala Exports to get Lem, Sallus, and Nick off the station," she said. "But how likely is that?"

"Not very," Anderson admitted. "But C-Sec is working on everything else so it's worth a try."

A group of rough-looking types scattered as Tark plowed through them and led his clients down a sloping ramp. A great deal of the Citadel had been reworked over thousands of years to keep it functional and to meet the needs of the millions who lived there.

But the lower they went the more Anderson was reminded of the station's true origins. The Reapers were responsible for the basic structure of it, including the invulnerable hull and the massive machinery that enabled it to open and close. But the hallways, ramps, and other structures that surrounded Anderson were the work of the various races that had chosen to occupy the Citadel.

The threesome were directly beneath one of the Citadel's major spaceports by that time, in an area that was thick with manufacturers, warehouses, and shippers. Spacers, business types, and all manner of dockworkers, technicians, and vendors were forced to make way as Tark took a right and led the humans down a gloomy passageway. A glowing sign could be seen at the other end. It read, "CAMALA EXPO TS."

Two batarians were slouched against opposite walls. They came to attention as Tark approached them and one issued a challenge. He was armed with a length of decorated steel pipe. "That's far enough, big boy . . . Who are you looking for?"

"*We're* looking for your boss," Anderson said as he stepped forward. "Tell him that a potential customer is here to see him."

The batarian blinked all four eyes at once. "What's your name?"

"Ray Narkin." There was a *real* Ray Narkin. A shady type who had been in trouble with C-Sec on numerous occasions but had never been convicted of anything serious enough to get him shipped to a prison planet. If Banca took the trouble to go online he'd see a list of Narkin's crimes right next to a picture of Anderson. It was a simple hack that was likely to go unnoticed unless Narkin objected and put it right.

"Wait here," the batarian said. "I'll see if Mr. Banca has time to see you."

"You do that," Anderson said casually. "But don't take too long. We don't have all day."

Tark and the second batarian spent the next three minutes trying to stare each other down, Anderson pretended to send messages via his omni-tool, and Kahlee took the opportunity to examine her makeup in a small hand mirror. Then the door slid open and the first batarian motioned for them to enter. "The boss will see you now . . . But the krogan stays outside."

Anderson shrugged. "Okay, no problem. Wait here Tark. We'll be out in half an hour or so."

Tark uttered a grunt of acknowledgment and remained behind as the humans entered a large but dingy office. There were three desks but only one of them showed any signs of recent use. It was located at the back of the room where a batarian was lit by the spill of light from a recessed fixture above. As they approached Anderson saw that Banca had a black patch over one of his four eyes. The rest regarded him with what looked like brooding suspicion. "Mr. Banca, I presume? My name is Narkin. Ray Narkin. And this is my assistant Lora Cole. Thank you for taking time to see us."

Banca made no attempt to rise. His head was tilted to the right, a sure sign of disrespect, and only one hand was visible. When the other appeared it was holding a semiautomatic pistol. The bore looked like the inside of a subway tunnel. "Sit down."

Banca flicked the gun barrel toward two mismatched guest chairs. And being unarmed, there was nothing Anderson and Kahlee could do but obey. "You aren't Ray Narkin," Banca growled. "He weighs well over three hundred pounds and the Torcs popped him yesterday. And they'd like to pop me too because we were bringing red sand in from Omega and selling it for less than they could. So tell me who you *really* are, and do it quickly, or I'll ship your dead bodies to a pet food factory on Hebat."

Kai Leng was in a good mood. The trip to the Citadel had gone smoothly, the apartment he had rented more than met his needs, and the people he'd been ordered to watch weren't home. He knew because he'd been across the way having tea in a stand-up kiosk when the garishly dressed couple left the building.

It was tempting to follow them, but Leng had a great deal of experience where such matters were concerned, and knew that the real priority lay elsewhere. So he finished the tea, paid the bill, and limped across the broad tree-lined pedway. His arrival was timed to coincide with that of a local resident. She entered the proper key code and Leng followed her inside.

It was a simple matter to ride the elevator up to the proper floor and take a quick look around. The hallway was empty. Leng hurried over to unit 306, where he rested the cane against the wall and activated the military-grade omni-tool on his left arm. A golden glow splashed the door as Leng ran a program that could get him through all but the most sophisticated of computer-controlled locks. The task took 5.6 seconds from start to finish. Leng heard a click, turned the handle, and entered the apartment.

The concierge, which had been fooled into believing that Anderson had entered, gave its usual greeting. "Welcome home. All systems are functioning properly. Two voice mails, sixteen text messages, and a holo are waiting."

Leng paused to savor his surroundings. He knew Anderson and Kahlee the way a predator knows its prey. They were amateurs insofar as he was concerned, and the battle on the Grissom Academy space station was proof of that. Anderson could have killed him that day. *Should* have killed him. But shot him in the legs instead. The wound in his left calf had healed fairly well, but the muscles in his right thigh were badly torn, and the prognosis wasn't good. Fortunately, his doctors were hard at work on a solution, one they claimed would make him better than new, even though he figured they were exaggerating.

But for the moment it was necessary to make do and that's where the cane came in. Leng could walk without the stick if necessary, but he still had a tendency to favor his right leg, and it was nice to have something to lean on from time to time.

So there was a score to settle. A need to even things up. And Leng knew that his chance would come. Not now, while he was under orders to watch the couple, but later, when it was time to leave for his next assignment. The only question was whether to kill them clean, or kneecap them and leave them to crawl around the floor the way he'd been forced to do.

The thought brought a grim smile to Leng's face as he took a long, slow look around. He was equipped with twelve wireless bugs, each of which had enough power to broadcast a signal for two weeks. And they were so small that only an electronic sweep would reveal their presence.

Would Anderson and Kahlee conduct such a sweep? It was possible. Anderson was employed by the Council and could call on their resources. But chances were they wouldn't think to look unless given some reason to do so. And Leng would do everything in his power to avoid that.

Working with the speed and certainty of the experienced operative that he was, Leng placed the pickups in locations that, when taken together, would provide complete coverage of everything that took place in the apartment. Then, having placed a wireless tap under the comm console, he was done. Or should have been done. But Leng was something of an adrenaline junkie and enjoyed being where he was.

That's why he checked the cupboards, located some cereal, and had breakfast before putting everything back exactly as it had been. It was *his* apartment now, meaning a place where everything that happened would be known to him, and to Cerberus. The thought pleased him and Leng was still smiling as he left.

Anderson felt stupid. The assumption that Nankin and Banca didn't know each other had proven wrong. Not only that, but it appeared that a gang called the Red Torcs were out to get both of them and had succeeded where Nankin was concerned. All he could do was come clean. "Okay, so I'm not Ray Nankin."

"But you *are* with the Torcs." Banca tilted the pistol up and a red dot wobbled across Anderson's forehead.

"No! We heard that you smuggle people off the Citadel from time to time. And we're looking for three people who might have been clients."

Banca opened his mouth to speak but was interrupted as a ceiling-mounted grill fell free and crashed onto one of the empty desks. A cloud of dust filled the air as Banca's pistol swiveled slightly and fired. Anderson turned in time to see a scrawny human collapse. The man wasn't wearing armor, the air duct had been too small for that, so the projectile went through him and hit the bulkhead beyond.

The first guard, the one with the section of iron pipe, ran over to look up into the duct and paid a steep price for his stupidity as someone shot him from above. The pipe made a clattering noise as it fell from a nerveless hand and rolled away.

The Torc in the shaft wasn't about to drop down into the room. Not after what happened to his buddy. But anyone who walked under the vent would catch a round.

There was a commotion out front as the door hissed open allowing Tark and the surviving guard to back into the office. They were fighting off waves of skin suit–clad humans, each of whom wore a red torc around his or her neck.

Banca stood, and was preparing to fire, when Kahlee threw a heavy desk clock at him. The batarian blocked it. But while he was doing so Anderson came over the desk at him. They collapsed in a tangle of arms and legs.

Kahlee went for the loose pistol, snatched it off the floor, and turned back toward the door. It appeared as though Tark had exhausted his stunner, or lost it in the fighting, because he was swinging his baton. There was a thump as it came into contact with a head and a Torc went down. "Close the door!" Kahlee ordered, "and lock it."

The batarian managed to do so, and was about to turn, when the krogan clubbed him as well. "Good work," Kahlee said. "Come back but stay clear of that vent. David could use a hand."

But the ex-navy officer didn't need a hand. Banca was not only down but unconscious. "He hit his head on the floor," Anderson explained matter-of-factly. "Four or five times."

"Pick him up," Kahlee ordered as Tark arrived. "Let's get out of here."

The krogan threw Banca over a shoulder as Kahlee went over to check the back door. A quick peek through a peephole revealed that the hallway was empty of Torcs. That was a surprise. Surely the gang's leaders were smart enough to cover the back entrance? But having met such fierce resistance it was possible that the drug runners had left. In any case, it was a way out and Kahlee was happy to take advantage of it. So she opened the door, motioned Tark through, and followed him out.

That was when she saw Lieutenant Varma. The C-Sec officer was standing a few meters away just outside the view from the peephole. Two heavily armed turians flanked her with their weapons aimed at Tark. "Put the batarian down," Varma ordered.

Tark obeyed but not in the way that Varma had intended. Rather than lower Banca to the ground he simply let go. There was a thump as the body hit. "Ooops . . . I lost my grip."

Varma was not amused. "Put your face to the wall with your hands on top of your head."

Tark obeyed. "I'm a licensed security officer."

"We know who you are," Varma said as she turned her attention to the other two. "Admiral Anderson . . . Miss Sanders . . . You have some explaining to do."

Anderson grinned sheepishly. "Yeah, I guess we do. How did you find us?"

Varma smiled grimly. "We have a lot of cameras, remember? And we had the Torcs under surveillance. You were fortunate. They killed a man named Narkin yesterday. We have video of them ejecting the body from an emergency lock."

Banca groaned and sat up. "Where am I?"

"In a whole lot of trouble," Varma replied. "Cuff him."

"There's a very real possibility that he smuggled Nick off the Citadel," Kahlee said.

"We'll know soon," Varma promised. "In the meantime I would appreciate it if you would surrender that pistol. You're going to jail."

FOUR

On the Citadel

Gillian was frustrated. Having been given the *Glory of Khar'shan* by the grateful quarians, she and a crew of freed slaves had flown the ship to the Citadel, only to be placed in what amounted to quarantine. The problem being that the vessel was registered to a batarian company that wanted it back. That raised issues of law having to do with jurisdiction, intragalactic slavery, and piracy.

And because of that the ship might have been stuck in legal limbo for months, if not years, had it not been for the fact that one of the newly freed slaves was a turian who'd been captured off the planet Palaven. He was a senior member of the turian Corps of Engineers, and thanks to his relationship with a high-ranking official, the *Khar'shan* was allowed to dock after only one day of legal haggling.

Hendel was pleased, as was McCann, not to mention the turian himself. But Gillian had no patience for anything that kept her from pursuing her new goal in life—which was to find the person responsible for her father's death and punish him. So she was still annoyed as the crew trooped off the ship to be processed through customs and released into the space station beyond.

The turian official was met by a gaggle of VIPs and swarmed by an army of reporters, but the rest of the crew were left to their own devices. And that was when McCann attempted to slip away.

Although he had every right to leave, McCann was an admitted member of Cerberus and the only link that Gillian had to that organization. So as the ex-slave pushed his way through the crowd of reporters, clearly intent on leaving the area as quickly as possible, the biotic gave him a gentle "shove." It was similar to a "throw" except less powerful and more focused.

Even so, the force of it was sufficient to topple the people to either side of McCann, making it appear that the fugitive had tripped and taken the others down with him. By the time McCann was back on his feet Gillian and Hendel were there to stop him. "What's the big hurry, Hal?" Gillian demanded. "It isn't nice to leave without saying good-bye. Especially since you'd be working in a mine if it wasn't for us."

"I'm not a slave," McCann objected. "I can go wherever I please."

"True," Gillian said soothingly. "Or at least it will be true. After we visit my friends. They knew my father and they're familiar with Cerberus. So I think it's safe to say that they'd love to hear your story. Then, once everyone is up to speed, you'll be allowed to leave. Okay?"

McCann dusted his clothes off. He looked resentful. "Okay."

"And one more thing," Gillian added. "If you try to run I will pick you up and slam you into a wall. After that Hendel will smash your knees. So save yourself some pain and come quietly."

Gillian's comments left Hendel feeling both proud and worried. Proud because of how confident she had become but worried because of the overriding anger that had taken control of her. Would he smash McCann's leg if she ordered him to? Of course not. So was she bluffing? Or did Gillian *believe* that he would? Some counseling was in order, but Hendel knew it would have to wait. "Come on," he said. "I know where Anderson and Kahlee live. We'll surprise them."

Anderson was sore—and for good reason. The batarian had gotten in some licks during their brief battle. And he was tired. Varma had held them for more than six hours while C-Sec investigators went over Banca's blood-splattered office with a fine-toothed comb. Fortunately their findings were consistent with the narratives provided by Anderson, Kahlee, and Tark. All of whom claimed self-defense.

Meanwhile Varma, and an officer qualified to translate the nuances of batarian body language, had been interrogating Banca. The businessman was reluctant to cooperate at first. But when Varma showed him video of Narkin's body being dumped into a lock, and threatened to put him in a cell with half a dozen Torcs, the batarian had a sudden change of heart.

Yes, Banca said, there had been three individuals, including a turian, a salarian, and a human. All bound for space station Omega. After paying with cash the biotics had been sealed into a specially designed cargo module. It was equipped with a life support system, cramped living area, and enough food for a short journey. A tray full of electronic components was on top of the compartment, directly under the lid. That was what customs agents would see if they opened the container. Not foolproof by any means, but sufficient to pass a cursory inspection. And with thousands of such modules arriving and departing each day, it was impossible to search each one of them.

So Anderson and Kahlee knew where they would have to go if they wanted to find Nick. But only after some planning and a good night's sleep. And that was foremost in Anderson's mind as Kahlee and he left a restaurant and went home. It had been dark for a while by then, so he didn't recognize any of the people waiting outside the building until they got closer, and Kahlee uttered a whoop of joy. "Gillian? Is that *you*? And Hendel . . . You're back! What a wonderful surprise."

Anderson shook hands with Hendel as the women hugged each other and a third male looked uneasy. "This is Hal McCann," Hendel said. "You won't believe how we met!"

"I like a good story," Anderson replied. "Come on, let's get you in off the street. How long were you waiting? Are you hungry?"

"About half an hour," Hendel replied. "And no, we had dinner just around the corner. We wanted to surprise you."

"Well, you sure as hell did," Anderson said, as he held the front door open. "Welcome to the Citadel."

* * *

Kai Leng was sitting at the kitchen table eating take-out food when the alarm began to buzz. The makeshift monitoring station was on the other side of the room. So he took his plate and went over to watch. The system incorporated motion detectors that selected which camera shots to record unless he took control. So as Leng stood there, spooning salarian curry into his mouth, he saw what he expected to see. Anderson entered the apartment first followed by Kahlee. The angle was from high up in a corner, which meant Leng had a good view of the door, and most of the living room.

Then something unexpected happened. Rather than close the door behind herself Kahlee stood off to one side and held it open. And that was when Hal McCann entered, followed by another man, and Paul Grayson's daughter! That was very surprising because McCann was dead. Or supposed to be, having been killed in the battle for the Cerberus space station, and disposed of by the turians.

The fact that McCann had survived was good news, or so it seemed to Leng, who'd been friendly with the man. But where had he been since the battle? And why was he on the Citadel? Leng put the bowl on the desk and sat down. A quick check confirmed that the auto record function was on.

The audio had a hollow quality but could easily be understood. There were three cameras in the living room. Leng took command of the system, which allowed him to zoom in and out. "Find a place to sit," Anderson said. "I'll get some drinks. We have a lot of catching up to do. Who wants to go first?"

Leng watched with interest as Gillian described the first part of the voyage on the *Idenna,* followed by the battle with the batarians, and the freeing of the slaves. Anderson and Kahlee were clearly fascinated. But McCann seemed to be nervous. Why? He knew how the story would end after all—which was happily for him. Or was there something more? Something McCann hadn't told Gillian? *Yes,* Leng thought to himself, *Hal is in a jam.*

"So," Gillian concluded, "once Hal told us that my father had been killed I wanted to learn more. Plus there was a shipload of slaves to consider, all of whom wanted to make their way back to civilization. So we came here. And I asked Hal to stick with us until we could meet with you. He has quite a story to tell. Don't you, Hal?"

Leng thought he could detect an ominous undertone to the question and watched McCann start to fidget. The story he told about his activities on the Cerberus space station and the turian attack was stripped to the bone. And Leng knew why. McCann didn't want Gillian to learn the truth, which was that he'd been a key member of the experimental lab team, and was partially responsible for the way in which Grayson's body had been modified.

Kahlee looked at Anderson as McCann completed his story and then to Gillian. "I'm so sorry, honey . . . But David and I know who killed your father and why. As you may or may not know, the head of Cerberus is called 'the Illusive Man.' He performed experiments on your father, but your father managed to escape, and went to the academy. We aren't entirely sure why . . . He may have been forced to do so by the

Reapers as part of an effort to gather information about our most promising biotics. There was a terrible fight—and a Cerberus assassin shot your father."

Tears were rolling down Gillian's face. "But you killed him, right?"

"No," Anderson answered. "We didn't. *I* didn't. But I could have and I should have. And for that I apologize."

But you shot me in both legs, Leng thought bitterly. *And you will pay.*

"Remember," Kahlee cautioned. "The assassin was a tool. The Illusive Man is the *real* killer."

Gillian wiped the tears away. "Then I need to find him. Where is he?"

"Nobody knows," Anderson said, "unless Hal can tell us. How 'bout it? Did the Illusive Man have a hidey-hole? A place to run to?"

McCann shook his head. "You know where I've been . . . Besides, that sort of information was way above my pay grade."

"Then we've got to focus on finding him," Gillian said as her chin quivered. "Then I'll kill him."

"That isn't realistic," Anderson said. "He's very well protected. And as important as destroying Cerberus is, there's something even more urgent to work on. And that's the need to stop the Reapers. The problem is the Council believes the threat has been dealt with. Maybe they should hear from Hal here."

McCann looked very uncomfortable but never got the chance to respond because Gillian was on her feet by then. "No! The Illusive Man is responsible for my father's death and I'm going to find him."

"Wait," Hendel said. "Let's talk about this."

But it was too late. Gillian was on her way out by then. Hendel stood as if to follow her but Kahlee held up a hand. "Let her go. She's upset and for good reason. Later, after she walks it off, she'll listen to reason."

That suggestion was followed by an uncomfortable silence that McCann broke by getting to his feet. "If it's all the same to you, I'll leave now."

Kahlee frowned. "He works for Cerberus. Maybe we should call C-Sec."

"And then what?" Hendel asked cynically. "The only proof we have is what McCann told us. And what's to keep him from changing his story?"

"What indeed?" Leng said out loud, as McCann made for the front door. "What indeed?"

Somewhere in the Crescent Nebula

The Illusive Man watched as a pale moon parted company with the jagged horizon and began another arc across the star-dusted sky. The satellite had been captured by the planet's gravitational pull millions of years earlier and been held prisoner ever since. The relationship was, he thought, somewhat analogous to the situation confronting the human race. They too had been forced to orbit something larger, in this case a galaxy-spanning society they couldn't control yet were increasingly affected by. So much so that he was beginning to wonder if the Systems Alliance, the organization that represented all of the human colonies in Citadel space, was truly human anymore.

The process of integration was often held up as a virtue. But the price for integration was compromise—

thousands of small, seemingly innocuous concessions, agreements, and "understandings" that combined to erode humanity's independence. And that was what made the situation so urgent. If Cerberus failed to act quickly enough the very thing it was created to save would be subsumed.

The Illusive Man's thoughts were interrupted by the sound of a tone. He swiveled to the right and the image of a heavily disguised Kai Leng blossomed in front of him. The background was out of focus. "I have a surprise for you."

The Illusive Man selected a cigarette from the case. "What kind of surprise?"

"Hal McCann is alive."

The Illusive Man lit the tube of tobacco and took the smoke deep into his lungs. "You're sure?"

"Positive. He showed up on the Citadel along with Grayson's daughter and the ex-security chief from the Grissom Academy. They met with David Anderson and Kahlee Sanders. I have all of it on a chip."

"Play it." The Illusive Man considered a dozen scenarios as he watched Gillian, McCann, and the rest of them interact. His mind was made up by the time the playback was over. "Unfortunately McCann has a self-admitted gambling addiction. It's just a matter of time before he gets into some sort of trouble. At that point he may or may not surface in front of the Council. They could use him to discredit Cerberus."

A brief moment of silence ensued. There was no discernible expression on Leng's face. But the Illusive Man had known the operative for a long time by then and recognized the slight tightness around Leng's eyes and a certain rigidity to the way he held his head.

"You were friends as I recall . . . Should I have someone else handle the sanction?"

"We had drinks together a couple of times. And played cards on the station. 'Friends' is too strong a word."

The Illusive Man blew a stream of smoke out toward the holo. The picture shivered. "So you're willing?"

"Yes."

"Good. That brings us to Grayson's daughter Gillian. On the one hand she seems like a somewhat overwrought teenager who is mourning her father. As such she deserves our patience and understanding.

"However," the Illusive Man continued as he tapped some ash into a tray, "passion is a very dangerous thing. Take your case for example. The Alliance arrested you for killing a krogan in a bar fight. A *krogan* for god's sake . . . With a knife. They should have given you a medal. Instead they sent you off to prison. And the injustice of that made you so passionate about the human cause that you were transformed from the equivalent of raw ore into a finished blade. So in considering Gillian's fate it's important to look beyond what she is to what she might become. And that is someone dangerous."

"Understood."

"So," the Illusive Man said, "enough about McCann and the girl. You were given a task. . . . Where is Grayson's body?"

A less confident operative might have flinched or offered a host of excuses. But not Leng. "I don't have control of it yet."

"That's disappointing."

"I'll work on it."

"See that you do. So long as the Council has custody of the body they can use it against us. Difficult days lay ahead. Our credibility will be important. And Kai . . ."

"Yes?"

"I'm told that you're using a cane. Take care of that leg."

The holo collapsed and the Illusive Man smiled grimly. The closing comment had been calculated to let Leng know that even *he* was subject to surveillance and to demonstrate that the head of Cerberus valued him. *Because it is,* the Illusive Man thought to himself, *important to be human.*

For the first time in her life Gillian felt free. Because for as long as she could remember she had been a captive. First of the Grissom Academy then of the quarian fleet. Now, having walked out on her minders she could do whatever she wanted. Even if Hendel and Kahlee disagreed with it.

But they weren't entirely wrong. Gillian knew that. The Illusive Man would be well protected. Just as they said he would be. But that was a problem which could be solved by taking her already considerable biotic powers and enhancing them further. It would take money of course, and fortunately Gillian had some. There was a large safe in the batarian slave ship. And after two failed attempts she'd been able to hack it, thereby gaining access to a stash of Beryllium slugs. Each of them weighed about one hundred grams and was worth a thousand credits. Most of the find was apportioned out to the *Idenna*'s crew, including Gillian, and the rest had been given to the freed slaves.

Gillian's first task therefore was to choose a supplier. A first-rate manufacturer with the resources to amp her overall effectiveness by at least ten percent. With nowhere else to go she checked into a boxtel. It was noisier than she preferred, but finally began to quiet down around 1:00 a.m., allowing her to fall asleep.

When morning came, and she awoke, it was to a renewed sense of purpose. Gillian took a shower, left the boxtel, and ate breakfast in a small cafe. From there it was onto a public shuttle and off to visit the high-rise building where the asari-sponsored Armali Council was quartered. The council represented a number of manufacturing guilds, one of which was dedicated to making and installing what many considered to be the finest biotic implants available in the galaxy.

Having exited the shuttle Gillian walked a short distance to the building and paused to look up. The structure was hundreds of feet tall and looked like a cluster of crystal shafts. They were of various lengths and joined together at the center.

The high-rise made Gillian feel small. But she gathered her courage, made her way up a flight of stairs, and followed a turian inside. The lobby was huge. An asari stood behind a slightly curved reception counter. Gillian thought of herself as homely and wondered what it was like to be so beautiful. The receptionist smiled politely. "Can I help you?"

"I would like to talk to a member of the Biotics Guild about acquiring some new implants."

The expression on the asari's face changed fractionally as if she was looking at Gillian in a new light. "Of course. Please proceed to the twelfth floor. I'll let them know you're coming."

An elevator carried Gillian and half a dozen other people up past transparent offices to the twelfth floor. An asari in a sleek ankle-length lab coat was waiting to greet her. "Welcome to the Biotics Guild. My name is Nomi E'Lan. And you are?"

"Gillian Grayson."

"It's a pleasure to meet you. I understand that you're interested in acquiring an upgrade. Is that true?"

"Yes."

"And you are a level?"

"Three."

"Excellent. Please follow me. The first step is to take readings on the implants you have now."

That made sense so Gillian allowed herself to be steered down a hall and into a well-equipped lab. "Please step behind the screen and remove your clothes," E'Lan said. "Then I'd like you to lay facedown on the table."

Like most biotics Gillian had a port in the back of her neck that could be used to access the tiny amplifiers that were located throughout her nervous system. They functioned to create the mass effect fields that enabled Gillian to manipulate dark energy. And some implants were better than others. So it wasn't unusual for biotics to buy upgrades when they could afford to do so.

Once on the table, with her hair pulled to one side, Gillian gritted her teeth as a probe was inserted into her neck port. There was a brief moment of pain, followed by a tingling sensation, and some involuntary muscle contractions as electronic impulses were sent to various parts of her body. Then E'Lan pressed small paddles against the points where implants had been inserted so that a computer could measure the amount of resistance in between them. The diagnostic process continued for about five minutes before the needlelike instrument was withdrawn from Gillian's neck port. "Okay," E'Lan said, "you can get dressed now. I have what I need. Thank you."

Gillian stepped behind the screen where she buckled the belt containing the Beryllium slugs around her waist before putting her clothes back on. "So," Gillian said as she emerged, "what do you think?"

E'Lan was standing in front of a podium-style terminal eyeing the data that scrolled in front of her. "It looks like you're equipped with solid Level Four implants complete with virtual intelligence chips. It's a good setup, better than average actually, but we can improve on it."

"By how much?"

"I think you could expect a ten percent or better increase in power—along with an equivalent improvement where duration is concerned. But I'll be able to give you a better idea after we receive a technical download from the facility where your amps were installed."

Gillian frowned. Would the academy cooperate? And if so, how much time would the process consume? "How long will that take?"

"Oh, a couple of weeks should do it," E'Lan said

breezily. "Then we'll put you on the schedule for an upgrade."

"You don't understand," Gillian said tightly. "I need the amps *now*. Today."

It wasn't clear how they had been summoned, but suddenly two additional asari entered the room, and they were dressed in matching suits of light armor. And even though nothing had been said Gillian sensed that they were biotics. *Powerful* biotics. E'Lan smiled gently. "Then I'm afraid we won't be able to help you. We require a full workup before we can perform an upgrade. The ethical guidelines we adhere to are very clear in that regard."

Gillian was down on the street ten minutes later. She was very disappointed. But not about to give up. "Where there's a will there's a way." That's what Hendel liked to say. And Gillian would find the way.

Kai Leng was going to kill both Gillian Grayson and Hal McCann—but had chosen to kill the ex-Cerberus employee first. Because McCann could leave the Citadel at any time and Leng figured the teenager would stick around for a while.

Then, once both sanctions were completed, Leng would go to work on retrieving Grayson's body. A much more difficult task since it was being held in the biological evidence section of C-Sec's Forensic Lab. A reality that the Illusive Man wasn't aware of or didn't care about. Not that it mattered because Leng took pride in solving such problems.

So as darkness settled over the Citadel, and most of the population went to their various homes, what Leng thought of as the night people began to take over. Some, like Leng, were predators. And some, like McCann, were prey. And finding them, especially on such a huge space station, would require patience.

Still, on most planets the wild game could be depended upon to visit a watering hole come sundown, which in this case meant a bar or club. The problem was that there were hundreds if not thousands of such establishments on the Citadel.

But as Leng left his apartment, and went down to the street, he had a pretty good idea of how to narrow the possibilities. McCann was an inveterate gambler. As such, he was likely to favor those establishments that offered games of chance as well as alcohol.

The first place on Leng's list was a club called Flux. It was easy to reach from the upper wards and was located near the markets. A cane was a sign of weakness. So Leng left it at home. Each step produced a twinge of pain. But a limp could attract the wrong sort of attention too—so he forced himself to walk normally.

Leng knew where he was going but stopped to consult a public terminal so he could check his six. It was silly. He knew that. But the comment about the cane had wormed its way into his head. Just as the Illusive Man had intended.

What made the situation so ridiculous was the fact that spotting the individual assigned to watch him wouldn't make any difference. He would still do what he had been assigned to do the way he planned to do it. But the fact that he could be watched without detecting the person carrying out the surveillance was not only an affront to his pride but dangerous, because Cerberus had enemies. Lots of them.

The effort was to no avail. Either the Illusive Man's operative was very, very good or had the night off. So Leng followed a steady stream of people toward the markets before taking the turn that led him to the Flux. It was a relatively new nightclub with a bar and dance floor on the main level and a casino on the mezzanine.

The music was loud, the place was packed with young professionals, and, as Leng entered the bar area, there was no sign of McCann. But that wasn't too surprising, because if the ex-Cerberus employee was present, he would probably be one level up. Still, it paid to be careful, so Leng checked the men's room before climbing the stairs to the casino.

It wasn't as crowded as the first floor, but was still doing a respectable business, judging from the fact that most of the tables were in use. At this point more stealth was called for because Leng had no way to know how McCann would react to the sudden arrival of a Cerberus operative. Would it be a case of hail-fellow-well-met? Or would the life support tech bolt?

Leng had left *all* of the Forbes identity back at the apartment, including the peel-off face that made him look fifteen years older than he actually was. But he couldn't wander around looking like himself, not if he planned to kill someone, so he was wearing a second disguise. One that had the effect of pushing his hairline back, flattening his nose, and emphasizing his cheekbones. It was a tough-looking face and appropriate for hanging out in bars. It was also attractive, to some women anyway, and it wasn't long before Leng felt someone touch his arm. "Hi, honey, it's good to see you again."

They had never met, and both of them knew it, but Leng played along. "You too . . . I like your dress. What there is of it."

The woman's hair was an unlikely shade of green and she was wearing a dress that consisted of two tubes of elastic cloth. One hugged her breasts and the other covered her hips. The fabric sparkled as light hit it. The compliment produced a smile. "Less is more."

"How true . . . Can I buy you a drink?"

"Yes, please. A Nova would be nice."

Leng left her standing next to a waist-high table and went over to the casino's bar. Then, as the bartender came over to serve him, he activated the omni-tool. The picture of McCann was ready. "Have you seen my buddy? We were supposed to meet up here."

The volus shook his head. "I've had no contact with that individual."

"Okay, thanks. I'll have a Nova and a shot of sake. Honzo if you have it."

Armed with the drinks Leng returned to the table. The woman's name was Marcy, and he let her natter on about her job as a hairdresser for a while, before punching up the picture of McCann. "This guy owes me two hundred credits. Have you seen him? He likes to gamble—so he might visit the casino from time to time."

Marcy looked at the picture and shook her head. "No, I haven't." When she looked up at him Leng realized that her eyes matched her hair. "What will you do to him?"

"I'll squeeze him until my credits come out," Leng responded.

"Squeezing can be nice."

Leng grinned. "We were made for each other. Will you be here tomorrow?"

Marcy looked disappointed. "Probably."

"Good. I'll have my two hundred credits by then and you can help me spend them."

Marcy brightened. "That sounds like fun."

"It will be," Leng promised, as he finished the sake. "Be careful out there." And with that he left.

The next place on Leng's list was the Dark Star Lounge. It was located on the twenty-eighth floor of a high-rise with a spectacular view of the Presidium ring. And as Leng made his way past a fancy restaurant and into a very quiet bar, he realized that the Dark Star was an unlikely habitat for a working stiff like McCann. Still, he was there, so it made sense to stroll between the gaming tables and eyeball the formally clad clientele. As expected, McCann was nowhere to be seen, and that included the casino area, where muted applause signaled a win.

So having checked the Dark Star Lounge, Leng left for what he hoped would be a more productive hunting ground. And that was the dive called Chora's Den. The trip took a good twenty minutes but the moment he walked inside Leng knew it was the sort of place McCann would gravitate to. There was a central bar with private booths all around the perimeter of the room. And each booth was equipped with a terminal on which a wide variety of virtual games could be played.

Slowly, so as to avoid attracting undue attention, Leng circled the room. But much to his disappointment McCann was nowhere to be seen. There were other bars. Lots of them. But rather than leave for the next place on the list Leng decided to rest his leg and hang around for a while. He took a seat that offered an unobstructed view of the main entrance and ordered a sake.

Some bars were set up to cater to a specific race, but Chora's Den had a very diverse clientele. And while Leng didn't like most aliens, there was no denying that the asari dancer who occupied the platform at the very center of the bar was fun to look at, and when she winked at him he winked back.

But in spite of the entertainment the next hour passed slowly, *too* slowly, and Leng was about to leave when Hal McCann walked through the door. Leng put his head down as the ex-Cerberus employee paused to look around. Then, having seen Leng but not recognized him, McCann made his way to an empty booth. After shoving a chip into the terminal he began to play. The light from the screen gave his face a bluish cast.

Now there was a decision to be made. Leng could sit down next to McCann, engage him in conversation, and slash his femoral artery. McCann would lose consciousness in about thirty seconds—and bleed out within three minutes. Plenty of time for an escape. But McCann might make noise and it was impossible to know how the other customers would react.

The other possibility was to wait for McCann to go to the men's room and take him out there. That could get complicated if the can was being used by others—but Leng figured he could schmooze McCann long enough to get him alone.

There should have been a *third* option, which was to follow McCann out onto the street, but Leng wasn't sure his leg was up to a brisk walk, never mind the possibility of a chase. So he ordered another shot of sake and settled in to wait. Fifteen minutes later McCann was still sitting in his booth and Leng needed to pee. So he went into the filthy men's room, and was standing in front of a urinal, when McCann stepped into the slot right next to him. Leng flushed and zipped his fly. "Hey, Hal, how're you doing?"

McCann turned to look at the stranger and frowned. "Do I know you?"

"It's your old friend, Kai Leng."

McCann had stepped away from the urinal by that time. The first expression to appear on his face was one of pleasure. The second reflected concern. "You're wearing a disguise. *Why?*"

"That's what I do," Leng replied lightly, as he placed himself between McCann and the exit. "You know that."

McCann's right arm was dangling at his side. There must have been a long narrow pocket on his pants leg, because the telescoping baton seemed to materialize out of nowhere. There was a loud click as four sections of spring steel shot out of the handle and locked themselves in place. "Don't try to spin me, Kai . . . The Illusive Man sent you."

"Okay, he sent me," Leng agreed, he eyed the baton. "So let's get this over with."

McCann raised his left hand, and Leng blocked the downward blow, but took a knee in the crotch. Or would have except he turned his hips at the last moment and took the blow on his right thigh. McCann charged him. The weight of the other man's body slammed Leng against the wall. He saw an opening, brought the heel of a hand up, and hit McCann's jaw. That sent the other man reeling. He hit the opposite wall and slid to the floor. Eager to finish the fight, Leng went after him.

Desperate to defend himself, McCann lashed out. The steel shaft made a whirring sound as it cut through the air and struck Leng's leg. His *right* leg. Leng heard himself scream as he fell. But even then his mind was working. Did McCann know about his wound? No, the location of the strike was a matter of bad luck.

Leng rolled onto his back as McCann struggled to stand. A professional would have delivered a blow at Leng's exposed head—or made good his escape at that point. But McCann was pleased with himself and wanted to savor the moment. "Well, well. So much for the famous Kai Leng. I know how you feel about aliens. How's it feel to roll around in their piss?"

"You tell me," Leng said through gritted teeth, as he pulled the knife out from under his waist-length jacket. The needle-sharp point passed down through the top of McCann's boot and hit the floor. McCann let go of the baton to grab his foot. A steady stream of swear words could be heard as he took two hops and fell.

Having recovered the baton, Leng pounced on McCann, pressed the steel rod down on his windpipe, and applied all of his weight. The other man's eyes bulged, and his back arched, as he tried to push Leng away. Then McCann jerked convulsively and it was over.

Leng rolled off the body, paused to recover the knife, and came to his feet. It wasn't easy to drag McCann's body into a stall, and prop him up on a toilet, but the effort was worth it. Chances were that it would be closing time before anyone discovered the body. And Leng would be long gone by then. So there was plenty of time to wash up, swallow a pain tab, and leave the premises. It was, all things considered, a job well done.

FIVE

On the Citadel

Having failed to obtain an upgrade from the asari Biotics Guild, Gillian was determined to get it somewhere else. And that was why she agreed to follow a man named Horst Acara down into the depths of the red ward. He was a bit overweight, dressed in a shabby business suit, and looked back occasionally as if to make sure that she hadn't deserted him. Each time he did so a smile appeared on his moonlike face. "Don't worry, we're almost there."

It had grown warmer for some reason, and as Gillian followed Acara down an ancient passageway the steady *thump, thump, thump* of what might have been a giant heart was at work somewhere nearby. There were no aliens to be seen. Just tired, hollow-eyed humans, lounging in doorways, sitting on stoops watching whatever happened to pass by. They had entered the ghetto known as Hu-Town. A place where humans who had been unable to find success with the Citadel's alien-dominated society often wound up. Their bitterness was plain to see on the graffiti-covered walls and in the professionally produced ads that crawled the walls. One of them read, "Cerberus will sound the call. Be ready."

Ready for what? Gillian wondered. Not that it mattered. Her purpose was to kill the man in charge of the organization. People like Anderson and Kahlee could worry about the politics of it.

"We're almost there," Acara said for the fifth or sixth time. "These quarters are just temporary mind you. We'll be moving up to one of the higher levels soon."

Gillian had met Acara in the markets, where the salesman had a poorly positioned one-man kiosk off in a gloomy corner. A spot so remote Gillian would never have noticed it if she hadn't been looking for an out-of-the-way place to eat her lunch. But having seen the sign that read CUSTOM AMPS, Gillian went to investigate. That was when Acara launched into his sales pitch. The problem, he claimed, was that all of the major providers were set up to force an entire suite of proprietary amps onto users, and then hold them captive by refusing to create cross-platform applications. A strategy aimed at building market share and limiting competition.

However, thanks to the virtual intelligence chips devised by Custom Amps, it was possible to mix and match implants from different manufacturers, thereby providing biotics with increased power and duration. That was music to Gillian's ears as was the company's willingness to service clients on a demand basis.

Did that mean they were hard up for customers? Yes, Gillian figured it did. But Acara's pitch appealed to both her rebellious sensibility *and* the need for additional offensive and defensive capability. "Here we

are," Acara said, as they turned into a side passageway. A sign that read CUSTOM AMPS winked monoto-
nously as the salesman entered a code into the keypad,
and the door hissed out of the way. The air that invaded Gillian's nostrils was tinged with ozone and the
faint odor of curry. Boxes of miscellaneous gear were
stacked against both sides of the entryway, leaving
very little room to walk.

The corridor opened into a reception area that
didn't have a receptionist but was furnished with a
rumpled bed. A salarian was flaked out on it sound
asleep. "Dr. Sani is a workaholic," Acara explained,
"so he sleeps here sometimes. Hey, doc, wake up. We
have a visitor. Gillian here wants to buy some amps."

Sani turned over, opened his eyes, and said something unintelligible. Then having spotted Gillian he
rolled onto his feet. The salarian had the long narrow
face typical of his race, a slightly downturned mouth,
and a slender body. Big luminous eyes blinked as he
spoke. "Welcome. No offense, but you don't *look* like
a biotic."

Gillian felt a sense of annoyance, shaped some of
the energy available around her, and gave it purpose.
"Whoa! Put me down," Acara insisted, as Gillian
lifted him up off the floor.

"You are more than you appear to be," Sani said
tactlessly, as Gillian put Acara down. "Please follow
me."

The lighting grew brighter as the salarian led the
way into what was obviously intended to be a lab,
but looked nothing like the sleek, well-organized facility that the Biotics Guild ran. Racks of equipment
lined the walls, cables ran every which way, and the

table at the center of the space looked like salvage from an old med clinic. "We don't go for the fancy stuff," Acara said by way of explanation. "That keeps the overhead down."

"Take your clothes off," Sani ordered, "and lay facedown on the table."

Gillian frowned. "What? No gown?"

"Sorry," Sani said, as he opened a locker. "Here."

The gown he gave her had clearly been worn before. Gillian looked from the garment over to Dr. Sani. "Are you sure you know what you're doing?"

The salarian's look of perpetual disapproval remained unchanged. "I can double your power—and triple the time available to use it."

There was a moment of silence. Gillian nodded. "If you gentlemen will step out of the room, I'll put the gown on."

The initial part of the process was quite similar to the examination at the Biotic Guild. Gillian experienced a moment of pain followed by a tingling sensation, and involuntary muscle contractions. That lasted for a good ten minutes or so as Dr. Sani used a variety of instruments to create a computerized map of Gillian's implants. The process was accompanied by Sani's barely audible narration. "Hmmm . . . Not bad. Uh-oh, it looks like amp 23 is starting to fade. Nexus 4.5 is suboptimal," and so forth until the process was complete.

"So," Sani announced, "I have good news for you. By tying equipment manufactured by HMBA and Kassa Fabrication together with our virtual intelligence chips, I will be able to provide you with a substantial improvement in performance. Shall we proceed?"

Gillian was still lying facedown on the table and wished she could see the salarian's face. Not that it would make much difference. His expressions revealed very little and she was mentally and emotionally committed by then. "Yes," she said into the table. "Let's proceed."

There were no medical exams or record checks. Dr. Sani went right to work. What followed was a grueling process during which the old implants were removed and new ones were installed. And, because each amp had to be tested, it seemed as if the ordeal would go on forever.

The stress of it took a lot out of her and Gillian found herself drifting in and out of consciousness after a while. There were shadowy dreams, all haunted by the same half-seen figure of a person who might have been her father, or the man responsible for her father's death. She couldn't tell which. Finally a voice summoned her back from the never-never land she had taken refuge in. "Miss Grayson? Can you hear me? The procedure is over."

It took Gillian the better part of five minutes to clear her head, roll over, and get off the table. All of the spots where the old implants had been removed, and new ones had been installed, felt sore. She staggered and Acara took her arm. "Careful," he said, "it will take awhile for your nervous system to adjust."

Gillian jerked her arm away. "I'll be all right," she insisted. "Give me some privacy."

So Acara and Sani stepped out into the reception area. It took Gillian longer than usual to get dressed.

Once the process was complete she called them back in. The belt containing six kilos of Beryllium slugs was dangling from her right hand. "What do I owe you?"

A preliminary fee had been set with Acara, but Sani had been forced to use more HMBA amps than anticipated, which made the final price higher. So once the transaction was complete Gillian found herself buckling a much lighter belt. Did she have enough slugs to reach Omega? She hoped so. "That's it? We're finished?"

"Not quite," Sani responded. "Computer readouts are one thing, but I would like to field test the entire system. Follow me."

The salarian led Gillian and Acara through a maze of passageways and onto an elevator that lowered them six levels and opened onto a corridor where the air was thick with the stench of garbage. "Where are we?" Gillian wanted to know.

"The garbage that can't be recycled ends up here," Sani replied. "It's dumped into bins which are loaded onto specially designed ships. They take the containers out to the Widow and drop them into orbit. Gravity takes care of the rest."

Gillian knew that the Widow was the nearest sun. She held her nose. It was necessary to shout in order to be heard over the sound of heavy machinery. "And we're here because?"

"Because of *this*," Sani said, as he led her onto a small observation platform. They were looking out over an enormous compartment. There wasn't much lighting, but dozens of firefly-like robotic drones could be seen, nosing about and sending video off to the computer that was in charge of the largely automated system.

Huge bins rattled, clanked, and rumbled as they were shuttled under funnels from which rivers of refuse flowed. Once a container was full the car that it was sitting on was pulled to the next station, where a lid was applied. Sparks flew as robotic arms came in to weld the top in place. Then it was off to a dimly seen lock through which the modules would have to pass before being loaded into the hold of a waiting ship. "Okay, now what?" Gillian inquired.

"Focus on the containers that are full. Then, once you're ready, create the most powerful singularity that you can."

As Gillian summoned all of her energy, she felt an additional surge, as her power was amplified to an extent never experienced before. It grew so large, and so powerful, that it was a struggle to contain it. Then, when it felt as if every fiber of her body might be ripped apart, she gave the energy purpose. And the results were nothing less than spectacular. *All* of the garbage in *all* of the open bins was sucked into what looked like a raging cyclone. Tons of refuse came spewing out of the vortex a few seconds later. It fell like stinking snow until the entire compartment was covered in a thick layer of the stuff. Something shorted, the system ground to a stop, and a klaxon began to beep.

Gillian, who was appalled by the extent of the destruction, took a step backward. "My god, did I do that?"

Dr. Sani nodded. And for the first time Gillian saw the hint of what might have been a smile on his face.

"You sure did. I don't know where you're headed, or what you plan to do," Sani said. "But I know this . . . You're ready."

Kahlee had spent the entire day looking for Gillian without finding a trace of her. In retrospect she realized that it had been a mistake to let the impetuous youngster leave. Now *two* of her ex-students were missing—and she felt miserable as she entered the apartment. Anderson and Varma were waiting for her.

Just the sight of the C-Sec officer was enough to give Kahlee a sinking feeling. Anderson shook his head. "I know what you're thinking. Gillian is fine. Or so we assume. C-Sec has pictures of her entering Hu-Town. Then she disappeared. Hendel is still looking for her and Lieutenant Varma wants to talk to us about someone else."

"That's true," Varma said. "I'm here because of Hal McCann. Someone killed him. And given the connection with Gillian I thought it would be a good idea to speak with you. Neither one of you had any contact with McCann after he left your apartment. Is that correct?"

Kahlee took a seat on the couch. "Yes, it is. McCann was very uncomfortable around us. And for good reason given the Cerberus connection. What happened?"

"He was killed in a gentleman's club called Chora's Den."

"I know the place," Anderson admitted sheepishly. "It's pretty rough."

Kahlee wrinkled her nose. "Men."

Varma smiled. "According to members of the club's staff McCann entered by himself, took a booth, and made use of the gambling terminal located there. Eventually he got up to visit the men's room. According to video captured by one of the bar's surveillance cameras, another human was already in there. For reasons we aren't sure of they got into a fight and McCann was killed. A janitor found his body sitting on a toilet hours later. The killer was long gone by then."

"So it could have been a random bar fight *or* a hit," Anderson mused.

"Exactly," Varma agreed. "Although I'd put my money on the second possibility given McCann's past."

Khalee frowned. "You think Cerebus was responsible?"

"I think that's a workable hypothesis," Varma agreed cautiously. "And one that is supported by the fact that once the killer left Chora's Den he did an excellent job of avoiding our cameras. The sort of thing one would expect from a professional."

The professional that Varma was referring to was nearby, sitting in his apartment, and watching as Anderson, Kahlee, and Varma discussed the way he had murdered Hal McCann. The hit hadn't been as clean as he would have preferred, but dead is dead, and McCann was extremely dead.

Ideally he would have followed up the McCann sanction by killing the girl named Gillian. But based on what he'd heard, the teenager had dropped out of sight. However, there was something he could do while waiting for Gillian to make an appearance, and that was to steal Grayson's body. Something the Illusive Man had been very insistent about. It wouldn't be easy however. Not according to the research he had carried out over the last day or so. Because the corpse was stored in C-Sec's Forensic Lab. A facility located underneath the Presidium and protected by a state-of-the-art security system.

Though less than perfect his right leg was better thanks to a liberal application of medi-gel and some rest. So having set the surveillance system to "record" and taken on a new disguise, Leng placed a brand-new camera into a small bag and set out for an address on the blue ward. There was plenty of time—and the fake sunlight felt good.

Wilbur Obey was a man of many habits. He always got up at six thirty and was at work by eight, so he could leave at five. Then came a stop at one of three restaurants for some takeout to carry home.

Someone else might have found such a routine to be stultifying, but Obey treasured it. Because unlike the rest of the things that occurred on the Citadel, he could control it. Obey took great comfort from organizing his day and keeping his studio apartment just so, with a place for everything and everything in its place.

So as he left Suki's wrap shop and made his way home, he was looking forward to a couple of days in splendid isolation. There were chores to do, a virtual pet to play with, and some favorite holo shows to watch. The doors to Obey's building parted to welcome him into an undecorated lobby. A short flight of stairs took him down to a landing and the door to his apartment.

Obey entered the pass code, waited for the barrier to slide out of the way, and stepped inside. It was dark and he was about to say, "Lights on," when he heard the swish of fabric. Obey had just started to turn toward the sound when the needle entered his neck and he felt a sudden stab of pain. Suddenly he was falling, but completely conscious and able to understand what was said to him, as he hit the floor. "This won't take long," a voice said conversationally.

"First, I'm going to tape your eyes open. Then I'll take pictures of your retinas with a special camera. That's a bother of course, but absolutely necessary because once they're removed from a body, retinas begin to deteriorate very quickly."

Obey tried to object, tried to struggle, but his body was paralyzed. Meanwhile his eyelids had been pulled back and secured in place. Obey knew his assailant was male from the sound of his voice, but couldn't see anything more than a shadowy presence bending over him, as some sort of device was pressed against his face. "It's a camera," the voice explained, as a series of flashes strobed Obey's eyes.

"There," the man said. "That should do it. I have what I need. Sorry about this, but we're fighting a war, and that means casualties." Obey was still thinking about that, still trying to make sense of it, when Leng cut his throat.

Leng liked to work by himself to the extent that such a thing was possible. But there were times when it was necessary to hire help. And the mission to recover Grayson's body was such an occasion. Not because Leng needed assistance to penetrate C-Sec's Forensic Lab. He could accomplish that by himself. No, the problem was that Grayson's corpse and the gas-filled chamber in which the remains were stored would be too heavy for one person to manage alone.

But where to find the kind of people he was looking for? A place like Chora's Den would have been ideal, but he couldn't go back there, so Leng chose to cruise some of the bars adjacent to Spaceport 5. The dives located around the inner ring were packed with all manner of spacers, mercenaries, and small-time crooks. Just the sort of people he was looking for.

Having ducked in and out of a mostly empty bar, and a place that catered to asari, Leng entered the Free Fall Club. It catered to a diverse mix of patrons including humans, salarians, turians, batarians, and a volus or two. And judging from the wary looks that were directed his way, plenty of deals were being done around the room.

A layer of blue smoke hung just below the ceiling, salarian techno music thumped in the background, and a zero-gee slam ball game could be seen on the wall screens. A cheer went up as the team from the red ward scored on their opponents.

Leng looked around, spotted a recently vacated table, and went to claim it. There were no stools. Just pole-mounted circular tables that could be raised or lowered according to need. Leng hadn't been there for more than a minute when a scantily clad asari arrived to take his order. "I'd like a Honzo," the operative said, "and a favor as well. The kind that could earn you a generous tip."

"We aren't allowed to have sex with customers," she replied.

Leng grinned understandingly. "No, I'm talking about a different kind of favor. I need to hire a couple of men. The kind who can lift a heavy load, avoid tripping over their own feet, and keep their mouths shut. Can you help me?"

The asari had beautiful green eyes. The right one winked at Leng. "One Honzo and two humans coming up!" Then she was gone.

The sake arrived a few minutes later. Leng was about halfway through his drink when an older man appeared next to the table. He had shoulder-length gray hair, two days worth of stubble, and the look of a man who had fallen on hard times. "The name's Hobbs. Rex Hobbs. I hear you're hiring."

Leng eyed the man. "That's right . . . Tell me a little bit about yourself."

Hobbs shrugged. "I've done a little bit of everything, but I got fired recently, and I'm broke."

"Broke enough to take a couple of chances?"

Hobbs produced a wry smile. "It wouldn't be the first time."

Leng took a sip of sake. "I'm looking for a couple of people who can help me recover an item that a certain organization has under lock and key. I have the means to get through security. But I'll need help hauling the object away."

"Sounds interesting," Hobbs replied. "What kind of object are we talking about?"

"A body."

"As in a *dead* body?"

"Exactly."

"Why?"

"Why not? I'll pay you a thousand credits for two days of work."

Hobbs gave it some thought. "You can get us in? And out? Without being caught?"

Leng shrugged. "There are no guarantees. But I'll be there throughout. Taking the same chances you do."

What might have been greed glittered in Hobbs's eyes. He nodded. "I'm in."

"Good. I'll buy you a drink. Let's see if the third member of our team shows up."

A man who was clearly drunk showed up at the table shortly thereafter and was rejected. Maybe he could get sober and stay that way, but Leng didn't have the time or the desire to find out.

Fifteen minutes passed before the next candidate appeared. Her name was Ree Nefari and she had dark skin, hair that hung in dreadlocks, and a lip piercing. The silver pin was clearly meant to be a replica of a human thigh bone. Leng frowned. "You are female."

Nefari smiled. "I can see that it's going to be damned near impossible to put anything over on you."

"I was looking for a male."

"Why?"

"The job involves lifting a heavy weight."

Nefari nodded. "I'll tell you what . . . I'll arm wrestle the ape here. If I put him down the job is mine."

There was a thin smile on Hobbs's lips. "Sure, bitch . . . Bring it on."

Leng shrugged. "Okay, it's a deal."

Leng could tell that Hobbs was in trouble the moment the two combatants locked hands. Nefari was strong, confident, and had clearly beaten men before. In fact, Leng had a sneaking hunch that she made at least part of her living putting suckers in their place. But it was too late for Hobbs to back out, so when Leng said "Go!" the other man put everything he had into forcing Nefari's arm down.

But it was a wasted effort. Nefari's arm was like a steel bar. She smiled beatifically as Hobbs's face turned red. "Is that it?" she inquired sweetly. "Are you all in?"

Hobbs answered with a grunt.

"Okay," Nefari replied. "Let's talk about how much you're going to pay me."

There was an audible thump as Hobbs's arm hit the tabletop. The team was complete.

"Gillian! Stop!" Hendel shouted, as the teenager entered a monorail car, and the doors began to close. But if the youngster heard him there was no sign of it as Hendel was forced to jump aboard the next car back or lose her entirely. A batarian swore but was forced to move when Hendel pushed his way into the crowd of passengers and the train left the station.

Hendel had been searching for Gillian for the better part of two days by then. He'd combed the streets of Hu-Town, checked dozens of hotels, and spent hours visiting the sort of restaurants Gillian preferred. All to no avail. So he had given up, and was on his way back to Anderson and Kahlee's apartment, when he spotted Gillian standing on a monorail platform.

Hendel felt mixed emotions as the train began to slow. Gillian was alive! And seemingly healthy. But why hadn't she called? And what about the suitcase she was towing?

The monorail came to a halt, the doors hissed open, and people flooded out. Hendel allowed himself to be carried along, craning his neck to see if Gillian was getting off too, and was relieved to see that she was. He shouted, "Gillian!" but was too far away to be heard over all the background noise, so he began to run.

There were lots of people forcing him to zigzag through the crowd. And that was when he accidentally bumped into a very short-tempered krogan. "Hey, human, watch where you're going!" The warning was accompanied by a blow that sent Hendel sprawling. By the time he picked himself up, and resumed the chase, Gillian was no longer in sight.

Hendel began to run, but was more careful this time, and managed to avoid additional collisions. All he could do was follow the main flow of foot traffic in hopes that it would lead him to his quarry. Then he saw the sign that read BOARDING AREA and realized he was closing in on Spaceport 4.

Desperate to see over the people in front of him Hendel jumped up onto the top of a flat-topped trash chute and stood on his tiptoes. That was when he spotted Gillian just as she passed through the first security check.

Hendel's legs absorbed the jolt as he landed on the pavement and ran toward the entry point. A turian C-Sec officer was stationed there and held up a hand as the human came to a halt. "Pass, please."

"The girl," Hendel said breathlessly. "The one who

just passed through. I need to speak with her. It's very important."

"Sorry. Please stand to one side so others can pass."

Hendel had no choice but to obey. His eyes went to the reader board on which flight information was displayed. His spirits fell. According to the sign the ship that Gillian was about to board was bound for a lawless asteroid that was home to all manner of criminals, outlaws, and mercenaries. And Hendel realized, as the last call for boarding came over the PA system, there wasn't a damned thing he could do about it. Gillian was on her way to Omega.

The better part of eight hours had passed since Leng had recruited Nefari and Hobbs. Now, having gone over Leng's plan, and dressed in the blue scrubs that Evidence Technicians wore, the trio was about to enter the C-Sec Forensic Lab via the subsurface employee entrance.

Leng had chosen to invade the facility at night when fewer people were on duty. But in order to do so they had to get past the retinal scanner mounted next to the steel door. And that was where the copy of Obey's retinal patterns came into play as Leng produced a black box and held it up to the reader. It should work. It had in the past. But his heart was pounding anyway.

The scanner sought a retina, found one, and sent the resulting image to a computer. It confirmed that the person with that pattern of capillaries was authorized to enter the facility and ordered the door to open. That allowed all *three* of the humans to scoot into the employee break room. It was empty except for some utilitarian furniture and a vid screen that sensed their presence and turned itself on.

Leng felt a sense of exuberance. The first hurdle had been cleared. The next step was to figure out where to go. "Sit down," he ordered. "And if somebody comes in you're on a break."

Nefari and Hobbs did as they were told while Leng went over to a pedestal-mounted terminal where he activated the omni-tool strapped to his left arm. The device was equipped with the finest hacking software that Cerberus could buy and made short work of the level-one security layer designed to prevent unauthorized personnel from accessing floor diagrams, personnel rosters, and emergency procedures. All of which were considered to be confidential rather than secret.

Having accessed the system it was only a matter of thirty seconds or so before Leng was able to download the maps he needed. The first gave him the location of the utility room in which carts, gurneys, and the transportable stasis tanks were stored. The second showed the most direct route to the Sentient Storage Section. And according to the listing it was there, in slot sixteen, that Paul Grayson's body was stored.

Leng broke the connection, called for the other members of the team to join him, and led them through a door into the sterile-looking hallway beyond. About ten meters down the passageway Leng spotted the door marked UTILITY 12, and took a right. The barrier slid open to reveal row upon row of gleaming conveyances.

Leng went over to the first tank in line. The transparent capsule was large enough to accommodate any species except a krogan. It sat atop a high-tech undercarriage that included a control panel, gas hookups, and sturdy wheels. The purpose of the unit was to prevent a body from decaying while C-Sec's investigators did their jobs. "Hobbs," Leng said, as he touched a button. "Hop in."

Hobbs frowned as the curved canopy whirred open. "Why?"

"So Nefari and I will have what looks like a dead body to push around. Now quit screwing off . . . The faster we get out of there the better."

Hobbs made a face, sat on the edge of the tank, and brought his feet up. Seconds later he was laid out with arms at his sides. There was the rustle of fabric as Nefari pulled a sheet over Hobbs in order to conceal his scrub suit. "Don't forget to keep your eyes closed," Leng said, as the canopy closed.

"He looked dead *before* he got in there," Nefari observed.

"I know," Leng said. "That's one of the reasons why I hired him. Okay, let's roll."

The tank was heavy but reasonably easy to steer. Together they pushed it down the hall and into a service elevator, where their luck ran out. A turian stood to one side. He was dressed in a lab coat and had the look of a doctor. "And who are you?" he inquired. "I don't believe that we've met."

"No, sir," Leng replied respectfully. "We hired on a couple of days ago. You know how it is . . . The new people always wind up on night duty."

That was a guess on Leng's part, but the turian made no effort to deny it. "I see," he said, as the lift started into motion. "What have you got there?"

"Most likely a heart attack," Leng replied. "They found him lying in a passageway behind a bar."

The turian nodded. But Leng, who was something of an expert at such things, could tell that the alien wasn't satisfied. Something, a small detail perhaps, wasn't right. Or maybe he disliked humans as much as Leng disliked turians. "Could I see your ID, please?" the turian inquired. "We have to be careful, you know."

"Sure," Leng replied lightly, as Nefari did her best to disappear, "here you go."

The ID card had been Obey's originally. But now it had a different name on it along with a picture of Leng. Not an image of his *real* face, but the one Hobbs and Nefari were familiar with, and had been captured by dozens of C-Sec cameras during the last twenty minutes.

The problem was that if the turian left the elevator, and slipped the card into a scanner, all hell would break loose. Of course, Leng would kill the doctor before he could do that. But a dead body would complicate things and reduce their chances of success. Time seemed to stretch. "Okay," the turian said as the elevator stopped. "Welcome to the team. I'll see you around."

Leng accepted the card, took a deep breath, and let it out again. "That was close," Nefari commented, as the doors closed and the elevator went down.

"Yes, it was," Leng agreed. The doors parted and they pushed the tank out into the hall. "But we're almost there."

And they were. After pushing the tank down a short corridor doors opened and allowed them to enter a long narrow room. The lighting was dim, the air was cold, and it was extremely quiet. Rows of evenly spaced stasis tanks lined both sides of a central passageway. Each bay was numbered so all Leng had to do was watch for slot sixteen. "There," he said. "That's the one we're after."

Having parked the stasis tank in the middle of the corridor Leng went over to look at Grayson. There was a grayish tinge to his skin. His eyes were open and a pair of blue-edged holes were still visible near the center of his forehead. Leng smiled. *We meet again,* he thought to himself.

"Okay," Leng said, as he turned to Nefari. "Disconnect the tubes and the power supply. These things can operate on their own for up to twelve hours. That's plenty of time in which to take him elsewhere."

Nefari went to work. There was a soft popping sound as each hose was disconnected followed by a momentary hiss of escaping gas. An alarm began to buzz as the power supply was disconnected and they pulled the unit out into the passageway. "Help me push the other tank in," Leng said. "Once we hook it up the alarm will go off." Hobbs had his hands on the transparent canopy by then and was trying to push it open.

"What about Hobbs?" Nefari wanted to know, as the man in question screamed soundlessly, and beat on the canopy with his fists.

"He'll have to stay here," Leng replied, as the tank came to a stop. "Otherwise someone will notice that the facility is one body short. Hook up the hoses—I'll take care of the power."

"You are one cold-blooded bastard," Nefari said

tightly, as the alarm fell silent. "What will the gas do to him?"

"I don't know," Leng said, as Hobbs began to turn blue. "But his pay will go to you."

Nefari stood with hands on hips. "Make the transfer *now*. All of it."

Leng started to object, thought better of it, and activated his omni-tool. "Give me an account number."

Nefari did so, verified the deposit via her tool, and nodded. "Let's get out of here."

Hobbs was quiet by then. His eyes stared lifelessly at the ceiling as the people responsible for his death left. Once they were gone there was nothing but the soft hum of machinery to disturb the otherwise perfect peace.

Ironically, Nefari's body wound up in a bay only six slots away nine hours later. Her throat had been cut, her pockets were empty, and nobody came forward to claim the body.

SIX

SOMEWHERE IN THE CRESCENT NEBULA

The Illusive Man sat silhouetted against a barren landscape as a young woman appeared in the door to his office. "You have a call from Madam Oro."

The Illusive Man looked up from his terminal. "Thank you, Jana." As he turned to the right an image blossomed over the holo-pad. The woman had black hair, large brown eyes, and a full figure. She was wearing a businesslike gray tunic. The Illusive Man smiled. "Margaret . . . It's good to see you."

Oro smiled. "You too."

"I look forward to hearing your report," the Illusive Man said. "The Hearts and Minds program is very important to me."

During the thirty-minute presentation that followed Oro brought the Illusive Man up to speed on the largely sub-rosa pro-Cerberus communications effort that she and her staff were engaged in. The purpose of the campaign was to counter the drumbeat of negative publicity that consistently found its way into the news. "At the moment we're working with the phrase, 'Cerberus will sound the call, be ready,'" she explained. "The mainstream media won't run our ads so we're using guerrilla marketing techniques to put the message out. That includes wall crawls in places like Hu-Town on the Citadel, pirate sites on the extranet, and a network of flesh-and-blood storytellers. All trained to tell tales about the rise of humanity."

"Well done," the Illusive Man said approvingly. "Our polling shows that even though members of the other races tend to have a negative impression of Cerberus, most humans feel we're a positive influence. And I know that your efforts play an important part in creating and reinforcing that impression."

Oro thanked him as the conversation came to a close. "Remember one thing," the Illusive Man said, as he prepared to say good-bye. "The biggest problem isn't the other races—even if they don't like us. The most significant challenge is apathy, social integration, and the passage of time. Because if humanity loses its identity the battle will be lost without a single shot being fired. So keep fighting Margaret . . . We have experienced some setbacks of late but things will get better."

Once the link was broken the Illusive Man turned to look through the oval-shaped window behind him. There were so many battles to fight. So many variables to control. The sound of a tone broke his chain of thought. "Who is it?"

"Kai Leng," Jana replied over the intercom.

As the Illusive Man turned back to his desk a slightly translucent Leng seemed to materialize out of thin air. The operative's face was expressionless as usual. "I have news."

"Of course you do," the Illusive Man said indulgently. "Where are you?"

"On the Citadel."

The Illusive Man was seated by then. He placed a cigarette between his lips. "I see. And?"

"And McCann is dead."

"Excellent. Things went smoothly?"

"For the most part, yes."

"And the girl?"

"That task has yet to be completed," Leng replied. "According to what Hendel Mitra told Kahlee and Anderson a few hours ago she boarded a ship for Omega."

The Illusive Man was disappointed but knew wet work could be very demanding. "How about the third task?"

"Completed. The body is aboard a ship on its way to you. What good is it anyway?"

A momentary flare of light lit the Illusive Man's face as he thumbed a lighter. "The body is a variable—and variables must be controlled. So you're free to follow the girl."

"Yes."

"Be careful." And with that the Illusive Man broke the connection. Then he blew a plume of smoke toward the center of the room where it shivered and began to dissipate. *Entropy,* the Illusive Man thought to himself. *The enemy of everything.*

On the Citadel

The elevator doors opened, and as Anderson followed Kahlee out into the lobby, his mind was churn-

ing. Varma had contacted them first, to let them know
that Grayson's body had been stolen and another left
in its place. Then, while they were still in the process
of absorbing that news, the salarian Council member's executive assistant had called to request a meeting that afternoon. Such "requests" were actually
more like orders, especially for Anderson, who was
employed by the Council.

The curving walkway took them past a statue and
clumps of trees to the base of the Citadel Tower. The
C-Sec office at the kiosk out front cleared them
through in what might have been record time. Moments later they were aboard the transparent elevator
that whisked them upward. The view was magnificent but Anderson's mind was on other things as the
lift stopped well short of the Council Chambers located high above.

They stepped out into a spacious lobby that was
decorated with abstract paintings, metal-framed furniture, and sand-colored marble floor. A salarian
came forward to greet them. "Hello . . . My name is
Nee Brinsa. Dor Hana is on a call at the moment, but
will be free shortly. Please follow me."

Anderson and Kahlee followed Brinsa into a small
but nicely appointed waiting room where they had no
choice but to sit on some salarian furniture. It was
uncomfortable. But true to Brinsa's word it was only
a matter of minutes before he returned to get them.
"Dor Hana is available now," he said as if announcing a minor miracle.

Hana's office was large and looked out over a
broad expanse of the Presidium and the wards beyond. But Anderson caught only a glimpse of the

spectacular view as Hana came around his desk to greet them. Anderson didn't know the salarian well but had met him a couple of times before. Kahlee waited to be introduced. Once that process was over Hana gestured to a low table and a grouping of fragile-looking chairs. "Please have a seat."

The salarian had large eyes, leathery skin, and a long face. He was dressed in a tight-fitting black suit that was broken up with artfully placed panels of white. Once the three of them were seated Hana got right to the point. "As you know, Paul Grayson's body was stolen from the C-Sec Forensic Lab."

"Yes," Anderson replied. "Lieutenant Varma told us. How is such a thing possible?"

Hana frowned. "The investigation is still under way, but it looks as though the thieves were able to identify vulnerabilities in the C-Sec security system and exploit them."

Anderson and Kahlee listened as Hana told them about how an employee named Obey had been murdered in order to access the Forensic Lab—and how a body had been left in Grayson's place. "The people who did this are cold-blooded murderers," the salarian concluded grimly. "The Council member is very upset."

Anderson knew that when Hana said "the Council member," the functionary was referring to *his* boss. The only Council member who counted insofar as he was concerned.

"I'd put my money on Cerberus," Kahlee said tightly. "They're the ones who experimented on Grayson—and they wanted to get the body back."

"That makes sense," Hana agreed. "In fact, it may

have been the presentation that you and Admiral Anderson made to the Council that triggered the theft."

That made sense and Anderson nodded. "What Kahlee said is true, but I believe there's more to it than that. We brought the body in front of the Council because of the modifications that had been carried out on it."

"Modifications that the two of you believe are somehow connected with the Reapers," Hana said. "Your opinions on the subject are well known. And even though I have been skeptical in the past, I'm beginning to wonder if you might be correct."

Anderson wasn't sure how to feel about that. It would be nice to be taken seriously for a change—if that was the case. But Hana had responsibility for the Council's intelligence operation and was known to be a notorious plotter. Did the salarian *truly* believe the Reapers were involved somehow? Or was he trying to gain Anderson's trust as part of an effort to better monitor the human's activities?

Anderson's train of thought was interrupted as Brinsa entered the office. "Lieutenant Varma is holding, sir. Shall I put the call through?"

"Yes," Hana replied, before returning to his desk in order to pick up the handset. "Please excuse me, but this call could have a bearing on the subject at hand."

The salarian had chosen to keep the call to himself rather than pipe it over the sound system. "Lieutenant Varma? Hana here."

The ensuing conversation was a one-sided affair in which Varma did most of the talking. Hana's responses were limited to comments like, "Really?"

"Interesting . . ." And, "Yes, double check to make sure that you got all of them."

Once the call was over Hana put the hand unit down and returned to his chair. "You'll be interested to know that the lieutenant is in your apartment."

"In our apartment?" Kahlee demanded. "She doesn't have a right to go in there."

"Oh, but she does," Hana replied coolly. "C-Sec officers can go anywhere they need to so long as they have permission from the right people. In this case *me*. And I authorized a search because the missing boy, McCann's death, and the theft of Grayson's body all share a common element. And that's *you*.

"No," the salarian said preemptively, as Anderson started to object. "I don't think you stole Grayson's body. I said that all of those events were related to you in some way. And that's why Lieutenant Varma was authorized to enter your apartment and sweep it for bugs. Her team found twelve of them. Someone was monitoring everything you did."

Kahlee blushed and Anderson swore.

"I agree with your sentiment," Hana said with the hint of a smile. "And it's apparent that someone is worried about what you might learn. That would suggest caution. A great deal of caution lest one or both of you wind up like McCann."

It was a sobering thought. Anderson looked at Kahlee and back again. "We'll be careful."

"Good. What do you plan to do next?"

Hana's eyes were as dark as the depths of space. Once again Anderson felt a sense of caution. Why did Hana want to know? It was a silly question. It was his job to know. "We're going to Omega."

"To find the boy?"

"To find the boy *and* Grayson's daughter Gillian," Kahlee put in. "She wants to find the Illusive Man and kill him."

"A noble ambition," Hana responded. "But wasted effort. So you'll try to intervene?"

"Yes," Kahlee replied. "And see what we can learn. Maybe Gillian will stir things up. If so we could find the kind of information we're looking for."

Hana stood. It was his way of announcing that the meeting was over. "Stay in touch," he said.

It could have been an invitation, or a way of conveying concern, but Anderson was a military man and knew an order when he heard one. "Sir, yes, sir."

THE PLANET THESSIA

The air was cool as Aria T'Loak stepped out of her bedroom and onto the veranda. It was protected by a roof supported by seven fluted columns. One for each of the city's softly rounded hills. Three of them were visible from that side of her house. Their carefully groomed slopes were home to hundreds of expensive houses and the early-morning light was reflected off broad expanses of glass, swimming pools, and weapons turrets. The hallmark of the rich.

But as Aria had discovered more than once during her long life, there were some things that money couldn't buy. One of which was peace of mind. Because the vision of her daughter's dead body was always there, always in the back of her mind, never letting go.

The Illusive Man maintained that Paul Grayson

was responsible for Liselle's death. And that made sense because they'd been lovers and he was a red sand addict. So perhaps there had been some sort of quarrel, Grayson had been high, and slashed Liselle's throat.

The problem was that T'Loak was a criminal and a very accomplished one. Many people believed she was the dominant force on Omega and they were correct. That, plus the fact that she was hundreds of years old, meant T'Loak had lots of experience where the act of murder was concerned. And something, she wasn't sure what, was wrong. *But I'll figure it out,* she promised herself, *and sooner rather than later.*

But it would have to wait. Because rather than cremate Liselle on Omega, it had been T'Loak's decision to bring her daughter home, where tradition said her spirit would join those who had gone before. T'Loak wasn't sure about that but hoped it was true. So she took a last look at the city she loved, then turned her back on it as she had so many times before, and went inside. The funeral was to begin in less than an hour.

In keeping with asari tradition, Liselle's carefully preserved body had been bathed, anointed with oil, and dressed in a white gown the evening before. Then it had been placed on a specially constructed platform at the center of the villa's spacious entry hall overnight. The four guards assigned to protect it were still on duty when T'Loak arrived.

She was dressed in a long gown with a formfitting bodice, as were the other asari who were awaiting her. There were eight of them and all were relatives. But not T'Loak's *only* relatives. She had hundreds of those. And most disapproved of the way she made her living. More than that, they blamed T'Loak for raising Liselle on Omega and allowing her to live there. And in retrospect the crime lord agreed with them. The fact that Liselle had fallen in with bad company was her fault. And the knowledge ate at her.

So as the guests came forward to lift the ornate stretcher off the platform there were barely enough of them to do the job. And as the mourners carried the body out through the front door to a long sleek hearse they were outnumbered by the heavily armed bodyguards positioned all around. *Bodyguards,* Aria thought bitterly. *How fitting.*

The funeral cortege consisted of four vehicles. A specially designed car that was equipped to ram vehicles and push them out of the way if necessary would take the lead. Next came the heavily armored stretch limo in which T'Loak and the other family members would ride, closely followed by the hearse, and what looked like a black delivery truck. Except it could open a pair of roof panels to fire missiles at air and ground targets. That was unlikely of course, especially on Thessia, but the price of power was powerful enemies. And T'Loak never took chances she didn't have to.

Once the vehicles were loaded the processional departed. No one spoke inside the limo. That was T'Loak's prerogative and she had never been one to share her feelings with others. So silence reigned as the vehicles wound their way down zigzagging streets, past hillside villas, to the flatland below. It was dense with clusters of high-rise buildings—many of which were bound together by delicate-looking sky bridges.

Lesser structures were gathered about the skyscrapers and represented self-governing neighborhoods. Some were quite nice and some weren't.

T'Loak was very familiar with the city's ugly underbelly because she had been raised in a twenty-square-block area called Hell's Waiting Room, where everyone lived by their wits, no one could be trusted, and crime was the norm. Her mother *hadn't* been raised there, but had been drawn to the flats for reasons T'Loak could only guess at, and never left. Since leaving home T'Loak had risen to what one of her more proper relatives called "an ugly prominence." Words that were supposed to hurt but didn't, because T'Loak saw her profession as being the natural expression of the way nature worked. Every planet had a food chain, predators were always at the top of it, and everything else was sentimental rubbish.

A row of stately evergreens blipped past on the left, each momentarily blocking the view of the sparkling river beyond, and the occasional groupings of homes along both banks. Then, as the highway followed a broad curve, the cemetery appeared in the distance. It had been in use for thousands of years and covered a vast tract of land. The seemingly endless maze of tombs, monuments, and markers came in every possible shape and size. Some looked like temples. Others took the form of soaring spires, statues, and pieces of abstract art.

The monuments surrounded the cortege as it followed a meandering street past a beautiful dome to the one-lane bridge that led out to the center of an artificial lake. The plot of land had been at the very edge of the cemetery back when T'Loak purchased it.

But thousands of monuments had been added since then, making the small body of water all the more remarkable. It was, some said, a moat. Put there to keep lesser beings at a distance. Others saw it as a testament to the size of T'Loak's ego, an effort to manage her own passing, and a sign of poor taste. *And all of those criticisms are correct,* T'Loak thought to herself, as the cortege came to a stop. *Not that it matters.*

The pyramid-shaped structure was made of black granite, and harkened back to a much younger version of herself, a person who had something to prove and thought that extravagance was the way to do it. It was the sort of immaturity typical of someone who is only a hundred years old and on the make. Now, as an asari matron, T'Loak thought the place was over-done. But to change it would be to apologize, to betray her younger self, and that was something she steadfastly refused to do.

T'Loak waited for the driver to come back and open the door before getting out and leading the other mourners to the point where they could remove the ceremonial stretcher from the back of the hearse. Liselle's eyes were closed. Makeup concealed the horrible cut across her throat and her hands were clasped in front of her chest. *I will not cry,* T'Loak thought to herself. *Crying is a sign of weakness.*

After lifting the stretcher the female pallbearers followed T'Loak down a steep ramp and into the circular chamber below. It was cool there. The lighting was intentionally subdued, and water gurgled as it spilled out of the vessel at the center of the room and cascaded into a pool.

Equally spaced chambers were set into the wall like spokes in a wheel. Some were occupied and some weren't. A capsule had been prepared for Liselle and was waiting. Slowly, using great care, Liselle's body was lifted up and in. Once the process was complete, T'Loak bent to kiss her daughter's cold lips. "I won't give up," she promised. "Not until I know the truth."

Then as the casket was closed and pushed into the wall, the woman who wasn't going to cry began to do so. Deep sobs racked her body as she stood head down in front of the name that had been chiseled into the marble. But none of the others dared embrace her, or to offer words of solace, because Aria T'Loak was the Pirate Queen. And to touch her was to die.

ABOARD THE FREIGHTER *PICTOR*

As the freighter *Pictor* shot toward the mass effect relay at a speed of nearly fifteen kilometers per second, it was little more than a momentary blur. Then there was a sudden flare of light as the ship's element-zero core was taken off-line and its mass effect fields were snuffed from existence. Like a projectile fired from a rifle the *Pictor* flew toward what looked like an evil eye floating in the blackness of space. Two communications masts stood straight up from a structure that consisted of two gigantic rings that rotated around a glowing sphere.

Slowly at first, and then with increasing speed, the rings began to spin as the ship closed in. Then, once the *Pictor* was about five hundred kilometers away, the relay fired and the freighter was consumed by a vortex of dark energy. It shimmered and disappeared.

But because Anderson was busy making love to Kahlee he missed the transition from one state to another. The big passenger liners didn't serve Omega. So anyone who wanted to travel there from the Citadel had to have a ship of their own or book passage on a freighter like the *Pictor*. Like most of her kind she was equipped to carry both cargo and a handful of passengers.

The fact that the emphasis was on freight rather than people meant that the cabins were so small and cramped that there was barely enough space to walk around the bed. So it was the natural place to sit. And once they sat on the bed one thing led to another and it wasn't long before the couple were on a journey of their own. A very pleasant interlude that was barely over when someone began to thump on the hatch. And that was necessary since neither the intercom nor the doorbell worked. "Yeah, yeah," Anderson grumbled, as he pulled his pants on. "Just a minute."

Having pulled the blankets up over her breasts Kahlee watched the hatch cycle open to reveal a portly volus. He was the ship's steward and none too pleased. "Your Earth friend is causing trouble."

"Hendel Mitra? Causing trouble? That's hard to believe," Anderson said.

"There was a fight in cargo hold two. Human Mitra attacked four crew members and two fellow passengers. Then he locked himself in the cook's storeroom. He refuses to come out."

Anderson swore and looked back over his shoulder. "Did you hear that? You know Hendel better than I do. What's going on?"

"I don't know," Kahlee said. "Close the hatch so I can get dressed. I'm coming along."

It took fifteen minutes to throw some clothes on and follow the steward down into the depths of the ship where some of the passengers and crew had been gambling and drinking in a half-empty cargo compartment. An overturned table and some mismatched chairs lay strewn about. "The fight took place *here*," the volus said accusingly, as if Anderson and Kahlee were responsible somehow. "According to witnesses the Mitra person attacked the others for no reason. Then, when they attempted to defend themselves, he ran."

Kahlee didn't believe a word of it. Hendel was one of the most disciplined and dependable people she knew. He had been born on Earth in the suburbs of New Calcutta. His mother had been accidentally exposed to element zero dust during her pregnancy and rather than the birth defects that some "dust" babies wound up with, Hendel was born with biotic powers.

His capabilities weren't on a par with what prodigies like Nick and Gillian could do, but were sufficient to qualify Hendel for Biotic Acclimation and Temperance Training, also referred to as BAaT. It was a rather draconian program that involved a conscious effort to alienate students from their families. A strategy that was so successful where Hendel was concerned that he refused to interact with relatives years after the BAaT program was shut down.

Subsequent to that Hendel enlisted in the Alliance military where he served with distinction prior to leaving for civilian life and a job as head of security for the Grissom Academy. Then, in an act of selfless loyalty, he volunteered to serve as Gillian's guardian during the time she was forced to hide aboard the quarian ship *Idenna*. "Save the bull for someone else," Kahlee said sternly, as she eyed the steward. "You said Hendel locked himself in a storeroom. Take us there."

The volus turned and led them into a passageway between two of the ship's holds. It led to an intersection. And that's where two crew members were waiting next to a hatch marked STOREROOM. One was turian, the other was batarian, and both looked as if they had been knocked around. "The bastard is still in there," the batarian rasped, as he slapped a palm with a shock baton.

"You get the door open and we'll make sure he gets back to his cabin safely," the turian said as if to mitigate his companion's words.

"I think you should return to your duties," Kahlee said sweetly. "I'm sure the captain could use your help."

The batarian opened his mouth but the steward preempted whatever he was about to say. "I will call for you should that become necessary."

There was some grumbling but the crew members did as they were told. Kahlee turned to the steel hatch. "Hendel? It's me . . . Kahlee."

There was no response. So she tried again. "Open the hatch, Hendel. I want to talk to you."

Five seconds passed followed by a whir as the lock was released. Anderson pulled the door open and Kahlee went in. Hendel was sitting on the deck with his head in his hands and his back against a shelving unit. His face was bloody and bruised. "There were six of them," he said dully. "I threw one against the bulkhead but the rest of them swarmed me."

"Passengers are not allowed in the storeroom," the volus said insistently. "You will remove him now."

"He'll be gone soon," Anderson said irritably. "Now shut up and get out."

"I will report your behavior to the captain," the steward responded importantly.

"You do that," Anderson said. "And while you're at it tell him that we plan to press charges against him and the crew members who attacked citizen Mitra."

The steward made a snorting sound and left.

Kahlee was kneeling next to Hendel by that time examining the cuts and abrasions on his face. "Were you drinking?" she inquired. Although the answer seemed self-evident.

Hendel winced as she touched a bruise. "I had a couple."

"More than a couple," Kahlee responded. "You smell like a brewery. This isn't like you Hendel. What's wrong?"

One of Hendel's eyes was swollen shut. The other one stared back at her. "Gillian."

"What about Gillian?"

"I failed her. It was my job to protect her and I didn't."

The truth was that Kahlee hadn't thought about Hendel lately. Or the effect that recent events might have on him. He was just *there*. Rock solid and eternally dependable. Until now. And as Kahlee looked at Hendel's badly battered face something occurred to her. Something she should have thought about earlier but hadn't. Hendel had spent his formative years in the strict BAaT program, followed by a career in the Alliance military, and a job as security chief for the Grissom Academy. All were jobs that provided him with context, purpose, and goals to strive for.

Then came the assignment to protect Gillian during her time with the quarian fleet, followed by what? Nothing. Gillian had departed without so much as a good-bye—and when Hendel went looking for her he had been searching for himself as well. "You mustn't blame yourself," she said. "Gillian is an adult. Legally anyway. You did all that anyone could."

"Come on," Kahlee said, as she motioned to Anderson. "Give me a hand. We'll take Hendel to his cabin and get him patched up."

"And sobered up," Anderson put in, as he came to help. "Damn, Hendel . . . you look like hell warmed over."

"Oh, yeah?" Hendel replied, as they helped him to his feet. "You should see the other guys."

"We did," Kahlee replied. "Some of them anyway. And they aren't very happy."

"Screw 'em," Hendel said thickly.

"See?" Anderson said, as he helped Hendel out of the compartment. "He's feeling better already."

Kahlee laughed. And together they shuffled down the passageway.

SEVEN

ON OMEGA

Nick was standing in front of a run-down building in the Gozu district just beyond the flow of foot traffic. The air was thick with the stench of uncollected garbage, ozone that was being emitted from a secretive shop a few doors down, and the combined odors of at least six food stalls located across the street. But he was happy. Because on Omega, for the first time in his life, Nick Donahue was a somebody.

That was evident in the light Level III Hydra Armor he wore, the Brawler pistols that hung low on both hips, and the fact that they were backups rather than his main armament. *That* was his ability as a biotic, which had earned him a place in the Biotic Underground.

The heavy-metal-rich asteroid was an important source of element zero, which was why many groups had attempted to control it over the years. None of them were able to hold it for very long, however, forcing them to share it or be displaced.

Now, thanks to both the element zero mines and its location deep inside the lawless Terminus systems,

Omega served as a tax-free port where pirates, mercenaries, slavers, assassins, and criminals of every race
could trade, rest, and enjoy their profits. And minus
a central government, the space station continued
to evolve in a haphazard fashion as various districts
were created, fought over, and reapportioned according to the whims of various crime lords.

The result was a place where 7.8 million people
lived in crowded and dangerous conditions, each looking out for him- or herself in a society where everything imaginable could be bought, sold, or stolen. So,
given that reality, it wasn't strange that the bubbling
cauldron which was Omega served as a refuge for
groups with political rather than criminal objectives.
Even if their methodologies were equally ruthless at
times.

And that had everything to do with why Nick and
a senior member of the Underground had been left to
help guard the front door of the low-slung building
where the Blue Sun mercenaries were headquartered.
A squad of armored mercs were present as well, all of
whom seemed bent on ignoring the biotics while leaders from both groups met inside.

Though not privy to the details of what was taking
place, Nick knew that the Biotic Underground hoped
to form relationships, which would enable it to overcome the most potent force on Omega. And that was
the asari crime lord named Aria T'Loak.

Nick's thoughts were interrupted as a commotion
was heard and the door opened. A human named
Cory Kim exited first. Her head swiveled left and
right as she checked to ensure that Arrius Sallus and
Nick were in position. Having confirmed that every-

thing was as it should be Kim spoke into a lip mike. "We're clear. Over."

As Kim stepped down into the street Nick knew he was supposed to scan his surroundings looking for threats rather than eyeballing other members of the group. But he couldn't resist watching Mythra Zon leave the building. She had a high forehead, wide-set eyes, and perfect lips. The asari was shapely as well.

However, Nick's infatuation with Zon was more than a case of teenage hormones run amok. There was an energy around the female. Something that emanated from deep inside her. Part of that could be attributed to her status as an adept. A level of biotic ability far superior to Nick's. Still, the attraction was more than that however. Zon's natural charisma was such that people of all races were drawn to her.

"We're headed home," Kim said over the radio. "Nick will take point. Sallus will bring up the rear. Keep your heads on a swivel—and don't forget to watch the upper stories."

Nick was young and inexperienced. And even *he* knew how dangerous the point position could be. Because if some group was laying in wait for the biotics, they would try to kill him first. But armed as he was with his talent and two pistols Nick couldn't imagine anything like that happening. What he *could* imagine was some sort of attack in which he would heroically kill the assailants, save Zon from mortal danger, and earn her undying respect. That would be a good thing, and as Nick led the way, his eyes roamed the area ahead, eager to spot any sign of danger.

The streets were crowded with salarians, turians, batarians, krogan, and even a few humans. The combined odors of their sweat and pheromones blended to form a stench so thick it caught at the back of Nick's throat.

Meanwhile, the sound of at least half a dozen languages, the unrestrained *thump, thump, thump* issuing from a nearby factory, and snatches of alien music all combined to create an unintelligible mishmash of sound. Foot traffic headed in the opposite direction was forced to part in front of Nick and the fifteen biotics following behind him. Most members of the crowd did so with the matter-of-fact nonchalance of water flowing around a stone. But a few took exception to the inconvenience and made a point out of passing close enough to deliver choice insults.

Such encounters kept Nick on edge because there was no way to know if and when one of them might escalate into violence. Then, as a pair of surly krogan passed, he saw the barricade up ahead. It was a temporary structure made out of beat-up cargo modules, some metal office furniture, and the lifeless remains of a Hosker II power loader. The junk was arranged in the shape of an hourglass so that pedestrians would have to pass through a narrow gap and pay a so-called street tax. Proceeds of which would go into some gang's coffers.

Such obstructions were annoying. However, so long as the thugs who manned them kept the toll down to a pittance there was very little reason for people further up the criminal food chain to take action against them. But was the barricade the real thing? Or a clever setup for an ambush? Because once the group entered the choke point they would be very vulnerable. Fortunately for Nick it was Kim's responsibility to make such decisions and her voice was hard as steel. "Clear that obstruction, Nick. We're coming through."

Nick felt both a sense of anticipation and fear as he began to gather the necessary energy. Anticipation because he *wanted* to use his power, but fear because he'd never been in such a position before. What if he botched it? Right in front of Zon? What felt like cold lead trickled into his belly as he raised his hands and directed a bolt of energy at the point where half a dozen street toughs were standing. The "throw" sent them flying and Nick felt a sense of satisfaction as the rest of the gang ran for safety. He'd done it! And all by himself too.

The pistols seemed to fill his hands of their own accord and he fired a shot from each. One of the slugs shattered a window in a building a block away and there was no way to know where the other went. The gunshots sent people scurrying for cover. "Enough," Kim said, as Nick entered the narrow passageway. "Pay attention people, we aren't home yet."

The rest of the trip was uneventful. But Nick was glad to see the building that the senior members of the Biotic Underground had chosen as the organization's headquarters. It was a blocky flat-topped affair separated from the structures around it by what Kim called "an air moat." By which she meant a gap invaders would have to bridge before they could attack roof to roof. Sentries armed with assault rifles could be seen on top of the building that was never left unguarded lest it be taken over.

Like all of the structures on Omega, the five-story building had been used for a variety of purposes over the years, but the large lobby, second-floor arcade, and multiplicity of small rooms suggested it had been built to function as a hotel. Which was nice because it meant that even the most junior member of the organization had his own quarters.

So that's where Nick was, trying to wipe some of the grime off his face and neck, when he heard a knock. He turned to see Kim standing in the doorway. He was pretty sure the security chief had at least some Asian heritage, although her hair was brown rather than black and she was almost as tall as he was. Having taken the point position and performed well Nick was ready for some well-deserved praise. "Cory . . . Come in."

But as Kim entered Nick saw the look in her dark eyes. And it was anything but friendly. She crooked a finger. "Come here."

Nick, who was suddenly very unsure of himself, obeyed. Then, once he was within arm's length, she slapped him across the face. *Hard*.

His first instinct was to strike back, but before Nick could send the necessary messages to the rest of his body a snicking sound was heard. The spring-loaded slip blade *looked* like a pointer, or a swagger stick, but was actually a very dangerous weapon. Suddenly Nick found himself standing on tiptoes as the slip blade's needle-sharp tip jabbed a point under his jaw. "Feel that?" Kim demanded. "All I have to do is push and the blade will go up through your tongue and the roof of your mouth into that tiny brain.

"There was no need to fire your weapons. The use of excessive force is stupid. And it has a tendency to piss people off. What if the round that went through the window hit a gang boss? Or her lover? Or their child?

"We'd be ass deep in trouble that's what. Trouble we don't need. All because some idiot fired a weapon he didn't need to. And that raises another issue. Using a firearm is one thing. Hitting a target is another. *You* are going to spend some time on the range. Got it?"

Nick swallowed the lump in his throat. "Got it."

"Good," Kim said, as she used the doorjamb to push the blade back into the weapon's handle. "And one more thing . . ."

Nick brought a hand up to touch the spot behind his chin. His finger came away bloody. "Yes?"

"Nice throw at the barricade. *That* was a thing of beauty."

Nick felt a sudden jolt of pleasure as Kim turned and left. It was, all things considered, a good day.

Having been forced to travel aboard a clapped-out freighter loaded with scrap metal, and share a claustrophobic two-bunk cabin with a woman who snored, Gillian felt a sense of exultation as she followed a handful of passengers out through the ship's lock and onto a causeway. It led them down a ramp to one of the docking arms that protruded spiderlike from the space station's bulk.

But the feeling of relief was short-lived. The first thing Gillian noticed was the absence of police officers at the entry point or any sort of customs inspection. Then came the realization that she was the only person in sight who wasn't armed. That, plus the suitcase she was towing, made Gillian a natural target for every sort of street scum. As she put the causeway behind her, and followed a graffiti-covered ped tube down into the asteroid, the locals took turns pitching her. "You lookin' for a place to stay?" a grimy-faced street urchin inquired. "You can flop with my mom for five credits."

That invitation was followed by one from a man who took Gillian's elbow and tried to steer her into a side passage. "Hey, baby . . . Need a job? Your face ain't much but that's a nice body. I can line you up for six humps a day. How's that sound?" A biotic nudge was sufficient to send him reeling away.

"Whoa!" a voice said, as Gillian increased her pace. "What's your hurry human?" a turian inquired, pacing along next to her. "You need some happy? They call me the sandman. And my stuff is red. *Real* red. Ten credits for some sweet dreams."

Gillian hurried to catch up with a pair of heavily armed batarians and fell in behind them. None of the hawkers, pimps, and dealers sought to bother *them*, which meant she was safe for the moment. But she was left to her own devices as the three of them arrived on the surface and the batarians entered a bar. "Hey, miss," a ragged-looking beggar said, shuffling forward with his bowl extended. "How 'bout a couple of credits for a homeless veteran? I fought for the Alliance I did, and I need a place to sleep."

Gillian gave him a credit. Now she realized that the suitcase was a liability. A magnet for all of the wrong kind of people. So having spotted a garishly lit pawnshop on the other side of the trash-strewn street she made her way over. A bell jangled as she pushed the old-fashioned door open and walked past a turian guard. Glassed-in display counters ran along both

sides of the room. And there, at the far end, the proprietor could be seen. He was human and appeared to
be in his sixties. His head was entirely bald and a pair
of high-mag zoom specs were perched on the end of
his nose. The expression on his face was carefully
neutral. "Yes, miss . . . What can I do for you?"

"I need a pack," Gillian replied.

"Yes, you do," he agreed. "There's nothing like a
suitcase to attract street flies. And you could use some
heat as well. I have a used Hahne-Kedar handgun I
could let you have for a reasonable price."

"How much?" Gillian inquired.

The man told her and she shook her head. "I can't
afford that much. Just a pack please."

So the shopkeeper gave her a nice pack, took five
credits off as an allowance for the suitcase, and placed
what looked like a very businesslike pistol on the
glass in front of her. "It's fake," he explained. "I sell
quite a few of them. Give me three credits and it's
yours. Make sure people can see it. Then come back
and buy the real thing when you can afford to do so."

It was a nice gesture and that gave Gillian the courage required to ask a pressing question. "Where's a
good place to stay?"

The old man frowned. "There aren't any good
places to stay. Not for a girl who can't afford a
weapon. The flophouses are dangerous. Especially for
young females."

Gillian wasn't unarmed. Not by a long shot. But
figured that it was best to keep her biotic capabilities
under wraps for as long as possible. As she began to
transfer her belongings from the suitcase to the pack,

an idea occurred to her. "Tell me something," she said. "Do the quarians have a presence on Omega?"

The man gave her a curious look. "We'd be better off without them if you ask me. But, yes, their ships come and go on a regular basis. So they maintain a warehouse a couple of kilometers from here."

"Can you give me directions? I'll pay."

That produced a snort. "Things are bad on Omega," he said. "But not *that* bad. I'll draw you a map. But don't let people see you look at it. Otherwise you'll attract the sort of attention you're trying to avoid."

Ten minutes later Gillian was back on the street wearing the fake pistol in a holster the old man had thrown in for free, and carrying her belongings in the sort of pack that locals used for everything from hauling groceries to carrying stolen merchandise. The good thing was that she had a destination. The bad thing was that it was a long way off.

But thanks to the changes Gillian had made to her appearance she was less noticeable now and no longer an obvious target for every hustler on the pedways. Having memorized the pawnshop owner's map she hiked east, or what she thought of as east, although Gillian wasn't sure the term meant much on the space station.

There was a lot to take in as Gillian marched along, not the least of which was layer after layer of architecture. She saw part of an ancient mining machine that had been incorporated into the side of a building, a long row of columns that rose to support something that didn't exist anymore, and a building so alien she wasn't sure that the free-form structure qualified as a building.

But strange though the sights were, there was an intoxicating energy in the air, a sort of communal buzz that filled her with a sense of hopefulness. Because if Cerberus was anywhere, it would have to be represented on Omega. And once she found that presence she would track it back to the Illusive Man.

Gillian's thoughts were interrupted by the rattle of gunfire somewhere up ahead and it was necessary to take shelter in a doorway as a flood of people rushed past. One of them was a salarian who stepped in next to her. "I hope you don't mind," he said mildly. "But stray rounds kill people every day."

"No problem," Gillian responded. "What's going on?"

"The Blood Pack is battling the Talons for control of the Noro district," the salarian answered.

His words were punctuated by the *pop, pop, pop* of rifle fire and a resounding *BOOM* as something exploded. Gillian knew it was dangerous to reveal her lack of knowledge regarding Omega but decided to take the chance. "Is there a way around it?"

"Yes," the salarian answered. "I have a business meeting to attend on the other side of the Haze. You can follow me if you'd like."

Gillian was confident that she could use her biotic powers to defend herself if it came to that, so she thanked the salarian and followed him into the maze of streets, pedways, and tunnels that was Omega. The sound of fighting could be heard in the distance as they zigzagged "north" and plunged underground to join the crowd using a defunct subway tunnel to pass beneath the disputed territory. Having surfaced next to a dry fountain the salarian said good-bye. "This is as far as I go . . . Good luck." Gillian thanked him and moments later he was lost in the crowd.

Gillian was a bit disoriented after the underground trip, and hungry as well, so she slipped into a noodle shop that was located in the corner of what appeared to be a block of apartments. That gave her an opportunity to eat a happy bowl *and* reorient herself using the pawnshop owner's map. After finishing her meal she was ready to complete the arduous journey.

A meandering pedway took Gillian past the headless statue of a krogan, across a trash-littered square, and up to a windowless building. It seemed to shimmer, as if shielded by a force field, and was protected by a low wall and plenty of enviro-suit-clad guards. Gillian went up to the nearest one. "My name is Gillian Nar Idenna. [Gillian child of the ship *Idenna*.] And I request sanctuary."

There was no way to know what was going on behind the quarian's reflective visor, but the prolonged moment of silence spoke volumes. "You're human," he said finally.

"That's true," Gillian replied. "But I am also a member of the *Idenna*'s crew. Why don't you check?"

The guard hesitated for a moment, said "Wait here," and entered the building behind him. A long ten minutes passed while Gillian was forced to linger in front of the warehouse with nothing to do. Finally, after what seemed like an eternity, the guard reappeared. He had a superior in tow—and she came forward to greet Gillian. "My name is Elia Vas Ormona. [Elia crew of the ship *Ormona*.] Your name is on the fleet list along with a photo and a list of your technical qualifications. Sanctuary is granted. Please follow me."

The teenager felt a sudden sense of warmth. Because here, for the moment at least, was a place of safety. Gillian had arrived.

Nick was in a faraway place making love to Mythra Zon when the door to his room flew open and banged against the dingy wall. "Hey, two guns," Kim said loudly. "It's time to earn your keep. We're going to a big meeting this morning. Be down front and ready to go in thirty minutes."

The door slammed closed and Nick groaned. Such outings had become common and often came without much if any advance warning. It was like being in the military. Or what he imagined the military might be like. Life at the academy looked easy in retrospect.

Nick swung his feet over onto the cold floor, made his way to the sink to brush his teeth, and from there to a shower that never produced anything more than a lethargic spray of lukewarm water. Then, having dried off, it was time to get dressed, strap the gun belt on, and hurry downstairs for a quick meal at the communal buffet. The food was brought in from a restaurant a block away and wasn't very good. But as Kim liked to put it, "You can eat this or go hungry. The choice is yours."

After gobbling a cold breakfast wrap, and been nailed with a piece of fruit that his friend Monar had "thrown" at him, Nick hurried out onto the street where what he thought of as "the processional" was forming up. Sometimes Zon and the other leaders were part of the very visible column of biotics and sometimes they weren't. In either case the parade was intended to be a display of confidence and power. Both of which translated to clout within the criminal hierarchy that ran Omega.

On this particular occasion it soon became apparent that Mythra Zon, and her second in command Rasna Vas Kather (Rasna crew of the *Kather*), were traveling separately from the rest of the group. The whole notion of parading through the streets for the sole purpose of building a reputation seemed silly to Nick. But people like Sallus assured him that it was necessary, since the Biotic Underground was largely unknown to Omega's population and needed to establish its credibility.

Nick was assigned to walk near the front of the twenty-person formation while carrying a pole topped by the group's lightning bolt–shaped sigil. Some of the other biotics referred to the symbol as "the bullet magnet," since bored guards stationed on surrounding rooftops had a tendency to use it for target practice. But Kim assured Nick that the position of standard-bearer was an important one. He wasn't so sure, but was forced to accept the role or look like a coward.

A new recruit led the way followed by Kim, Nick, and all the rest of them. Every single person in the group had biotic powers, but many of the rank-and-file members were Level 1 or Level 2, which meant they would have to rely on conventional weaponry in any sort of serious battle. So, having been reclassified as a Level 3 *and* having been chosen to carry the sigil,

Nick felt a natural sense of superiority where the other rankers were concerned.

The route selected for the procession passed within two blocks of the heavily fortified building that functioned as headquarters for the Eclipse Mercs. A well-established group that was said to control roughly twenty percent of that deck. The idea was to get their attention without pissing them off.

A projectile tore through the lightning-bolt sigil, and caused the pole to shiver in Nick's hands, but the rest of the journey went smoothly. Fifteen minutes later, having followed a twisting-turning course through Omega's serpentine streets, the biotics arrived in front of a huge crawler. The mining machine was at least three stories tall, and although the tracks had been removed was still very impressive. The vehicle had been taken over by a group called the Grim Skulls. Some of them were posted in prepared positions around the behemoth. They were dressed in skull-shaped helmets and medium armor that was painted to make them look like skeletons.

Having been assigned to guard duty before, Nick assumed he would be ordered to remain outside. But much to his surprise Kim told him to collapse the telescoping sigil and follow her inside the ship. Although the crawler was clearly hundreds of years old the interior was in surprisingly good shape. Power had been restored to the wreck and Nick could see what looked like batarian stencils on the bulkheads, along with an overlay of colorful graffiti and Grim Skull artwork.

After being led through a series of passageways Nick found himself in what had once been a cargo hold judging from both the layout and fittings. Two tables were in place, one for the biotics, and one for the Grim Skulls. They were separated by about three meters of steel decking and lit from above.

Kim ordered Nick to stand near Zon's right arm directly across from the Grim Skull who was holding *their* sigil, which consisted of a turian skull mounted on a metal pole. Even though he didn't know the particulars of what was taking place, Nick could tell that Zon and her negotiating team had entered into some sort of agreement with the Skulls.

Their leader was a fierce-looking turian named Sy Tactus. The left side of his face was badly scarred, as if by fire, and his right hand was missing. In its place was a chromed grasper. Light twinkled off the prosthetic as he made a gesture. "So we have both an objective and a date. That leaves the issue of how the spoils should be divided. Given the fact that the Skulls will have to do most of the heavy lifting we should receive a larger share. With that in mind a seventy-thirty split is appropriate."

When Zon laughed it had a harsh quality. "I love your sense of humor," she said. "You know what we'll be up against. The place will be lousy with powerful biotics. How many do you have anyway? One? Two? And how strong are they? Not very is my guess. I'll tell you what, Tactus . . . I'll put my weakest follower up against the best biotic you have. If my man wins we split the loot fifty-fifty. If yours wins we'll go with a seventy-thirty split. What do you say?"

The metal pincer produced a loud clang as it hit the metal table. "A fight to the death! You're on."

Nick was watching Zon out of the corner of his

eye. He saw her frown and realized that the asari had miscalculated. She'd been visualizing a test of biotic skill similar to those that Nick and his friends engaged in all the time. But Tactus had a different type of contest in mind. And Zon couldn't back down without looking weak. So one of the Level 1 or Level 2 grunts was about to get a workout. Nick wished him or her well. That was when Zon turned and looked straight at him. "Nick, give the sigil to Kim, and your pistols too. Don't toy with whoever they put up against you. Kill them quickly."

All sorts of thoughts and emotions collided inside Nick's head. First, he was amazed to learn that Zon knew his name. Then came the sudden realization that she planned to trick Tactus by sending her *youngest* rather than weakest follower into battle on the theory that the turian would mistakenly equate age with power. Finally, there was the stomach-churning knowledge that he was supposed to kill someone. The very thing he had been looking forward to—but suddenly realized that he didn't want to do. "Go get 'im killer," Kim said, as she took control of the sigil. "And don't screw around. This ain't no game."

One minute later Nick found himself at one end of the space that separated the two tables. Directly across from him was a willowy-looking salarian female rather than the turian he expected to face. And while Nick was busy thinking about that his opponent plucked him off the floor and threw him against a steel bulkhead. It knocked the air out of him and left him gasping for breath as he fell to the deck.

A roar of approval went up from the Skulls as Nick struggled to regain his feet. He heard Kim yell "Kill the bitch!" as he struggled to focus. It felt as if every bone in his body had been broken, but logic told him that couldn't be true since he could stand. Painful though the surprise attack was, it helped to the extent that it made him angry. And scared, because had the salarian been any stronger, Nick knew he would have been dead. Now he had two or three seconds at most in which to respond or she would hit him again.

So Nick raised his hands, gathered the energy necessary to pick the Skull up off the ground, and hold her there for a moment. Then, as her feet kicked helplessly, he slammed her down. The salarian uttered a cry of pain, and was clearly injured, because as she got to her feet she couldn't put much weight on one of them. But she was game and, as her hands came up, Nick knew he had only seconds in which to prevent a counterattack.

A solid "throw" might have been sufficient. But Nick was angry and conscious of the fact that people were watching. So he employed a shockwave instead. Rapid pulses of dark energy surged across the compartment, pummeled the other biotic like a series of physical blows, and knocked her off her feet. There was a sickening thud as the salarian fell and her head hit the metal deck.

At that point a Skull went over to check her pulse, looked to Tactus, and shook his head. The turian made a face. "All right, a deal is a deal. We'll split the loot fifty-fifty."

That wasn't the end of it. Not by a long shot. Because even as the dead biotic was towed feetfirst out of the compartment, Tactus and Zon were already in discussions about how and when the loot would be divided.

Meanwhile, Nick, who felt decidedly sick to his stomach, had been forced to resume his duties as standard-bearer. And the reality of what he'd done continued to weigh heavily on him even as Zon led her delegation back onto the busy street.

But rather than be left alone to deal with his emotions Nick soon found himself on the receiving end of congratulatory backslaps, celebratory man hugs, and a compliment from Kim. "Good work two guns—but strike *first* next time."

It was heady stuff. And one aspect of Nick's personality enjoyed it. But nothing could dispel what felt like a dark place deep inside of him. Because while it would have been one thing to defend himself against street thugs, he had allowed himself to be used as a pawn in a business dispute, and a person had been killed as a result.

Once the group arrived home Nick slipped away, went to his room, and locked the door. Then, while lying on his bed and staring at the ceiling, Nick thought about his parents. He should contact them— and Kahlee too. Or maybe he shouldn't. What would *they* think about what he'd done? The thought followed him into a troubled sleep, and a place where people fought each other for reasons they didn't understand, as part of a war that nobody could win.

EIGHT

ON OMEGA

The ship was small, fast, and registered to a Cerberus-controlled company. Just the thing for moving agents, prisoners, and cash from place to place. And thanks to the high-priority fee already paid to Aria T'Loak's docking facility, the sleek little vessel was able to enter a berth without delay.

A beautifully dressed woman and two heavily armed men left the ship twenty minutes later. And because she was clearly in charge, those who were paid to monitor such comings and goings saw what they were *supposed* to see, which was a female executive followed by two bodyguards.

None of the street scum who haunted the docks were stupid enough to approach the woman, so the trio was able to make it down and into the space station very quickly. A mixed force of humans, turians, and batarians were waiting for them and were quick to surround the executive with a wall of protection.

And it was during that interlude when one of her original bodyguards slipped away. Moments later Kai Leng was lost in the crowd. A bounty hunter perhaps, or a merc, on some errand or other. Omega was populated with thousands of such individuals. His leg was feeling better and he set a brisk pace.

Leng's duties had required him to spend a great deal of time on Omega over the years, but conditions on the space station were always in a state of flux. Favorite restaurants had disappeared since his last visit, what had been through streets were blocked off, and the Blue Suns were running the area he was in. Something that could be discerned from how many of them were on the streets—and the absence of street thugs.

Fortunately there was one thing Leng could count on and that was the Cerberus safe house waiting for him. After Leng murdered Liselle, and Grayson fled Omega, it had been necessary to close all of the organization's hidey-holes on the assumption that the entire network had been compromised.

New safe houses had been established since then, but Leng didn't know what to expect as he followed a narrow street into a district favored by upper-class criminals. Security people stood on corners, in doorways, and on roofs. All watching as the operative made his way up to a nice three-story building that was protected by a blast wall, metal gates, and a brace of krogan. They eyed Leng suspiciously as he paused for a scan and turned their backs on him when the gate rolled open.

Another scan was required before Leng could enter the building. After taking a lift up to the third floor it was necessary to enter a four-digit code into the keypad to open the door. The apartment was what Leng had expected it to be. And that was a hotel-like one-bedroom, one-bath suite with a small sitting area and kitchenette. The whole thing was comfortable but impersonal. Even the air had an institutional flavor to it. But that was fine with Leng, who didn't intend to stay there for very long.

Like any large organization Cerberus was dependent on a small army of functionaries. People who could arrange for the sort of distraction that allowed Leng to slip away, rent safe houses for operatives to stay in, and carry out dozens of other activities that were critical to success. And Leng was reminded of their role as he went over to examine the items that had been left on the coffee table.

There were toiletries, all according to his preferences, and three sets of clothing. He was already wearing a very serviceable set of light armor, and carrying a Kassa Fabrications Razer pistol. But, per his request, a Sokolov shotgun and a Vesper sniper rifle had been left for him. Boxes of ammo and two cleaning kits were available as well. It was the sort of service that only a top operative could expect and Leng took such things for granted.

A tone signaled an incoming call. But from whom? The answer was obvious. The Illusive Man. It was a reminder that Leng was still under surveillance. He turned to the apartment's holo-pad. "Accept call."

A swarm of light motes materialized in the air and flew together to form an image of the Illusive Man. A frozen wasteland had been visible in the background the last time Leng had seen the Illusive Man. But now his superior was silhouetted against a rusty red planet. It appeared that he was on an errand of some sort, the purpose of which would remain unknown. "I'm glad to see that you arrived safely," the Illusive Man said.

"Thank you."

"Hendel Mitra, Kahlee Sanders, and David Anderson are on Omega or will arrive there shortly."

Leng shrugged. "That's to be expected. They're looking for Nick Donahue and Gillian Grayson. I'll kill them when I have time."

The Illusive Man was holding an unlit cigarette. He caused it to twirl through the fingers of his right hand and back again. "Just before they left the Citadel Kahlee and Anderson were summoned by Council member Dia Oshar."

"Interesting."

"Very. The obvious question is why? But, until such time as we know the answer, I want you to leave them alone."

"I understand."

There was a moment of silence as the Illusive Man looked off camera. Then his steely blue eyes came back to meet Leng's. "Gillian Grayson wants to kill me. And I think it's safe to assume that Oshar and other members of the Council would like to see that happen."

"Probably," Leng agreed levelly. "But I'll find Gillian, and when I do that part of the problem will be solved."

"Now that your other assignments have been carried out you can turn your full attention to the matter," the Illusive Man replied as he lit the cigarette. "There is a great deal of work to do Kai . . . Wrap it up as soon as you can." And with that he disappeared.

Having broken the link Leng spent a few minutes at the apartment's computer terminal prior to loading the shotgun and returning to the street. The purpose of the heavy artillery being to serve as a deterrent to street thugs and to give him an edge if forced to defend himself against a gang.

The krogans were still out front, and everything looked normal, as Leng set off to visit the Beggar King. His name was Hobar, he was a volus, and something of an institution on Omega. The title stemmed from Hobar's position as the proprietor of a large network of professional and semiprofessional beggars, all of whom paid the volus ten percent of their daily take in return for what he liked to call "management services." That included the assignment of a corner or other location where a particular beggar was authorized to ply his or her trade, the "protection" payments that had to be made to the various gangs in order to operate in their constantly shifting territories, and some rudimentary medical care.

But Hobar had a secondary line of business as well. His network of beggars was so ubiquitous that they saw everything worth seeing. And there were those who were willing to pay good credits for information about their enemies, business associates, and in some cases their friends. A capability that Leng planned to take full advantage of.

Hobar's headquarters were located at the back of a cafeteria-style eatery where the emphasis was on quantity rather than quality—a surefire business model where many of Omega's residents were concerned. And thanks to his long-term patronage, not to mention that of the beggars who came and went each day, Hobar's favorite booth had been modified to accommodate both his rotund body and the power chair that stood in for his missing legs.

No one knew how or why the bilateral amputation had taken place, although there were dark rumors that the volus had his legs removed in order to look more pitiful. If so the strategy had been successful, because Hobar had taken the money given to him by passersby and parlayed it into a successful if shabby empire.

Leng, who had made use of the Beggar King's services before, entered the steamy embrace of the restaurant and followed a long warming table loaded with bins of food back to where Hobar's chair was parked. The table in front of him was strewn with half-eaten plates of food, printouts, and other bits of office paraphernalia. In spite of the environment suit he wore, the rank odor of unwashed flesh tainted the air. A sleek computer terminal sat to Hobar's right and two guards were leaning against the wall behind him—one was human, the other batarian, and both were well armed. They were watchful but made no attempt to intervene as Leng hung the shotgun on a wall hook and took the bench seat opposite Hobar.

The Beggar King was known to have an excellent memory and that was apparent as he spoke. "Mr. Manning . . . It has been awhile. Your last endeavor went well I hope?"

During his most recent mission to Omega Leng had broken into Grayson's apartment and murdered Liselle T'Loak. The Manning persona had been useful then and could be again. "Yes, thank you."

"Good. How can I assist you?"

"I'm looking for a young woman. A human. Chances are that she arrived on Omega during the last few days."

"You have a picture?"

"I do," Leng said, as he slid a chip across the table.

Hobar scooped it up. "That will be five thousand credits if we spot her and provide you with a location."

"Two thousand five hundred."

"Four thousand—and not a credit less."

Leng smiled thinly. "Three thousand."

"Three fifty."

"Done."

Hobar's facial expression if any was hidden by the mask that covered most of his face. But Leng could tell that he was satisfied. "Your contact information?"

"It's on the chip."

"Excellent. Have a nice day, Mr. Manning. And don't forget to give to the poor."

With the exception of those on guard duty all of the members of the Biotic Underground were gathered in the old hotel lobby or up on the mezzanine level where they could lean on the rail and look down onto the main floor. There were seventy-three of them including Nick, who was on the mezzanine standing next to Lem.

Nick was feeling a little bit better by that time, but still regretted killing the biotic the Grim Skulls had sent against him, even if such deaths were, as Mythra Zon liked to put it, "an unfortunate but necessary part of the revolution"—meaning the process by which the biotics would eventually supplant the Citadel Council. That would take money of course. Large quantities of it. Which was why the biotics and the Grim Skulls were going to rob a bank.

And not just *any* bank. But a bank owned and operated by none other than Aria T'Loak. The Pirate Queen. A daring act, which, if successful, would not only provide the Underground with some much needed capital but lift the organization up into the middle ranks of Omega's criminal hierarchy. "So," Zon was saying as her eyes roamed the faces all around, "the bank is heavily guarded. The Skulls will provide most of the conventional firepower. But we should be ready to assist them if necessary.

"That being said," she continued, "our primary task will be to confront and defeat T'Loak's biotics. Based on information collected by both the Skulls and our people it looks like we'll be up against at least twelve Level Three or better practitioners."

"No problem," one of the men on the main floor said. "We'll have them for lunch." The comment was followed by a chorus of supporting comments.

"Yeah, that's right!" "Bring 'em on." And, "We'll crush the bastards."

"Talk is cheap," Zon responded critically, "and overconfidence is stupid. Plus I would remind you that we will have to leave a third of our people here to defend the hotel. Because within an hour of the robbery, two at most, T'Loak's forces will attack this building. And the Skulls' headquarters as well. So we'll send about fifty people. Roughly ten of whom will be prime talents like Nick Donahue." The comment produced a round of applause.

Was Zon aware of his doubts and trying to pump him up? Nick didn't know. But when the asari looked straight at him, and said his name, the teenager felt a sense of pride so intense he would have done anything for her. And that included robbing a heavily defended bank.

The meeting continued for another fifteen minutes as Zon and second in command Kathar went over the battle plan, communications protocols, and the post-robbery exit plan. Because breaking in was one thing—getting home with the loot was another.

Then it was time for the biotics to leave the hotel and make their way to the bank, which was about three kilometers away. But rather than march through the streets in an effort to draw attention to themselves as they had in the past, the biotics were divided into three teams, each of which was to follow a different route to the objective. Nick was in the third group under the command of Arrius Sallus.

The ten-hour-long artificial night was almost over as Sallus led his subordinates through the nearly deserted streets following a route that he had checked the day before. In spite of the early hour other predators were out and about. They could be seen lurking here and there, eternally ready to roll drunks, mug those on their way to work, or prey upon each other should the opportunity present itself. But they knew better than to attack the heavily armed group as it jogged through alternating pools of light and shadow.

Eventually, having arrived at a predetermined assembly point, it was time to integrate the Skulls with the biotics and make final preparations for the assault. There was one team for each point of T'Loak's triangular bank building. It had been a temple originally, built by members of a long-forgotten cult and surrounded on all three sides by pedways and streets. The open spaces made it impossible for people to sneak up on the structure—and provided what amounted to a free-fire zone all around.

And making the objective that much harder to take were the weapons emplacements—one at each of the building's three corners. They had been added by T'Loak seventy years earlier, and used only once, when a defunct gang called the Black Jacks attacked the "east" side of the bank. Not a single one of the attackers had been able to enter, or so legend had it, which explained why none of Omega's many criminal organizations had attempted to break in since. So the direct approach was out, as was some sort of underground assault, because T'Loak had defenses down there as well.

Simply put, T'Loak's treasure trove was impregnable. That's what the Pirate Queen believed anyway, although the assumption was about to be tested. And Nick was going to be part of the combined team that would either succeed where the Black Jacks had failed or die trying.

"Okay," Sallus said, as about thirty biotics and Skulls came together. "You know the drill. Teams one and two will fire on the northwest and northeast corners of the building from positions on the opposite side of the street. Our job is to drop the hammer on the 'south' end of the bank. How 'bout it, Skulls? Are the charges ready?"

"They're preshaped and ready for placement," a helmeted noncom said stolidly.

"Good," Sallus responded. "Now remember . . . Once the path has been established it will be important to go in *fast*. If the weapons emplacement is still in operation we'll take it out. If it's out of commission we'll head for the control center. Meanwhile the defenders at the other end of the building won't be able to respond without exposing their sectors to a possible breach. There will still be plenty of opposition though, so keep your heads on a swivel. Okay, follow me."

Nick felt his heart start to beat faster as he followed Sallus and the Skulls between two nondescript buildings to the base of a fifty-meter-tall column. There were dozens of them all across Omega and this one was positioned directly across the street from T'Loak's bank. "Place the charges," Sallus said, as he consulted his omni-tool. "Detonate on my command."

The Skulls placed the charges and motioned for the rest of the team to back away. Sallus nodded knowingly as the sound of gunfire was heard to the north— and held up a three-fingered hand lest one of the Skulls trigger the explosives early. Timing was critical. And it was his responsibility to give T'Loak's quick response team enough time to reinforce the part of the bank that was under attack *before* blowing the column. "There," he said, as sixty seconds elapsed. "Blow it."

Artificial daylight was starting to fade in by that time, so Nick could not only hear a series of resonant booms as the charges went off, he could feel the ground shake under his feet and see the column start to fall. The process began with puffs of pulverized debris that shot sideways from the structure's base. Then came the strange moment when the column began to fall in what seemed like slow motion, followed by an explosion of dust as it hit the south end of the bank and crashed through the top two floors of the three-story building. The force of the impact caused the weapons emplacement at the south tip of the badly damaged structure to fall outwards and collapse onto the street beyond. There might have been survivors but not many.

"That's it!" Sallus roared. "We have our bridge . . . Follow me."

An enormous cloud of dust was still billowing upward as Nick followed a dimly seen Grim Skull up over a pile of debris and onto the top surface of the column. It stretched across the street to the point where the top of it was buried in T'Loak's depository. The curved surface was difficult to walk on, and a scream was heard as a Skull fell, but most of the attackers managed to keep their balance. It was a mad moment in which all of Nick's senses were alive in ways they never had been before, and his only concern was to perform well and earn additional respect from Zon. He wasn't sure where she was, with Tactus probably, but he knew she would receive detailed reports.

Devastating though the attack was there was plenty of opposition. That became apparent as the sound of gunfire was heard and a Skull staggered under the impact of multiple hits. But thanks to the fact that he and the rest of the lead team were wearing heavy armor he was able to stay vertical and fire back. The so-called heavies were relatively slow, however, which was why the people immediately behind them were clad in medium armor and carried lighter weapons.

Nick had elected to stay with his light armor and the additional freedom of movement it allowed him. Flashes of light appeared all around as the bank robbers jumped down off of their makeshift bridge and opened fire. Nick considered throwing a biotic barrier up to protect his team but wasn't sure who would wind up inside of it. So he shaped the energy required to create a singularity and willed it into existence. The effect was spectacular. Suddenly all of the defenders were sucked together along with loose pieces of furniture, chunks of debris, and a dead turian.

Then, as T'Loak's people floated helplessly in front of them, the Skulls opened fire. The defenders were a mixed group of salarians, batarians, and humans. They jerked spasmodically as hundreds of projectiles struck, beat their kinetic shields down, and left them vulnerable. Moments later all of them were dead, and as Nick allowed the singularity to collapse the bodies fell to the floor. "Well done!" Sallus shouted. "The control center is next. Follow me."

Nick wasn't sure how leadership had been able to find out about the control center and its location, but suspected that a bribe had been paid to someone on T'Loak's payroll. A person who, if they were smart, had left Omega for parts unknown.

Sallus led the team to a set of emergency stairs and from there down to the first floor. Nick knew that taking over the control center was critical to opening the vaults. But if Nick knew it then so did T'Loak's employees. And those that hadn't been sucked to the north end of the building by the diversion were wait-ing as Sallus cleared the stairwell and was hit with a hail of high-velocity pellets.

That made Nick angry. He sent shockwaves down the hallway. Then, having pulled the pistols, he began to fire as he marched forward. Skulls moved forward to add their fire to his. A pile of bodies lay just outside a door labeled CONTROL CENTER.

A klaxon was bleating as one of the Skulls aimed a shotgun at the door lock and fired twice. The spray of projectiles tore the locking mechanism apart, allow-ing one of the biotics to slide the barrier out of the way. Overhead lights threw pools of light down onto the floor of the room beyond, and three people were standing about eight meters away, with their backs to a curved console.

Nick was the third person to enter the room and knew he was up against an adept right away. The asari stood with hands raised. The barrier in front of her sparkled as high-speed particles hit it. That meant the biotic and the technicians sheltered with her were momentarily safe from the Skulls.

But that didn't apply to Nick, who knew that a bi-otic charge or a melee attack could penetrate the de-fensive screen. So he went in hard, felt a momentary resistance as he passed through the barrier, followed by the sensation of wading through quicksand. Then came the moment of release as Nick lumbered for-ward.

The asari was worried by then. He could see it on her face. Once they collided, and the defender lost focus, the screen would fall. That would open the controls to the salarian who had been hired to hack the bank's security system. He was bringing up the rear and should arrive at any moment. All of that flashed through Nick's mind as a projectile slammed into his right shoulder, turned him around, and sent him reeling. The floor came up to meet him and suddenly Nick was laying facedown as a searing pain stabbed his body. The light armor had been a mistake.

Fearful that he would take a round in the back Nick managed to roll over. That was when he saw the top of the asari's head fly off as one of the Skulls shot her. Nick shouted, "Don't kill the technicians!" but they were dead by that time. And that meant success would rest on the shoulders of the salarian.

Nick was propped up on his good side as one of the weaker biotics paused to slap some medi-gel on his wound and help him to stand. She was about his age and dressed in medium armor. "You have to walk," she insisted. "The Skulls aren't likely to carry you—and I'm not strong enough."

Nick knew she was right and struggled to his feet. He'd been shot before, back at the academy, but that didn't make it feel any better. He felt dizzy, swayed uncertainly, and felt grateful when the girl ducked under his left arm in an attempt to steady him. But wounded or not he had the satisfaction of seeing the salarian sitting in front of the control panel and heard a reedy cheer as one of the vaults opened.

Then Zon appeared with Tactus in tow. They passed Nick without so much as a sideways glance, went straight to the control panel, and remained there until the other vaults cycled open. That was when Kathar rushed in. Judging from the damage to his armor he'd been in the thick of the fighting. Nick was close enough to hear as the quarian spoke to Zon. "T'Loak's people are streaming in from all over. We've got to get out of here."

"We'll enter vault one," Sallus said grimly. "Then we'll clean it out, blow a hole through the west wall, and exit that way. I'll order team one and team two to reposition themselves and provide covering fire."

The plan made sense and Zon was smart enough to recognize that. "Fair enough," she said calmly. "We'll redirect our people accordingly. I'm sorry there won't be enough time to loot vaults two and three, but something is better than nothing."

Seconds later Nick found himself in a column of walking wounded that snaked out into a corridor, leading them to a blown door and the long narrow space labeled VAULT ONE. A muffled *THUMP* was heard as the Skulls blew a hole in the back wall and a biotic began to yell, "Take a pack! Take a pack!"

The backpacks were cheap and flimsy but that was fine since they would only be used once. Time was of the essence and all of them knew it as they shuffled through the vault toward the ragged hole in the back wall and the artificial sunlight beyond. Those who had been wounded weren't required to wear a pack, but the others were, so that predesignated "loaders" could dump small ingots into each one of them. Most of the galaxy's commerce was carried out digitally, but such transactions could be tracked, so criminal enterprises were forced to use other forms of currency, Beryllium being one of them.

The process was slow at first, but the line began to pick up speed as the loaders became more efficient, so

it wasn't long before Nick and his escort were step-
ping through the newly created door into a chaotic
firefight. It seemed teams one and two had successfully repositioned themselves to provide covering fire,
but T'Loak's people were infiltrating the area, and
snipers were firing from all around. "Come on!" the
girl said, as they began to cross the street. "Run!"

Nick couldn't run. Not really. But he did the best
he could as the battle grew more intense and projectiles pinged the pavement all around them. Then they
were across the street and entering the narrow passageway that separated two buildings. The sound of
fighting began to fade at that point and Nick thought
they were safe until a batarian stepped out of a door
eight meters in front of them. The merc was armed
with an assault weapon that he leveled at them.

Nick was reaching for a pistol with his good hand
when the girl shook him off. She was Level 2 at best,
but there was nothing wrong with her "throw." It
pushed the batarian backward and ruined his aim. A
burst of high-velocity particles flew over Nick's head
as he pulled the trigger three times. The time spent on
the range paid off as two of the three rounds pulped
the merc's unprotected face.

Then it was time to shuffle past the body and clear
the area as quickly as possible. It was clear that the
plan to re-form and return to the hotel as a unified
force had come apart and each biotic was on his or
her own. And the girl knew that. "We aren't going to
make it back to headquarters," she said grimly. "Not
before T'Loak's people attack the place."

"Leave me," Nick said. "I'll be fine thanks to you.

All I need is a place to hole up until the fighting dies down."

The girl looked up into his face. She had a broad forehead, wide-set eyes, and a nice mouth. It was set in a firm line. "No. I won't leave you."

Suddenly Nick saw something that was entirely new to him. There was a protective look in her eyes. And something more as well. A level of devotion he didn't deserve. Nick smiled. "Thank you. Come on . . . There's a hotel up ahead. You can check in for both of us. T'Loak's people will be all over the place looking for stragglers pretty soon. We need to get off the street."

The hotel was on lockdown and for a very good reason. The last thing the owner wanted was to get involved in a raging gang war. But the girl was determined. She beat her fist on the door until the manager opened it a crack. Then having gotten his attention she told a reasonably convincing story about how she and her husband had been walking past T'Loak's bank when all hell broke loose. He had been hit by a stray round and all they wanted was a place to take refuge until the craziness died down. Fortunately the manager was human and inclined to help a member of his own race.

The twosome were inside a minute later, and entering a shabby room shortly after that, as the fighting began to decrease and traffic noise increased. Gun battles were common, people had to work, and life went on. For most people that is, the exceptions being those who had been killed during the robbery.

Nick sat on the bed, fought to suppress a groan as

the girl lifted his feet up off the floor, and lay back against the pillows. "Tell me something."

The girl sat down next to him. Her eyes were brown and very serious. "What would you like to know?"

"Your name."

"It's Marisa. Marisa Mendez."

"My name's Nick. Nick Donahue."

"I know. Everyone does."

"I want to thank you, Marisa. You saved my life."

Marisa looked down. "It was nothing."

Nick brought his left hand up under Marisa's chin. Her eyes met his. He meant to say something but wound up kissing her instead. Her lips were soft, she smelled like soap, and the pain in his shoulder was momentarily forgotten. It felt good to be alive.

NINE

On Omega

Aria T'Loak was furious. She had returned from Thessia only to learn that her bank had been robbed the day before. Though a very small part of her net worth, the loss was irksome and might signal weakness. And that was never a good thing on Omega. The fact that the heist had been carried out by a low-rent gang like the Skulls, and a heretofore unknown group called the Biotic Underground, meant a loss of face. Both of the offending organizations had already been punished with reprisal attacks, but neither had been wiped out. That meant further efforts would be required in order to deal with them.

So as the asari stood across from the bank and looked at the damage, she was angry. But something more as well. T'Loak was worried. Because when she climbed up onto the broken column that led across the street and straight to her bank she realized how elegant the plan had been. Not the sort of thing she expected from the Skulls. Had the idea originated with biotics then? Yes, she thought so. It seemed that there was a new and potentially dangerous player on Omega. One that would have to be watched.

Fortunately her people had been quick to react to the attack. So while the bank robbers had been able to remove the contents of one vault the other two remained untouched. Still, the loss of material worth 2.5 million credits was nothing to sneeze at, and someone would have to pay. Even if T'Loak was partially to blame for failing to anticipate the way in which the column could be used. It was a lesson learned and one that would be applied to all of her other holdings. Anything that could be used as a giant club would be seized or purchased and destroyed.

A very frightened batarian was waiting for T'Loak inside the building. Later, in the wake of the robbery, he had been apprehended trying to board a freighter bound for Khar'shan. That was why a pair of armed turians were positioned behind him. His name was Obo Pol and he'd been in charge of the bank on the day of the attack. T'Loak faced him across two meters of debris-strewn floor. "You're alive," she observed. "*Why?*"

"They attacked without warning," Pol answered lamely. "I thought they were going to try and enter through the north wall so I sent the quick response team there. That's when they blew the column. And they had biotics. Lots of them."

"Excuses won't cut it," T'Loak said harshly. "The column was a surprise. I'll grant you that. But once it hit you should have rushed reinforcements to the control center, yet you failed to do so. Not to mention the fact that you attempted to run rather than remain here and take responsibility. That's why they're going to hang you. And right out front too . . . So people can see the connection. Take him away."

Pol tried to run but the turians were ready. They stunned him, and with help from two additional mercs hauled the batarian away. The hanging wouldn't repair the damage done to T'Loak's reputation, but it couldn't hurt, and would provide Omega's citizens with free entertainment.

Tann Immo had risen through the ranks of T'Loak's syndicate to become one of her most trusted advisers. And that was why he had been brought in during the aftermath of the robbery to sort things out. Once Pol had been carried away he took the opportunity to speak. "We have three prisoners."

"Good," T'Loak said irritably. "Hang them too."

"If you say so," Immo said gravely. "But one of them claims to have been present when your daughter was murdered."

What felt like ice water trickled into T'Loak's veins. "Where is this person?"

"The prisoners are in a secured area at the north side of the building."

"Take me there." T'Loak followed Immo down a passageway toward the center of the bank. Having left the column and the impact zone behind, things looked normal. They passed the offices associated with T'Loak's profitable loan-sharking operation, and a data center that also functioned as a backup for computers located elsewhere, before entering the maze of small rooms that the guards lived in.

One section of the residential area had been put to use as a medical clinic where the wounded were being cared for at T'Loak's expense. Because she felt that just as incompetence should be punished, loyalty should be rewarded, which explained why the turnover rate in her organization was relatively low. "The prisoners are being kept here," Immo said, as they passed a pair of guards. "They were wounded and left behind when the attackers were forced to withdraw. Two of them are Skulls. The third is a member of the Biotic Underground."

T'Loak nodded. "Which one claims to know about Liselle's death?"

"A Skull named Shella. She's in the last room on the right."

A batarian was stationed at the door and came to something resembling attention as T'Loak approached. She gave him a nod and entered the room. It was empty except for a bed and the human female laying on top of it. She appeared to be about thirty or so and wore her hair in a military-style buzz cut that served to show off the elaborate tracery of tattoos on her scalp. She was skinny, her face had a pinched look, and T'Loak was struck by the look of defiance in her eyes. The human was sitting up with a pillow under her right knee. It was wrapped with bandages. "So," T'Loak said, "your name is Shella. Do you have a second name?"

"Yes," the woman said. "It's Shella."

T'Loak might have smiled on some other occasion but not now. "I see. Okay, Shella . . . I'm told that you murdered my daughter."

"*No,*" Shella said emphatically. "I said I was present when your daughter was murdered. There's a big difference. The killing came as a complete surprise to me."

"I find that hard to believe," T'Loak replied. "But go on—convince me. And while you're at it tell me who slit her throat. More than that, make me believe it."

"I'll tell you," Shella promised. "But only if you allow me to live. Otherwise the name of the person who killed your daughter dies with me."

T'Loak didn't like being forced to do things. And the fact that Shella had been among those who robbed her made the demand that much harder to stomach. But she wanted the information and wanted it badly. "Maybe I'll agree to your proposal," she said, "and maybe I won't. I'm going to ask you some simple questions. The kind you'll be willing to answer if you want to live. Then, if I like what I hear, the deal is on."

"Okay," Shella replied cautiously. "Depending on what you ask."

T'Loak battled to maintain her composure. "Where did the killing take place?"

"In Paul Grayson's apartment. You knew him as Paul Johnson."

That was true. And Aria felt a slowly rising sense of excitement. Maybe Shella *did* know who the killer was. The Illusive Man claimed Grayson was responsible for Liselle's death, and T'Loak had assumed the same thing, but was it true? "Something was removed from the apartment after the murder," T'Loak said. "What was it?"

Shella didn't hesitate. "A large quantity of red sand. *Your* red sand."

That was enough. T'Loak believed her. The woman *had* been present. Maybe she was the killer and maybe not. She would agree to the deal. Then, if there was proof that Shella had been holding the knife, the asari would kill her. *Personally.* "All right . . . Start talking."

"So we have an agreement?"

"Yes."

"How do I know you'll keep your word?"

"You don't," T'Loak replied grimly. "But you know my reputation. Everyone on Omega does. When I make a deal I honor it."

Shella clearly had her doubts but was in a jam. All she could do was take her best shot and hope for the best. "Okay, I'll tell you everything I know. Before joining the Skulls I was a freelancer. Cerberus hired me."

T'Loak was already paying close attention. And the mention of Cerberus heightened her interest even more. "You worked for Cerberus? In what capacity?"

"I was a communications tech working for an operative named Manning. The Illusive Man sent him here to collect Grayson and bring him in. I have no idea why. They don't tell freelancers things like that."

If the Illusive Man was in any way responsible for Liselle's death T'Loak wanted to know about it. "Go on."

"We found a way to get past the security guards out front. Then we managed to enter the apartment. Your daughter was present. One of our team members knocked her out with a tranq dart. Grayson was next. And that was when Manning did what he did."

T'Loak tried to swallow the lump in her throat. "Which was?"

"He had a knife. From the kitchen. He used it to slit your daughter's throat. He hadn't gone there with the intention of killing her. Or so it seemed to me. But Manning is the only person who would know for sure."

T'Loak was determined not to cry. Not until later. When she was alone. She cleared her throat. "So, Manning is alive?"

Shella shrugged. "How would I know? But yes, probably. He's a survivor."

"Describe him."

So Shella described the man she knew as Manning, the way he handled himself, and his relationship with the Illusive Man, which she described as "close."

T'Loak's perfectly shaped eyebrows rose. "How close?"

"It's like I told you," Shella replied. "I wasn't involved in high-level meetings. But I know Manning had direct access to the Illusive Man, and that's rare."

"Yes, it is," T'Loak said thoughtfully. She knew a thing or two about the Illusive Man, having dealt with him on a couple of occasions, and Shella's description was consistent with what she had observed. "All right. You kept your word—and I'll keep mine."

Having turned to Immo, the asari said, "Have her delivered to the Skulls."

Immo nodded. "And the other prisoners?"

"They were interrogated?"

"Yes."

"Do the biotics or Skulls have any of our people?"

"No."

There was a long pause. Finally, just as the silence was becoming very uncomfortable, the Pirate Queen spoke. "Release them. There has been enough killing." And with that she left the room.

Omega's streets were filled with people as another artificial day neared its end and the light began to fade. Most of the pedestrians were headed home but others were just starting to stir as Gillian left the ordered world within the quarian warehouse for the chaotic environment beyond. She had been pounding the pavement for two cycles by that time, searching for a way to connect with Cerberus, and ultimately the Illusive Man. But it wasn't easy. Those who didn't know were eager to sell her lies and those who knew, or *probably* knew, were very tight lipped.

It was frustrating. Extraordinarily so, and Gillian was running out of options, not to mention money. But there was one more possibility. A long shot to say the least—but something was better than nothing. And that was the nightspot called the Afterlife. It was everything to everyone. It was said that the rich and powerful gathered there as well as the station's common folk because, regardless of social standing, all of them were interested in the same things. And that included music, sex, and drugs. None of which had any appeal for Gillian.

No, *her* interest stemmed from the fact that the Afterlife was owned by Aria T'Loak. The asari crime lord who was said to be the most powerful person on Omega. But more important, from Gillian's perspective at least, was the fact that there was a connection between T'Loak, her father, and the Illusive Man. Because according to Kahlee the asari had agreed to kill Paul Grayson on the Illusive Man's behalf. She hadn't been able to do so, but the arrangement suggested some sort of ongoing connection, which Gillian hoped to take advantage of. The problem was how to get an audience with T'Loak, and if she managed to obtain one, how to pry the information out of her. These complexities explained why the visit to the Afterlife was the last item on Gillian's to-do list rather than the first.

So as Gillian let the flow of foot traffic carry her along, the plan was to buy some cheap street food and kill time before making her way to the nightclub. T'Loak typically arrived there about nine, or so people claimed, which meant there was no point in showing up earlier.

Gillian had acquired some street smarts by that time and knew how to avoid the hustlers. One of the most important tactics was to keep moving. But as she walked past a store specializing in armor, she felt a strange tingling sensation between her shoulder blades, and paused to look around. It wasn't the first time. Gillian had experienced a similar feeling the day before. Was someone watching her?

The simple answer was "yes." Everyone was watching everyone on Omega. Either in hopes of taking advantage of them somehow or in an effort to protect themselves from harm. So, having scanned her surroundings without identifying a specific threat, Gillian continued on.

Though still in the process of learning her way around the space station Gillian had been on Omega long enough to develop a list of favorite street carts. One of which sold spicy pastry-wrapped sausages that were not only delicious but affordable. So after waiting in line Gillian collected her dinner, and was headed for the cluster of tables that a number of food vendors shared, when she experienced the tingling sensation for the second time. She turned quickly, caught a glimpse of a face she thought she'd seen before, but couldn't place. Then the man was gone, swallowed up by the crowd. Gillian was inclined to write the episode off to the jumpiness she felt, but resolved to keep a sharp eye out just in case.

She ate a leisurely dinner, washed it down with hot tea purchased from a neighboring cart, and sat with her hands wrapped around the warm cup. As she watched the people sitting at the other tables, and the couples strolling past, Gillian felt the way she always did, which was lonely. She had always been an outsider. First at the academy where the other children tormented her, then on the *Idenna* where acceptance only went so far, and now on a very dangerous habitat.

There had been moments though . . . Brief moments when her father had come to visit. *Gigi*. That was his pet name for her. He was the only person who had bothered to give her one. And outside of Kahlee the only person she could speak freely to. In bursts usually, separated by periods of silence, during which Grayson sat beside her and waited. He'd been neatly dressed on such occasions, but gaunt, as if starving to death.

Gillian's right hand went to the green jewel that was hanging around her neck. The gift from her father had arrived shortly before she left the academy. The handwriting on the card had been shaky. "Dear

Gigi," it said. "Something pretty for a pretty girl. Love, Father."

Grayson wasn't her *real* father, but he loved her anyway. And that meant a lot. So much that she felt compelled to do what any good daughter would do: avenge his death. The problem being that the person responsible was very hard to find.

Her drink was cold by then, but Gillian felt warm, and ready to take the next step on the path she had chosen. The teenager was filled with a renewed sense of determination as she got up, dropped the cup into a disposal chute, and set off for the Afterlife.

There were a number of reasons to feel frightened. The first was natural but would have seemed silly to her more worldly peers back at the academy. Gillian had never been in a nightclub before. And based on its reputation the Afterlife was a nexus for all of the things that Kahlee and Hendel had warned her against. Plus Gillian didn't know how to behave in such a setting. There were bound to be norms, just as there were on the streets of Omega, but what were they?

That uncertainty was bad enough. But making the situation even *more* difficult was the nature of her mission. Logic dictated that T'Loak would have plenty of bodyguards. How to break through? The question was still nagging at Gillian as she arrived in front of the nightclub.

There were lots of people. Some entering, some leaving, and some just milling around. And as was the case everywhere on Omega the presence of so many people was a draw for vendors, street performers, and petty criminals. Although the latter were quickly identified by T'Loak's uniformed mercs and chased away.

Having gathered the necessary courage Gillian threw her shoulders back and made for the front door. She was wearing the best outfit she had. A red waist-length jacket, broad belt, and gray pants. Nothing compared to what the women entering ahead of her were decked out in but it was the best she could do.

Massive krogans stood to each side of the entrance. They eyed Gillian as she passed between them but made no attempt to stop her as she was funneled through a weapons detector and onto the main floor. Dance music pounded Gillian's ears, the smell of artificially flavored tobacco wafted through the air, and the lighting was dim.

Being unsure of where to go, or what to do, Gillian paused to orient herself. There was a stage at the center of the room on which three asari dancers were swaying to the music. All of them were beautiful, nearly naked, and mesmerizing to look at. Having never been exposed to something like that before Gillian found the scene to be both fascinating and embarrassing at the same time. She couldn't imagine doing what the asari were doing—and was surprised at how nonchalant the other customers were. In fact, many of those gathered around the bar that circled the stage were busy talking to each other rather than looking at the dancers. And there were *more* performers as well, dancing on a ring that was suspended from the ceiling, and hung level with the second floor. "Care for a drink?"

Gillian turned to discover that a waitress was

standing half a meter away from her. The asari was dressed in a slightly luminescent top, short skirt, and high-heeled shoes that glowed green. She was holding a tray with two empty glasses on it and had an expectant look on her face. Unfortunately Gillian had no idea what to do. Was it necessary to purchase a drink? Could she afford to do so? And what would she order?

The waitress smiled engagingly as if to allay Gillian's discomfort. "Have you been here before?"

Gillian shook her head.

"Right then," the asari said. "Perhaps you would enjoy one of our nonalcoholic drinks. A Zesmeni Blush perhaps. That's a blend of fruit juices with a touch of mint."

That helped Gillian find her voice. "Yes, thank you. And there's something else as well. I would like to speak with Aria T'Loak."

If the waitress was surprised there was no sign of it on her beautiful face. "One Zesmeni Blush coming up . . . And I'll pass your request along." With that she left.

There was an empty table nearby, so rather than stand at the edge of the circular walkway, Gillian made her way over to it. The closest customers, a trio of batarians, turned twelve eyes in her direction. Having registered her presence they resumed their conversation.

Time passed and Gillian began to feel increasingly awkward since she had no drink and no one to talk to. Then, after what seemed like an eternity, the waitress returned. "Here you go," she said, and placed a tall glass on the table. It was filled with an amber-colored liquid and topped off by a slice of fruit and a glittering stir stick. "That will be ten credits."

Gillian fumbled for the chips, found three of them, and placed them on the tray. She didn't know how much to tip and hoped five was enough. Judging from the asari's smile it was. "Thank you," she said. "Miss T'Loak isn't available but Mr. Immo has agreed to see you. He is one of Miss T'Loak's senior staff members— and will be able to answer any questions you may have. Wait here and he'll drop by as soon as he can."

Gillian didn't want to see a senior staff member and knew he wouldn't be able to answer her questions. But maybe she could talk the Immo person into facilitating a meeting with T'Loak. So she said "Thank you," and watched the waitress walk away. Could *she* sway her hips like that?

The question remained unanswered as Gillian took a sip of the drink, found it to her liking, and went back to watching the people who passed by. A half-drunk spacer paused at her table a few minutes later, called her "honey," and was about to sit down when she gave him a biotic "push." The nudge was sufficient to put him on his ass, much to the amusement of the batarians, who laughed and made what were probably rude comments in their own language.

The human got up, told them what he thought of "bats," and stumbled away.

Five minutes later a salarian appeared, paused to look around, and spotted Gillian. Then, having approached the table, he produced the salarian version of a smile. It looked more like a grimace. "Hello . . . My name is Tann Immo. May I join you?"

Gillian nodded. She felt impatient but slightly

hopeful. "Please do. Thank you for taking the time to speak with me."

"It's my pleasure," Immo responded as he sat down. "How can I help?"

"I wish to speak with Aria T'Loak," Gillian replied.

"Regarding what?" Immo wanted to know. "Maybe I can handle your request."

"*No,*" Gillian said tightly as the tension began to build inside of her. It was the wrong approach. The teenager knew that with her brain but her emotions were taking over. It was a problem that plagued her in school as well. But there was more than a lack of self-discipline involved. If she told Immo what she was after, and he told T'Loak, she would lose the only advantage she had. And that was the element of surprise. "I want to talk to T'Loak regarding a private matter," she said. "And I wish to do so in person."

It appeared as though Immo was about to respond when a disturbance was heard off to the left. Two mercs appeared, closely followed by an asari, and two additional bodyguards. Their client had lavender-colored skin, and her face was decorated with a pair of lines that arced between her eyes, as well as a heavier line that ran from a well-formed mouth to the bottom of her chin.

There was an immediate buzz of conversation from the surrounding customers and Gillian knew who the closely guarded personage was without being told. "Aria T'Loak!" Gillian shouted, as she came to her feet. "I want to talk to you!"

The asari crime lord kept walking and didn't bother to turn her head. But three of the four bodyguards stopped, turned toward what they perceived to be a threat, and began to draw their weapons.

Gillian was amped up both emotionally and physically. Her response was as natural as breathing. Her hands came up, energy flowed, and surged outward. The "reave," as biotics referred to it, was used to target an opponent's nervous system. And because the guards were standing so close to each other, Gillian was able to hit all three at once. They dropped their weapons, doubled over, and collapsed. That was when all hell broke loose. People screamed and some of them stampeded out through the front door.

Immo launched himself at the biotic, but lost all forward momentum as a stasis field locked him in place, and Gillian turned back to the task at hand. And that was to catch up with T'Loak. With that in mind Gillian left the table, stepped out onto the walkway, and was just about to go after the nightclub owner when what felt like a hammer hit her. It was a shockwave. And the force of the biotic blow knocked her down.

But rather than remain on the floor she rolled right, scrambled to her feet, and found herself confronting *two* asari biotics. They were blocking the path that led toward T'Loak. Gillian felt a sudden surge of anger, raised her hands, and drew a picture in the air. As thought was transformed into purposeful energy three rapidly shifting mass effect fields came into existence. The "warp" tore the asari biotics asunder. One moment they were there, and the next they weren't, as chunks of raw meat flew in every direction.

The resulting blood mist was still floating in the air

and would remain so for a few seconds as the half-executed "pull," which the asari had been creating at the moment of their deaths, lost its coherency. But there was no time to think about that or anything else as a burst of projectiles whipped past Gillian and tore into the bar. Glassware shattered, wood splintered, and someone shouted "Kill her!" as the teen turned to face a new set of attackers.

Gillian had seen the krogan guards standing outside of the main entrance and now the monsters were marching her way firing as they came. But the biotic barrier she had thrown up was sufficient to protect her for a few seconds. Gillian had surrendered all hope of talking to Aria T'Loak by then. Her only objective was to escape as she took dark energy in, routed it through her customized amplifiers, and gave it purpose.

What happened next came as a complete surprise to the krogan as Gillian triggered the biotic power called "charge." Rather than running away from the guards Gillian pounded straight at them. Within the space of three steps her body became a blur and she could feel additional strength coursing through her body as she hit one of the reptiles and sent the brute flying. The krogan smashed into a wall, fell onto a table below, and crushed it under his weight. His partner uttered a roar of rage, Gillian ran for the door, and time seemed to slow.

Kai Leng had an excellent view of the Afterlife from a darkened third-floor apartment on the opposite side of the street. The window was open and the Vesper sniper's rifle was resting on a table he had positioned in front of it. All the Cerberus operative had to do was wait. Because after learning of Gillian's location from the Beggar King he had followed her from the quarian warehouse to the Afterlife and had watched her enter.

It would have been preferable to kill her quietly, in bed perhaps, or a dark alley. But the quarian warehouse was very well guarded, and even if it had been possible to sneak inside, Leng would have been incredibly obvious. So that meant he would have to carry out the sanction in public. Something that was easier to do on Omega than it would have been on the Citadel. But it still entailed some risk, since all of the people on the street were not only armed, but paranoid. And likely to return fire on the off chance that he was shooting at them.

Leng's thoughts were interrupted by the sound of muffled sobs. He glanced over his shoulder. The woman who lived in the apartment was crying again. Tape covered her mouth and she was tied to a chair with lengths of cord. Leng frowned. "Shut up. Remember what I told you. Behave yourself and live—or cause trouble and die. The choice is up to you." The sobbing stopped.

Leng turned his attention back to the scope and the scene below. Nothing had changed. The question, in his mind at least, was why Gillian had gone into the Afterlife at all. She didn't seem like the nightclub type. Not that it mattered because his job was to kill her, not understand her.

The minutes crawled by. People came and went. There was a scuffle between two prostitutes. T'Loak's mercs chased them away. *More* time passed. Finally,

just as Leng was about to pee in the vase he had selected for that purpose, something happened.

There weren't very many private vehicles on Omega,
so whenever one appeared it was a sure sign that a
VIP was inside. As an armored limo emerged from a
side street Leng swung the rifle around to cover it.
There was a gun turret mounted on top of the armored vehicle, and four uniformed mercs on the running boards, all of whom were ready to jump down
and clear obstacles should anyone or anything get in
the way.

Aria T'Loak? Coming to work? Leng thought so.
And that hypothesis was confirmed as the vehicle
pulled up in front of the Afterlife and an asari got out.
Leng couldn't see her face, and wouldn't have been
able to take a shot had that been his intent, because
the limo was in the way. That was no accident. But
the extremely deferential way that the guards were
treating her said it all. The Pirate Queen had arrived.
All of which was entertaining but otherwise meaningless.

The limo left, the activity died down, and Leng was
starting to think about his bladder again when something strange occurred. Suddenly, for no apparent
reason, the krogan door guards turned and went inside. That piqued Leng's interest and caused him to
re-center his crosshairs on the door.

Nothing happened at first. But then, seconds later,
Gillian appeared. And she ran straight at him. Her
exit was so sudden, and so unexpected, that Leng
barely had time to adjust his aim and squeeze the trigger. There was a soft pop as the silencer did its job,
the rifle butt kicked his shoulder, and the projectile

spiraled down toward its target. The particle was small, but thanks to the rifling in the gun barrel, and the extreme muzzle velocity that the weapon produced, it packed a big punch.

But Gillian was moving *fast*. And instead of hitting her the round struck the krogan who was chasing her. A mixture of blood and brains flew as the fast-moving projectile punched its way through an eye and buried itself in the mercenary's skull.

The body was still falling as Leng swore, depressed the rifle, and scanned for Gillian. But it was too late. His target had disappeared.

That left Leng with no choice but to pack up and leave. He paused long enough to open a flick knife and cut the cords that held the woman in place. "Thanks for the hospitality. Sorry about the mess. Have a nice evening." There was a hiss as the door opened followed by another as it closed. The night was young. And life, such as it was, went on.

TEN

On Omega

Kahlee and Anderson had been to Omega before. But Hendel hadn't. And even though he'd heard about conditions on the space station, hearing and seeing were two different things. Thanks to the fact that they were armed and clearly knew what they were doing the threesome had been able to clear the docking area without incident and make their way inside the habitat.

Once in the thick of things they headed for the Tra-Na hotel. It was a nice hostelry, and the rates were relatively high as a result, but Anderson had a government expense account and saw no reason to stay in a flophouse. Especially given all the security concerns.

It was almost dark when they arrived. After they had eaten it was time to retire to their individual rooms for the night. The occasional sound of gunfire made it difficult to sleep, so none of them were completely rested as they came together for breakfast. "What's on the agenda for today?" Hendel inquired as he finished his second cup of caf.

"There aren't any public newscasts on Omega,"

Anderson replied, as he buttered a piece of toast. "But there is a private subscriber-based service run by a man who sends occasional stories off to the Citadel. I'm told that he can give us a picture of what's been taking place here—and that could be very helpful."

The others agreed and once breakfast was finished they set off for a destination that was a brisk twenty-minute-walk away. Anderson and Kahlee led the way with Hendel bringing up the rear. The office they were looking for was located in a shopping arcade sandwiched in between a Laundromat and a tiny cafe. The sign above the door read GALACTIC NEWS SERVICE. A name that suggested something a lot larger than the one-man operation inside.

As Anderson, Kahlee, and Hendel entered they saw what they presumed to be the proprietor at the other end of a long narrow room with his back turned to them. He was seated in front of three flat-screen monitors. And as video appeared and disappeared it became clear that he was editing a story. When Anderson said "Mr. Nix?" the human turned.

Implants of various types were common on Omega, the Citadel, and throughout known space. And many of them were custommade according to the requirements of the individual customer. So seeing them was an everyday occurrence. Still, there was something shockingly unexpected about the zoom lens that protruded from Nix's right eye socket. The device whirred softly as it brought the visitors into focus. Was it connected to a neural chip? Enabling Nix to record what he saw? Anderson would have been willing to bet on it. The rest of the reporter's face had a slightly cadaverous appearance. He had wispy hair, a bent nose, and skin that was pitted as if from some disease. "Yes?"

The actual question was forthright enough, but Anderson thought there was a good deal that *hadn't* been said, such as: "I'm busy. What the hell do you want?"

He forced a smile. "My name is Anderson. David Anderson. This is Kahlee Sanders and the gentleman on my right is Hendel Mitra. We arrived yesterday. According to people on the Citadel you know everything there is to know about the situation here. It's our hope that you'll agree to a briefing."

The expression on Nix's face changed subtly. "David Anderson as in *Admiral* David Anderson?"

"Yes."

"Please sit down," the newsman said eagerly. "I'm Harvey Nix. Oops! I only have two guest chairs. Sorry about that. Mr. Mitra, is it? Perhaps you would be willing to pull that gearbox over. Exactly, well done. So, Admiral . . . What brings you to Omega?"

Anderson could see where things were going and held up a hand in protest. "I can't give you an interview, but I would be happy to pay for an hour of your time."

Money was tight judging from the look of Nix's office and Anderson saw what might have been a glint of avarice in the reporter's real eye. "Yes, of course, I understand. My hourly fee is five hundred credits."

Anderson didn't believe that Nix had an established fee. Much less one that was so high. He smiled. "Two fifty."

"Done," Nix agreed quickly. "What would you like to know?"

"Give us the headlines for the last couple of weeks," Kahlee put in. "Then, assuming we hear something interesting, we'll ask for more details."

So Nix sat back and launched into a very service- able summary of the major events that had taken place on Omega during the last fifteen days. Most of which was of very little interest to his audience. But when Nix mentioned that the Grim Skulls and a new organization, which called itself the Biotic Under- ground, had combined forces to rob a bank owned by Aria T'Loak, all sorts of mental alarms went off. An- derson pressed the reporter for details. And Nix pro- vided all the information he could, including the fact that the batarian who had been in charge of the de- pository had been hung from a lamppost and subse- quently used for target practice.

Once the account was complete Kahlee turned to her companions. "The Biotic Underground. That's the group Nick joined."

"It sure is," Anderson replied. "How very interest- ing."

"If the bank robbery is of interest to you," Nix put in, "then you might want to know about what took place last night."

Anderson, Kahlee, and Hendel listened with inter- est as Nix described how a female biotic had gone crazy inside the Afterlife nightclub. A number of T'Loak's employees had been killed including a pair of biotic adepts who had been torn to pieces. It was a big deal and everyone on Omega was talking about it. Hendel was the first to respond. "Do you have a pic- ture of her by any chance? That is, the biotic who took the place apart?"

"As a matter of fact I do," Nix assured them. "Hold on a sec."

Anderson, Kahlee, and Hendel looked at each other, then at the screens on the back wall, as Nix's fingers flew over the keys on his controller and video swirled. "This is surveillance video from the Afterlife," Nix said with his back turned to them. "Aria T'Loak's staff sent it over in hopes that I would include it in my daily feed. The Pirate Queen is offering ten thousand credits for the girl dead or alive."

Kahlee held her breath as the video locked up and prayed that the biotic she was about to see was a complete stranger. Then her heart sank. Because there, on all three screens, was a very familiar face. Gillian was looking straight into the camera with hands raised and a grimace on her face. Then the video cut to a reverse over-the-shoulder shot as a pair of asari were ripped to pieces. The little girl Kahlee had known was no more. A killer had been born.

Having learned that the Biotic Underground had taken part in the bank robbery, Anderson, Kahlee, and Hendel went looking for it on the theory that an entire organization would be easier to find than a single individual. And thanks to the high profile the biotics had created for themselves, the threesome was able to get information about where the group was headquartered in a matter of hours.

But when they arrived at the old hotel it was to find that the Biotic Underground had abandoned the much abused property and a street gang was moving in. They were a scruffy-looking bunch who wore face paint, were dressed in mismatched pieces of armor, and rode power skates. They were called the Lightnings and were known for their hit-and-run-style robberies.

Hendel crossed the street to speak with one of the sentries posted around the building. Judging from all the damage that had been done to it, the place had been attacked in the very recent past. The guard had purple hair, orange facial markings, and teeth that had been filed into points. "That's far enough, pops," the thug said. "Don't make me stomp you."

"Take it easy," Hendel said, as he stood with palms out. "All I want is some information. And before you stomp me take a look at your chest."

The Lightning looked, saw the red dot, and knew what it meant. Someone was aiming a weapon at him. From the other side of the street most likely. He could see a pile of debris that would provide good cover. The sentry looked up. There was no fear in his eyes but the tone was slightly conciliatory. "So, pops, what's on your mind?"

"We were told that the Biotic Underground was headquartered here. But you're moving in. What happened?"

The Lightning shrugged. "The biotics were stupid enough to rob a bank owned by T'Loak. She sent a small army over to punish them. But, according to the locals, it was pretty much of a draw. The biotics were expecting trouble. So they put up a stiff fight. And once the battle was over they moved out."

"Where did they go?"

"Beats me . . . Now take a hike before I tell the guys on the roof to put a rocket into the pile of trash where your buddies are hiding."

Hendel nodded. "Roger that . . . I like the teeth by the way. Nice touch."

And with that Hendel turned his back on the Lightning and crossed the street. Anderson and Kahlee were waiting for him. "No luck I'm afraid," Hendel said. "They don't know where the biotics went."

"Damn," Anderson said. "We're back to square one."

"How about Gillian?" Kahlee inquired. "Maybe we should look for her at this point."

"Sounds good," Anderson allowed. "But *where*? There's a price on her head. So she'll be in hiding."

There was a moment of silence before Hendel spoke. "I have an idea. Do the quarians have a presence on Omega? If so they would take her in if she requested sanctuary."

"Brilliant!" Kahlee exclaimed. "They're bound to have a facility here. And that's exactly where she would go. Come on. Let's find the quarians."

The lights were dim and the air inside the warehouse was cool. Sounds had a tendency to echo off the walls as teams of bio-suit-clad quarians worked to move a pile of outward-bound cargo modules to the loading dock. Tar Vas Sootha's office consisted of some movable partitions located in a corner of the cavernous room.

Tar was in charge of the warehouse and known for his no-nonsense style. Gillian was seated on the opposite side of his utilitarian metal desk and she was frightened. And for good reason. After going to the Afterlife in hopes of speaking with Aria T'Loak she had gotten into a fight and been forced to flee. Then, having spent a night tossing and turning on her cot, she had been ordered to meet with Tar. And he wasted no time getting down to business. Gillian couldn't see the expression on the quarian's face but the extent of his displeasure was clear.

"Gillian Nar Idenna," he said sternly, "to say that I am disappointed in you would be an understatement. You came seeking sanctuary. And based on your status as a crew member of the *Idenna,* plus your valor in defending that vessel from pirates, sanctuary was granted.

"So, how do you return that favor?" he demanded. "By entering the Afterlife and killing a number of Aria T'Loak's guards. Video of your exploits came in via the news feed this morning. And T'Loak put a ten-thousand-credit price on your head.

"Do you know what that means? The lesser gangs, not to mention each and every street thug, will be out looking for you. Not only to score the reward but to earn favor with the Pirate Queen. And someone knows where you are. You can bet on that . . . So, if we allow you to stay they'll come after *us*. And most of the people on Omega dislike our race already."

"I'm sorry," Gillian said contritely. "I really am. All I wanted to do was talk to T'Loak. But when I tried to do so her guards attacked me. I had to defend myself."

"Which you did very well indeed," Tar replied crossly. "Well, it isn't for me to judge. And we have no interest in collecting the reward. But you can't remain here. Trouble is bound to find you and we can't afford it."

"But where can I go?" Gillian inquired plaintively.

"You should have thought of that earlier," Tar replied coldly. "Collect your belongings and get out. Your name will be struck from the *Idenna*'s list of crew members and you are no longer welcome in the fleet."

Gillian rose, made her way to the area set aside for single females to sleep in and began to pack. Somehow, without meaning to do so, she had ruined everything. And she knew that Tar was right. Just about everyone would be gunning for her. And with no allies to depend upon her life expectancy could be counted in hours rather than years.

But she wouldn't die easily . . . Whoever came after her would be forced to pay a price. The thought was accompanied by a sense of grim determination as Gillian made her way to the door. Eyes were upon her. She could feel them. And Nar would be informed the moment she left.

The door opened, Gillian squinted as the artificial daylight hit her eyes, and the incessant roar of life on Omega assailed her ears. Her heart was racing and she was beginning to feel the effects of the adrenaline that was entering her bloodstream as she walked away. The voice came from her left. "Miss . . . I don't know your name. But I know who you are . . . And I want to help."

Gillian whirled, hands raised, and ready for combat. There was no need. A woman with dark hair was standing with hands held away from her sides. "My name is Cory Kim. I'm a member of the Biotic Underground. Nick Donahue told me to say 'Hi.' He'd like to see you."

"Nick? Really?"

"Yes, really. We know about the fight at the After-life. Everybody does. And we'd like you to join our organization."

"How did you find me?" Gillian demanded suspiciously.

"That was easier than you might think," the other woman responded. "Aria T'Loak is offering ten thousand for you. Dead or alive. We offered fifteen thousand but only if you were alive. A street vendor saw you enter the warehouse last night."

"You have that kind of money?"

"Yes, we do," Kim replied cheerfully. "We withdrew it from T'Loak's private bank! And she came after us. But we're still around. Here, put this stuff on, and keep the hood up. Nobody will recognize you that way. And we need to lose your tail. He's watching from a passageway on the other side of the street. No, don't look. Let him think we're in the dark. That will help us give him the slip."

"A bounty hunter?" Gillian inquired as she pulled the lightweight robe on over her clothes.

"No," Kim replied. "Kai Leng and I spent time in an Alliance prison camp together. Cerberus got us out. He stayed in the organization; I left it."

Gillian felt a sudden flood of hope. *Cerberus!* Here was a possible link . . . But she would have to be careful. Mistakes had been made the night before. Stupid mistakes. And she didn't want to repeat them. "Do you know where this Leng person lives?" Gillian inquired, as she pulled a pair of goggles over her eyes.

Kim frowned. "One of our people will follow him. Why?"

"Oh, nothing," Gillian replied. "Thank you, Cory. Please lead the way."

Kai Leng had been watching the quarian warehouse from the other side of the street for hours and had nothing to show for the effort. He was still upset with himself for missing the kill the night before. The way Gillian Grayson had come charging out of the club caught him by surprise, but he was supposed to be better than that.

As a self-imposed punishment for the failure Leng resolved to wait outside the warehouse until his target emerged, even if that took a full day. But he was tired, hungry, and his resolve was beginning to fade.

Suddenly Leng's pulse quickened as the door to the warehouse opened and a human female emerged. Was it Gillian? Leng brought the sniper rifle up for a quick look and, as the crosshairs floated over the woman's face, he saw that yes, his target was right there in front of him. Should he take the shot? And risk return fire from the quarian guards? Or follow Gillian until she was well clear of the warehouse?

Then, before a decision could be made, a *second* female stepped in to block his shot. Leng swore, then swore again, as the shock of recognition registered on his brain. Because he *knew* the second woman. Or had during the time both of them were confined to an Alliance prison. She was a biotic named Cory Kim, and more than that, an ex-lover. But that was ancient history. What was she doing on Omega? And why was she talking to Gillian?

Leng was still trying to come up with a plausible hypothesis when both women walked away. His first impulse was to follow. But what if Cory had backup? A person or persons assigned to watch her six? Anything was possible. So Leng forced himself to take thirty seconds and scan the area around him for anyone or anything that looked suspicious. Not an easy task on Omega where just about everyone could constitute a threat. But the effort was fruitless.

It would have been nice to take more time, but if he did there was a good chance that Cory and Gillian would lose themselves in the crowd. And judging from the pack on the teenager's back she wasn't planning to return. So Leng collapsed the rifle, slung it across his back, and took up the chase. The key was to stay back, but not *too* far back, lest he lose the women to a sudden twist or turn.

There was plenty of foot traffic, which worked in his favor part of the time, but also made it difficult to see, thereby keeping Leng on edge. Although they were mostly healed his wounds were still painful at times. Fortunately neither of the females seemed to be concerned about the possibility of a tail, and never took the time to glance back over their shoulders.

Such were Leng's thoughts as a group of ten or fifteen youngsters surged out of a side passageway in front of him. They were chasing another teen, or so it appeared, as they shouted incomprehensible gobbledygook and their quarry led them in a circle. Then, just as quickly as they had appeared, the youngsters were gone. And as Leng looked up the street he realized that the two women had disappeared as well. Was that a coincidence? Or had he just witnessed some street theater staged for his benefit? There was no way to know.

Leng sighed. He would go back to the safe house, get some rest, and visit the Beggar King in the morning. Having located Gillian once he was confident he could do so again—if a bounty hunter didn't find her first. The possibility of that brought a smile to his face and made him feel better. Positive thinking. That was the key.

It was late afternoon by the time Anderson, Kahlee, and Hendel arrived at the quarian warehouse. The trip had taken longer than any of them would have preferred because there weren't any addresses on Omega, some of the streets were blocked off, and others led to dead ends. All of which made for a very frustrating and time-consuming journey.

Finally, having arrived in front of the warehouse, Hendel went forward to seek admission. A guard listened to his request and chose to enter the building rather than radio the request to her superior. A sure sign that she thought the matter was sensitive and didn't want Hendel to hear her end of the conversation. The quarian returned five minutes later. Her voice was neutral. "Follow me, please."

"Can my friends come as well?"

"Yes."

Hendel, Anderson, and Kahlee followed the slim, slightly built female into the dimly lit building and over to an informal office where a second quarian rose to greet them. "Welcome," he said. "My name is Tar Vas Sootha. I'm in charge here . . . I understand you have some questions regarding Gillian Nar Idenna. Please sit down."

Hendel had given his name to the guard but reintroduced himself and his companions. Tar nodded. "You are listed in our records as Hendel Vas Idenna. And you are considered to be an honored member of the ship *Idenna*. Were it not so I would have refused to meet with you."

"Thank you," Hendel replied. "As I told the guard, we are looking for Gillian Nar Idenna. She came to Omega on her own—and might have sought sanctuary here."

"She did," Tar said gravely. "And we were happy to have Gillian here until she entered the Afterlife club and got into a fight with Aria T'Loak's bodyguards. Are you aware of that?"

"Yes," Hendel said soberly. "We are."

"Then you know that Gillian killed a number of people, fled the premises, and that T'Loak put a ten-thousand-credit bounty on her head."

"That's very regrettable," Hendel allowed, "but I *know* this girl. If she killed people it was in self-defense. Is she here? We'd like to speak with her."

"No," Tar replied. "She isn't. *You* say she acted in self-defense. And that's what Gillian claims. But what else would she say? T'Loak's spokesperson called the attack 'unprovoked.' And we have no way to know what the truth of the matter is. But having lived and worked among us you know that many people despise our race—and that makes our presence here on Omega rather tenuous. So Gillian was asked to leave."

Hendel jumped up out of his chair and drew his pistol. It was aimed at Tar's head. "You rotten bastard! You knew there was a price on Gillian's head and you put her on the street. Not because she had done anything to you but in order to kiss up to T'Loak and the rest of the scum on this worthless pus ball. I should blow your frigging head off!"

"Hendel," Kahlee said, as she rose to intervene. "Please put the gun away. Killing him won't solve anything. *Please . . .* What's done is done. We'll find her."

Slowly, incrementally, Hendel allowed Kahlee to push his gun arm down. And a good thing too . . . because two heavily armed quarians had arrived by then—having been summoned by a means unknown. "You'd better hope that Gillian survives," Hendel said, as he holstered the pistol. "Because if she doesn't I'm going to come for *you*."

"Show them out," Tar said coldly. "And inform the guards. If any of these people show up again, shoot them." The meeting was over.

It was evening, Afterlife was starting to fill up, and T'Loak was in a bad mood. And for good reason. Though superficial in nature, residual issues related to the bank robbery and the rampage the night before had taken up time and energy that would have been better spent on other things. Such were the crime lord's thoughts as Immo entered the U-shaped enclosure reserved for her on the second floor and waited for the asari to acknowledge his presence. Aria was well aware that Immo had thrown himself at the deranged biotic the night before and knew that kind of loyalty was hard to come by. She forced a smile. "Yes, Tann. What's up?"

"Some customers would like to speak with you."

T'Loak raised an eyebrow. "None of them are crazy biotics I trust?"

It was a joke but Immo wasn't known for his sense of humor. "No, ma'am. One of them is a human named David Anderson. The other is a female named Kahlee Sanders."

T'Loak knew both individuals fairly well, having held them prisoner on Omega during the widespread search for Paul Grayson. She had been acting on behalf of the Illusive Man at the time, as well as herself, on the theory that Grayson was responsible for Liselle's death.

Now, in the wake of the bank robbery and Shella's account of what actually occurred that night, it seemed likely that a Cerberus operative named Manning had slit her daughter's throat. Because he enjoyed such things? Or on orders from the Illusive Man? Given the extent of their involvement Kahlee and Anderson might have relevant information. T'Loak nodded. "Send them up."

Immo hadn't met the humans before and looked surprised. Or as surprised as he was capable of looking. "Armed? Or unarmed?"

"They can keep their weapons. I have no idea what they want. But they aren't assassins."

Immo said, "Yes, ma'am," and disappeared.

T'Loak took a sip of the drink at her elbow and looked out at the asari dancers on the ring beyond. They were young. And hungry. The way she'd been back when the nightspot's original owner hired her as an exotic dancer. That had been a mistake because what had been his club then was *her* club now. Was that how it would end, she wondered? Would one of the lithe females performing on the ring in front of her find a way to bring her down? Maybe. But not yet. Not for quite a while.

There was a slight disturbance as Immo arrived with the humans in tow and ordered T'Loak's body-guards to let them pass. The crime lord was seated on a curving bench-style seat. She waved the visitors over. "Please . . . sit down. It's been awhile."

"Yes, it has," Anderson agreed. "The last time we were on Omega your hospitality was a little over the top."

T'Loak laughed. "There were locks on the doors. I admit that. But the rooms were nice."

"Much nicer than where we're staying now," Kahlee allowed. "Let us know if you have a vacancy."

"I'll keep you in mind," T'Loak said. "So, what brings you to the Afterlife? Or is this a social call?"

"I wish it were," Anderson said soberly. "We're here regarding Paul Grayson's daughter."

T'Loak allowed an eyebrow to rise. "What about her?"

"Her name is Gillian," Kahlee replied. "And she's the biotic who killed your employees last night."

T'Loak frowned. "You're serious? That was Gray-son's daughter?"

"Yes," Kahlee said. "It was. Not his biological daughter, but his daughter nonetheless. Gillian demonstrated biotic abilities at a very young age. The Il-lusive Man became aware of her and ordered Grayson to play the part of her father and enroll her at the Grissom Academy. Grayson did as he was told, but at some point over the years he came to care for her the way a *real* father would, and a bond was formed.

Meanwhile her biotic abilities continued to develop, and based on what took place here, we believe that she had new amps installed."

"She killed two of my best biotics," T'Loak said sourly. "And she's going to pay for that."

"That's why we came," Anderson put in. "We know about the price on her head—and we're hoping that you would be willing to remove it. Then, if we can find her, we'll make sure that she gets the help she needs. Gillian is very impetuous—and determined to kill the Illusive Man. In fact, if I had to guess, I'll bet that is why she came here. She's looking for a way to find him."

That piqued T'Loak's interest. "Why?"

"Because the Illusive Man killed her father," Kahlee answered. "She wants revenge."

T'Loak thought about that. Ironically enough it seemed that she and Gillian Grayson had some complementary goals. The girl wanted to strike back at the Illusive Man, and assuming that Shella was telling the truth, so did she. But rather than share that with Anderson and Kahlee, T'Loak chose to keep the information to herself. "So there's something you want," T'Loak said. "And, as it happens, there's something I want as well. Perhaps we can come to some sort of an agreement."

Kahlee frowned. "What, exactly, are you looking for?"

"Information," T'Loak replied. "Grayson wiped his computer just before he left Omega. But there was evidence that he sent a copy of everything he had to someone off-station first. Do you know who that person was?"

* * *

As it happened, Kahlee *did* know who that person was. Because just prior to running for his life Grayson had sent a copy of his hard drive to her. And she still had the information. Files that Grayson had been updating for years. Notes that included everything he knew about Cerberus. That included lists of agents, the location of key facilities, and safe houses on a dozen planets. All compromised with a single keystroke. "Yes," Kahlee answered. "Grayson sent the contents of his computer to me."

T'Loak smiled. "Of course he did. And, being a thrifty sort of person, you still have that information."

"She does," Anderson acknowledged. "But while it was an incredible intelligence coup at the time, the data is meaningless now. The Illusive Man knew how unstable Grayson was—and knew he was desperate. So agents were warned, codes were changed, and safe houses were closed. All within a matter of days. I'm reluctant to say that, because we'd like to arrange some sort of trade, but the truth would soon become apparent."

"You're very forthcoming," T'Loak said with only a trace of sarcasm. "And I appreciate that. However, even though the operational data is no longer accurate I'm looking for historical information. And history is what it is. The Illusive Man can't change that."

T'Loak was investigating something. An event of importance to her. But *what*? Kahlee saw no harm in asking. "What are you after? Maybe we can help."

"It's a private matter," T'Loak responded dismissively. "For the moment anyway. But I see the makings of a deal here. Can you access the Grayson files from Omega?"

Kahlee gave the matter a moment's thought. "Yes, if I can get a link to the extranet on the Citadel, I'll be able to pull them up. Once I do it should be a simple matter to download them here."

"Excellent," T'Loak said. "If you have no objection to working with one of my communications specialists we can make sure that the process goes smoothly."

"Okay," Anderson said cautiously. "But you mentioned the possibility of a deal. What sort of terms did you have in mind?"

T'Loak nodded. "Here's my proposal . . . I will order my people to put out the word. I still want Gillian Grayson, and am still willing to pay ten thousand credits for her, but only if she's alive and in good health. In the meantime you will download the files."

Kahlee shook her head. "No way . . . Once you have Gillian in custody I will download the files. Not before."

T'Loak smiled thinly. "That's what I *meant* to say."

Kahlee didn't believe that. Not for a minute. But she was quite satisfied with the terms of the deal. The agreement meant they were much more likely to find Gillian than if they tackled the job by themselves. Kahlee forced a smile. "Yes, of course."

"But remember," T'Loak said gravely. "You must promise that if I deliver Gillian Grayson into your hands you will keep her confined. Should you fail I would be very angry."

"We'd like to avoid that," Anderson said dryly.

"See that you do," T'Loak said sternly. "Now, can I buy you a drink?"

ELEVEN

ON OMEGA

Gillian was impressed by the smooth manner in which a street gang had been used to block the Cerberus agent who had been following her. Because of her father? Yes, probably, although Gillian wasn't sure what the Illusive Man hoped to gain. It wasn't as if she had access to secret information. However, if the biotics were able to track the man called Leng perhaps Gillian would find a way to take advantage of the situation.

Before she could consider such a possibility it would first be necessary to deal with the Biotic Underground. They wanted her. That's what Cory Kim claimed. But did Gillian want *them*? Not that she had a great deal of choice given the need to hide. Such were Gillian's thoughts as she followed Kim through the surreal cityscape that was Omega.

The fake sunshine had started to fade as a computer somewhere began to dim the lights for the comfort of races that were diurnal or nocturnal and still required alternating periods of light in order to get sufficient rest. So as the women followed an ancient sluiceway west, all sorts of lights and signs began to blink on. There were shadows, lots of them, which gave predators a place to hide. Gillian knew that and couldn't help but feel a sense of concern.

Not Kim though. She maintained a steady stream of chatter as they walked along, most of which was centered on Nick's exploits, and seemed to be unaware of the danger that lurked all around. That struck Gillian as strange until a trio of street toughs appeared up ahead. They positioned themselves to block the path and the one in the middle did the talking. The turian was wearing armor and carrying an assault rifle. "Good evening, ladies . . . We're collecting donations for a good cause, which is to say ourselves."

The batarian and the human thought that was very funny and guffawed loudly. Kim spoke from the side of her mouth. "I'll take the four-eyed joker on the right. You handle the others. Let's slam them."

After proving herself in the Afterlife Gillian felt confident of her ability to carry out the order and was already in the process of gathering the necessary energy. Having brought her hands up Gillian plucked her targets off the ground. When the street toughs came down it was with considerable force. The human uttered a yelp of pain as both of his ankles shattered. Meanwhile the turian fired a burst of rounds into the air as he landed on his back. He struggled to get up, and was about to do so, when Kim dropped the batarian right on top of him. A shockwave followed and put both out of action.

Kim spit on the batarian as they passed the heap of bodies. It was an act of contempt that both repelled

Gillian and thrilled her at the same time. Because in keeping with the guidance received from Kahlee Sanders and Hendel Mitra she was accustomed to downplaying her biotic abilities in order to be accepted by society at large. So to see an individual like Kim using her talents openly, even proudly, was a revelation. Suddenly she realized that other people should be afraid of *her*, not the other way around.

It was almost dark by the time the women arrived in front of a much-abused steel door. Alien hieroglyphics had been etched into the barrier and looked to be very, very old. A human male and an asari were standing out front and in spite of their casual demeanor Gillian could tell that they were guards. The asari palmed a switch and the door rumbled upward to reveal the tunnel beyond.

The way the guards were looking at her made Gillian feel uncomfortable as Kim took her inside and the barrier closed behind them. "Why were they staring at me?"

"You're famous," Kim replied, as they followed a set of partially buried metal tracks through the wide, dimly lit tunnel. "Here on Omega anyway. More than that you're a living example of biotic superiority." That was a new idea to Gillian, who had always thought of herself as a freak rather than a person to be admired.

Three dusty gyrocycles were parked off to one side of the passageway, along with an open cart and a beat-up ground car. The tunnel came to an abrupt end in front of another heavily guarded door and this one appeared to be new. Even though the heavily armored biotics knew Kim, she was still required to pass a retinal scan. Gillian was asked to remove everything from her pockets and stand with legs spread and arms raised. A loud beep was heard as the guard passed his wand over her chest. He glanced at the terminal located next to him. "The jewel is a data storage device. Please remove it."

Gillian was confused. "It's a what?"

The guard ignored her response. "Do we have your permission to check the storage device for malware?"

Gillian looked at Kim and back again. "Sure, I guess so. Honest . . . I had no idea that it was a storage device."

The guard accepted the jewel, dropped it into an opening on his terminal, and eyed the words that appeared on the screen. "No encryption, and no malware. You're good to go."

The jewel popped up out of the receptacle and was returned to Gillian. She zipped both it and the chain into a pocket and made a mental note to open the storage device as soon as she got the chance. "It was a gift," she said to Kim. "From my father. But I had no idea there was a message on it."

Kim smiled. "How nice. You have something to look forward to. Come on, people are waiting for us."

They passed through the checkpoint and into the area beyond. It was a great deal more than the played-out mine that Gillian expected. Solid rock had been removed to create a sphere-shaped chamber with a flat floor. The interior surface of the cavern was pockmarked by rows of symmetrical holes, all fronted by a succession of ledges and connected via a spiraling path. As Gillian looked upward she could see people coming and going.

There was a dome-shaped structure at the center of the vast room, and as Kim led her toward it Gillian thought it looked as if it had been built by a race other than those responsible for the hollowed-out sphere, although there was no way to be certain. "We believe the original cavern served as a nest," Kim volunteered, as they crossed an open area. "Not that it matters. The main thing is that this place is safe. Or as safe as anything can be on this turd ball. The hotel where we were headquartered earlier was okay, but when this came on the market we jumped on it. And, thanks to the money we stole from T'Loak, we were able to pay cash."

There it was again. An unabashed statement of confidence and power. And Gillian couldn't help but be impressed. The structure in front of them consisted of a roof supported by fluted columns. Judging from appearances it was being used as both a communal meeting room, dining room, and kitchen. There were about fifteen people lounging about and all of them turned to look at the newcomers as Kim led Gillian through the facility and toward the other side of the cavern. And that was when she heard a male voice. "Gillian! It's me! Nick."

Gillian turned to see a familiar figure coming her way. Except that Nick seemed taller somehow, his right shoulder was swathed in bandages, and he was wearing two pistols. That was the sort of thing she would expect of him, as was the big grin, and the kiss on the cheek. "Damn girl, it's good to see you."

And suddenly, after all the days of feeling as if she

was alone even when she wasn't, Gillian felt that she belonged. "Nick," she said, "your shoulder. What happened?"

"We were inside T'Loak's bank making a withdrawal," he said. "And I zigged when I should have zagged. And speaking of fights . . . Have you seen the footage of the battle inside the Afterlife? T'Loak's people sent it out and I recognized you right away."

"Zon would like to meet you," Kim put in. "Nick, you're welcome to join us if you'd like to."

After leaving the dome they crossed an open area to one of the cavelike rooms at ground level. Gillian thought it might be larger than the ones on the levels above but couldn't be sure. The unconventional space was furnished with conventional furniture, including a round table and six matching chairs. Both of the people who were seated at it rose. The asari who came forward to greet Gillian had blue skin, widely set eyes, and was dressed in a sleek pantsuit. "Welcome! My name is Mythra Zon."

Gillian could sense the power of the other woman's personality and was enveloped by the heady perfume she wore as they exchanged asari-style air kisses. The air crackled with static electricity as the biotics came together and parted. "Please allow me to introduce Rasna Vas Kathar," Zon said, as she turned to an enviro-suited quarian. "He's our number two and in charge of technical operations."

Gillian shook hands with the quarian, wondered why he had left the fleet, and what his former crewmates would think about his current activities. "Greetings," she said. "My quarian name is Gillian

Nar Idenna. Or it was. According to Tar Vas Sootha it will be struck from the rolls as of today."

The quarian shrugged. "I know Tar and he's a fool. But even as your name is removed from one list, perhaps it will be added to another."

"That's correct," Zon said smoothly. "Why don't you drop that pack and have a seat? Perhaps Cory and Nick would like to join us."

Both were quick to accept the invitation and Gillian wasn't sure if that was because they wanted to do so or felt they had to. She got the distinct impression that people didn't say "no" to Zon very often.

"Now," Zon said, once all of them were seated. "We would like to provide you with some information about our organization. It's called the Biotic Underground and our goal is to replace the Citadel Council with a biotic meritocracy."

Gillian looked at Nick and he smiled. "Welcome home, Gillian. This is where you belong."

Unlike the luxurious passenger shuttles Kai Leng had been privileged to fly on from time to time, the transport had the feel of a stripped-down military assault boat. All of the fittings were practical in nature and no effort had been made to please the eye. A pair of human cargo masters were strapped into fold-down seats on the other side of a pile of well-secured crates. They were playing some sort of game on their omni-tools and one of them said "Gotcha!" as he scored points on the other.

The load process was already under way when Leng had arrived at docking Station 22, been scanned, and allowed to board. The crates were unmarked so there was no telling what they contained. Weapons? Tech? Cash? It was impossible to know.

What Leng *did* know was that he was very, very tired. After losing track of Gillian he had returned to the safe house to discover that a message was waiting. The Illusive Man wanted to see him aboard the Cerberus vessel *Spirit of Nepal*. And there was very little time in which to reach the correct docking arm and board shuttle SN-2. The purpose of the trip being unknown, to Leng at least, although he could hazard a guess. The Illusive Man was in the neighborhood and wanted to discuss the Gillian Grayson sanction. Or the lack of one.

Leng's thoughts were interrupted as the pilot made a brief announcement, the shuttle slowed, and stopped shortly thereafter. Leng knew that the SN-2 was inside the *Spirit of Nepal*'s hangar bay at that point, but couldn't see anything, because there weren't any viewports.

But before he could leave the shuttle it was necessary to seal the bay and pressurize it. A process that would consume at least fifteen minutes. So Leng allowed himself to doze off. He awoke with a start when metal clanged. It felt as if only seconds had passed, but a quick check of his omni-tool revealed that he'd been asleep for half an hour, and during that time all but one of the crates had been unloaded. Leng hit the release on his harness, got up, and left via the rear cargo ramp. The bay was large, but still crowded, thanks to the presence of another transport, this one labeled the SN-1.

Leng wound his way between stacks of cargo modules and various pieces of equipment to a personnel hatch that opened to admit him. It took a couple of minutes to cycle through the lock and enter the passageway beyond. And there, her face expressionless as always, was Jana. If the Illusive Man's assistant disapproved of his tardiness there was no sign of it on her finely chiseled face. She said, "Please follow me," and walked away. Her heels made a staccato rapping sound as they hit the metal deck and Leng wondered how human she really was.

After following the woman through a maze of passageways and up two levels he was shown into a spacious compartment equipped with a large viewport. Omega could be seen floating beyond. The outer surface of the space station was alive with glittering navigation beacons that made the asteroid look like a royal orb. An irony not lost on Leng.

Jana said, "Kai Leng is here, sir," and left. Her heels made a clicking sound that faded away. The Illusive Man was seated with his back to the hatch. When he turned there was a smile on his face. "Thank you for coming. I know you've been busy. Please . . . sit down.

"As I'm sure you're aware," the Illusive Man said, "Aria T'Loak was anything but pleased when Gillian Grayson went on a rampage inside the Afterlife. So she put a price on Gillian's head. Ten thousand credits dead or alive. Then something interesting happened. T'Loak ordered her people to modify the offer. She's still willing to pay ten thousand for the girl . . . but only if she's alive and in good health. The question is *why*?"

Leng was surprised to hear it. And concerned as well. Because if Aria's mercs wanted to keep Gillian alive that would make killing her that much more difficult. "I have no idea," he said levelly. "But I did witness an incident that might have a bearing on the situation. After trashing the Afterlife Gillian took refuge in a warehouse occupied by the quarians. And when she came out, a woman was waiting for her. A biotic named Cory Kim."

"So you know her?"

"We were in prison together. As you know, a Cerberus recruiter arranged for our release. I stayed but she left. In any case, Kim spoke with Gillian and they left together. I was hoping for a clean shot but never got one."

"That's interesting," the Illusive Man observed. "Especially the part about Kim being a biotic. She's a biotic, Gillian is a biotic, and an organization called the Biotic Underground is on the rise."

"Maybe they want to recruit Gillian."

"That seems likely," the Illusive Man mused. "If they do, and Aria's people want to protect her, your job will become even more difficult."

"So my orders are the same?"

"Yes," the Illusive Man said. "Find Gillian Grayson and kill her *before* someone hands her over to Aria. There's no way to know what our asari friend is up to, but I doubt it will benefit Cerberus."

Leng rose to leave. "Understood."

"And one more thing . . ."

"Yes?"

"Kahlee Sanders and David Anderson were seen meeting with Aria in the Afterlife. Chances are that the conversation had to do with finding Gillian Grayson and Nick Donahue, but maybe not. Keep your eyes peeled. Don't forget . . . Anderson has been in touch with the Council, so there's a chance that one or more of the members are involved somehow." The chair whirred and the Illusive Man turned his back on the room. The meeting was over.

On Omega

The scope of what the Biotic Underground hoped to accomplish was truly staggering. Rather than simply work their way up Omega's criminal hierarchy they wanted to take control of *everything*. And that included both the Citadel and the Council.

It was difficult to believe that such a thing could be possible and some of Gillian's skepticism must have been visible on her face as Mythra Zon smiled from the other side of the circular table. "It sounds crazy. I know that. But hear me out.

"The Citadel Council has been in place for thousands of years, and what have they accomplished? Nothing," Zon said, "other than dealing with new races such as your own and perpetuating the status quo. Remember, the Citadel, the relays, and all the rest of it were in place *before* the Council came into being.

"Nothing lasts forever nor should it," Zon continued. "We believe that the time for new leadership has arrived. And who better to provide it than biotics? We represent all of the various races, aren't vested in the existing system, and have extraordinary powers. The kind of abilities that will help us seize control and keep it."

Gillian had been a good student while at the Grissom Academy. And one of the axioms that had been drilled into her was "that absolute power corrupts absolutely." So to replace the multiracial council with a biotic meritocracy struck Gillian as a stupid thing to do. Unless you were Mythra Zon and likely to wind up in charge. So Gillian wasn't buying the bill of goods that the asari was selling.

She *did* need a place to stay however—and a way to get her hands on the Illusive Man. And that raised an important question: Could the Biotic Underground be used? That remained to be seen. The key was to hide her true opinions and say the things Zon wanted to hear. It was the sort of duplicity that she'd seen all around her since leaving the academy for the adult world. "It's a very audacious plan," Gillian said brightly. "But how can we make something like that happen?"

"The process is already under way," Zon answered confidently. "First we worked to raise our profile. Then we robbed T'Loak's bank. Nick was critical to our success where that endeavor was concerned. The robbery provided us with an operating budget and the sort of respect normally reserved for larger, more entrenched groups. Now we're going to consume or destroy other organizations until we have complete control of Omega. Once that has been accomplished we will go after the Council. And *you* could play an important part in making it happen. You're famous thanks to the battle in the Afterlife and the bounty on your head. That could come in handy."

"I'd like to help in any way that I can," Gillian said earnestly. "Can I make a suggestion?"

Gillian saw what might have been a look of caution

appear in Zon's eyes. The asari had a need to recruit troops, especially Level 3 biotics, but wanted to retain leadership. She couldn't say that, however, and was forced to acquiesce. "What did you have in mind?"

"There are lots of organizations on Omega," Gillian began. "And by tackling the most prominent one right off the top the Underground was able to gain instant credibility."

Gillian had been listening. Zon nodded approvingly.

"So that raises the question of which group to tackle next," Gillian continued. "Conventional wisdom might suggest the Blue Suns or a similar gang. But I would like to suggest an alternative. I'm thinking of a secret organization that has more reach than the Suns do, is a clear threat to all but one of the Council races, and if defeated would clear the way for the Biotic Underground to gain more influence."

Zon appeared to be genuinely intrigued. "And the name of this organization is?"

Gillian smiled grimly. "Cerberus."

"It *sounds* good," Kathar said, as he spoke for the first time. "But unlike the Suns, Cerberus has no clearly defined presence on Omega. What would we attack?"

"The best way to kill a monster is to cut off its head," Gillian said grimly. "And in this case that means the Illusive Man."

Gillian was watching Zon's eyes to see how she would react and saw a succession of emotions flicker through them. Doubt, fear, and greed. Because in spite of everything Zon knew, Gillian was correct. If the Underground managed to destroy Cerberus it would be a very big deal indeed. And a natural lead-in to eliminating Aria T'Loak. "Okay," the asari said hesitantly. "But *how*?"

It was the question that Zon was supposed to ask—and Gillian felt a momentary sense of satisfaction. Then, based on a plan that seemed to create itself as she spoke, Gillian told the biotics how they could kill the Illusive Man.

Most of the people on Omega knew about the After-life club and the fact that T'Loak could often be spotted in a private enclosure on the second floor. What they *didn't* know was that her real office was in a heavily secured basement underneath the nightspot, along with a sophisticated communications center, an armory, and two escape tunnels. Neither of which had ever been used. And that was where the crime lord was, seated behind a nearly transparent desk, when a chime sounded. She said, "Video on," and the text on her flat screen was replaced by an image of Tann Immo. "The files have been deencrypted," he said. "They are ready for review."

T'Loak said, "Thank you," and ordered her in-box to appear. The item she'd been waiting for was right at the top of a lengthy list. She smiled grimly. Kahlee Sanders was either naive, a fool, or both. Once T'Loak knew where Grayson's files were located she wasn't about to wait around for someone to turn Gillian in so she could access them.

Within minutes of the meeting with Kahlee and Anderson T'Loak had issued orders to operatives on the Citadel. And two hours later they hacked into

Kahlee's computer via the extranet, sucked it dry, and went about the delicate task of opening her files without triggering the self-destruct program designed to defend them. That took some doing, but T'Loak's techs were up to the task, and now the information was hers.

Rather than delegate the task of going through the data to an underling Aria was determined to read all of it herself. Because what she was looking for would be buried in the details. The kind of thing that only she would recognize as being important.

So T'Loak read, and read, until she was couldn't read anymore. Then she took a nap on the couch that took up most of one wall. Two hours later she got up and read again. Meals came and were removed. Messages went unanswered. All so T'Loak could accomplish one thing—and that was to identify Liselle's killer.

Finally, after more than twenty hours of unrelenting work T'Loak found what she'd been looking for. Having compared Shella's description of the man who slit Liselle's throat with actual surveillance footage of the assassin who killed Grayson, and a snapshot taken from the murdered man's files, she had a name: Kai Leng. A Cerberus operative just as Shella had said. The knowledge gave T'Loak a deep sense of satisfaction and fed her ever-growing desire for revenge. Leng was going to die.

But where was the killer? On Omega? Or somewhere else? There was only one way to find out and that was to ask the Beggar King. A request went to Hobar, who replied a scant ten minutes later. Not only had the volus seen the person in question, the man was a client, and currently searching for a human female. The *same* female dozens of groups and bounty hunters were looking for—the biotic who had gone on a rampage inside the Afterlife.

T'Loak felt her heart start to beat a little bit faster. Things were starting to come together. The offer she sent to Hobar was extremely generous and it wasn't long before every beggar on Omega was looking for Kai Leng. And one hour and sixteen minutes later they found him.

After the meeting with Von and the rest of the biotics Gillian had been shown to her quarters, which consisted of a cavelike room on the second level. The furnishings included a bed, a footlocker, a chair, and a very small table. But it was the terminal that sat on top of it that captured her attention.

Gillian sat down, hurried to free the green jewel from its chain, and dropped it into the universal port located on top of the machine. Then, like a specter from the past, Paul Grayson appeared. He looked ill but managed a smile. "Hello, Gigi. So now you know . . . The jewel was more than a pretty bauble to hang around your neck. There's no way to be sure when you'll see this. But I'm likely to be dead by then. And at some point you'll wonder what happened to me and why. It's all here. Every bit of it. All taken from Cerberus. But I warn you that some of the footage is difficult to look at. I love you, Gigi . . . And I'm sorry I wasn't a better father."

That was when the image of her father disappeared and the rest of it began. There were hundreds of pages of reports, thousands of sensor readouts, and one extremely disturbing holo. As Gillian watched the footage sobs came from somewhere deep inside her. And by the time the segment was over she felt sick to her stomach. *You will pay for what you did,* Gillian thought to herself, *and the price will be very, very high.*

Having been returned to Omega's surface Leng had elected to visit one of his favorite restaurants rather than return to the safe house. He was tired, but hungry as well, and there was very little food in the apartment.

The restaurant was called the Blue Marble and specialized in Earth cuisine. Leng was partial to Mexican food so he ordered an enchilada, some tacos, and a shot of Honzo. The Marble was packed and that was one of the reasons why he liked the place. Leng spent a great deal of time by himself. And it was depressing to eat alone. So with drink in hand he settled in to watch the crowd. And that's what he was doing when it began to dwindle.

Leng wasn't alarmed at first, and why should he be? Groups of people entered and departed the restaurant all the time. But then he noticed something strange. At first it looked like the proprietor was simply making the rounds, slapping backs, and schmoozing his regulars.

Then Leng realized that shortly after speaking to the owner the Blue Marble's patrons got up and left. Even if they hadn't finished their food or paid for it. And that was when an alarm began to sound in the back of his mind. The man in the greasy apron was systematically emptying his own restaurant. *Why?*

Because the rotten bastard knows something I don't, Leng concluded. *Something bad is about to happen and he wants his customers to survive.*

There was a back door. Through the steamy kitchen. Leng knew that because he never ate in a place that lacked one. But if he was correct, and something bad was about to happen, then it would be covered.

So rather than try for it Leng chose what he considered to be a better alternative. And that was to shoot the restaurant owner in the head. Partly as an act of revenge, but mostly to trigger a stampede, which he did. The report sounded unnaturally loud in the enclosed space, blood and brains splattered one of the customers, and she screamed.

That brought the rest of them to their feet as all but one of the patrons sent chairs and tables flying as they sought to exit through the front door. The single exception was a long lean piece of work who believed that he could kill the problem and finish his dinner. His pistol had barely cleared its holster when Leng shot him in the throat. Blood flew sideways, he backpedaled into a wall, and was dead by the time his butt hit the floor.

At that point Leng joined the stampede. He was just about to exit through the front door when the shooting began. Leng concluded that a turf war was under way, or the attackers were trying to kill a particular customer, and didn't care how many innocent people were gunned down in the process.

But what would have worked on one of the more civilized planets wasn't so easy on Omega where *everybody* went armed. And that included the armor-clad Blue Sun mercenary who was directly in front of Leng and already returning fire. He was a big man and that worked to Leng's advantage as he took shelter behind the soldier and looked for a way out.

The attackers were all around, firing from cover, and riddling the front of the Blue Marble with hundreds of rounds. Half a dozen hapless customers had already been cut down and Leng knew the Blue Sun wouldn't be able to remain upright forever. So he did a pirouette as if he'd been hit and went down. Then, by elbowing his way between a couple of bodies he was able to gain the cover of a badly overflowing dumpster. It was made of steel and Leng could hear a steady *ping, ping, ping* as he took refuge behind it. Projectiles were passing through the container but were too high to hit him.

Finally Leng had the seconds necessary to retrieve the rifle that was slung across his back and put it to work. It was dark but by firing at muzzle flashes he was able to score three hits in less than a minute. That had the effect of reducing the amount of incoming fire and intimidating however many survivors were left. Could they summon reinforcements? Leng figured they could and took advantage of the interlude to slip away.

Then, having moved shadow to shadow, he cleared the area where the Blue Marble was located and pursued a zigzag course toward the safe house. He was hungry, but not enough to start over with another restaurant, so whatever was available at the apartment would have to do. Halfway home he started to limp. It had, all things considered, been a bad day.

TWELVE

ON OMEGA

What light there was came from the cracks between projectile-proof shutters, store signs, and the slightly-out-of-focus ads that slip-slid across vertical walls. Visibility was poor so Kai Leng checked his back trail twice on the way home, even going so far as to stand in the canyon of blackness between two buildings for a full five minutes before following the narrow street to the safe house where he was staying. Guards were positioned in doorways and on roofs, but none of them cared what Leng did, so long as he didn't cause trouble for their upper-class clients.

A new set of guards were stationed in front of the Cerberus safe house. But that wasn't unusual because the company the mercs worked for had to rotate their personnel three times per day. One member of the two-person team was salarian and the other was a turian. Both viewed Leng suspiciously as he paused in front of the scanner on the gate but turned their backs as the barrier began to open.

A second scan was required before Leng could enter the building. Then he took the elevator up to the third floor where it was necessary to enter a four-digit code to enter the apartment. As the door began to open Leng was looking forward to a snack and eight hours of sleep. But as he stepped people with strong hands grabbed him from both sides. Within a matter of seconds both his rifle and pistol were taken from him. Then a person he hadn't seen in a long time stepped into view.

Cory Kim smiled. "You know the drill, Kai . . . Lock your hands behind your neck. And don't try anything. We'll slam you against the wall if you do."

Leng had no choice but to obey. He could hear the comm set chiming as Kim circled around behind him. Leng felt her pat him down, take the knife from his right boot, and withdraw. He grinned. "Everything is just the way you left it."

"Which is to say limp," Kim retorted, as she completed her task and circled back in front of him. "So, Gillian," Kim added, "have you seen him before?"

Leng felt a sudden shock of recognition as he realized that the girl he'd been sent to kill was standing right in front of him! She was wearing a hood, which she threw back. She saw the look on his face and nodded grimly. "Yes, I think so . . . Just glimpses. But he looks familiar."

Leng's mind was racing. How much did the girl know? All he could do was keep his composure and wait for some sort of opportunity. His eyes were locked with Gillian's. "So you're part of the Biotic Underground."

"In a manner of speaking, yes," Gillian confirmed. "It turns out that we have certain goals in common."

"Such as?"

Kim spoke before Gillian could reply. "There will be plenty of time to talk later. Sweet dreams, Kai."

Leng frowned. "Sweet . . ." He never got to finish the question. The dart gun produced a soft *phut* and he felt a sharp pain in his neck. That was followed by a brief moment of dizziness. Then, as his knees gave out on him, everything went black.

"Nice shot," Kim said, as Leng hit the floor and Ocosta Lem holstered his weapon. He'd been sent along to hack the Cerberus security system and provide backup.

As Kim spoke into a lip mike Gillian knew she was communicating with the guards out front. "Bring the car as close to the front door as you can. Citizen Leng is a big boy. No point in carrying him any farther than we have to. And keep our eyes peeled. Odds are that the guards on the surrounding buildings will sit this one out. But if they start to get interested let me know."

Gillian knew that the *real* guards, the ones employed by Cerberus, had been neutralized earlier because she'd played a role in taking them out. It felt good to be treated as an equal for once. "Come on," Kim said, "let's get to work."

Kim was right. Leng weighed at least eighty kilos, and it took all three of them to drag the Cerberus operative into the elevator and move him down to the main floor. That's where two additional biotics were waiting with a cart. Such conveyances were common on Omega and used for a wide range of purposes. So once Leng was loaded and covered with a tarp, the biotics would be able to move him to the waiting car.

* * *

Of course that didn't mean there weren't any witnesses. There were. At least a dozen guards and neighbors were watching as the scene played out in front of them. People who, on a civilized planet, would have reported the abduction to the police, but couldn't since there weren't any. Plus, to interfere would be to violate the credo "mind your own business" and run the risk of making what could be a powerful enemy. So with the exception of Mara Mott none of the onlookers were going to take action.

But she was, and for good reason, because it was Mott's job to keep Cerberus informed of Kai Leng's activities. And Mott was good at what she did, which consisted of watching, following, and taking care of certain tasks. Not wet work, because that wasn't her specialty. No, her job and the jobs of other people who did similar work, was to ensure that operatives like Leng remained loyal and had all of the things required to carry out their various assignments. That included making arrangements for safe houses, delivering special weapons, and bailing them out of trouble.

Having lost track of Leng during the battle at the Blue Marble, Mott had returned to the safe house in time to see him arrive. And being in charge of the guards she knew the ones posted out front were fake. So she called Leng's apartment in hopes of catching him as he entered, but he hadn't picked up. Now she knew why. The people who were loading Leng into the car had been waiting for him. And they wanted the operative alive—because why haul a dead body through the streets?

Well, no matter, Mott thought to herself, as she eased out through the front door of the apartment building across from the safe house. *I'll follow them and call for reinforcements.* The lighting was dim, but she could see the car and the people gathered around it. And as Mott watched the group did something strange. They formed a circle around the car and faced out. Then they raised their hands as if to signal peace, and one of them said, "Now!"

The three-hundred-sixty-degree shockwave surged in every direction, struck all of the witnesses who were located at ground level, and threw them backward. Mott's body slammed into a wall, the back of her head made contact with solid concrete, and she went down hard.

ABOARD THE *SPIRIT OF NEPAL*

The Illusive Man was asleep. And wanted to stay that way. But the chime wouldn't allow him to do so. It was a pleasant sound, intentionally so, but he had come to hate it. Because none of his staff were allowed to disturb him unless there was some sort of emergency. And emergencies were all too common. Other than for some indicator lights it was pitch-black inside his sleeping cabin. He rolled over to slap a button. "Yes?"

"We have a problem, sir." Jana's voice was flat but the Illusive Man could tell that she was worried.

"What sort of problem?"

"Kai Leng has been abducted. I have his handler online. She witnessed what occurred. Would you like to speak with her?"

The Illusive Man swore. "I'll be there shortly." He ordered the lights to come on, donned the synsilk robe that was draped across the back of a chair, and stepped into a pair of slippers. Two minutes later he was seated behind his desk with Jana standing to one side. A hot cup of coffee was waiting for him. He took a tentative sip, opened a case, and selected a cigarette. His lighter flared and he took a drag. "Her name is Mara Mott," Jana said. "I assigned her to Leng after the Grissom Academy shootout and she has performed well."

The Illusive Man knew Jana and knew she was trying to manage him. He could be aloof, not to mention abrupt, and Jana didn't want him to demotivate one of her subordinates. He smiled. "Message received."

The image that materialized in front of the Illusive Man was that of an average-looking woman. Nothing about her appearance was remarkable. Not her black hair, nor her dark skin, nor her clothes. And that the Illusive Man knew was intentional. Mott's job was to be present but nearly invisible. He forced a smile. "I don't believe we've met. But Jana says you're doing a good job and I appreciate that."

Mott looked surprised. Because she didn't expect to see him? Because she rarely heard praise? It didn't matter. "Thank you, sir."

"So tell me about Leng . . . What happened?"

The Illusive Man listened as Mott described the manner in which she had been separated from Leng during the attack on the Blue Marble, and her realization that something was wrong when she spotted the substitute guards. That was followed by Mott's account of how Leng had been loaded onto a car—and she had been momentarily disabled by a biotic shock-wave. "They were gone by the time I came to," Mott finished. "So I entered the safe house and that's where I am now."

The Illusive Man took some smoke deep into his lungs and blew it out. "The biotics . . . Was Gillian Grayson among them by any chance?"

"It was dark," Mott replied, "but yes. I think she was."

"So the Biotic Underground took Leng. The question is why?

"One thing *is* clear," he continued. "Leng was following Gillian, and they were too, which is how they spotted him. Did you notice anything suspicious?"

Mott shook her head. She had missed the biotics and felt badly about it. "No, sir."

No excuses. The Illusive Man liked that. "Okay . . . Here's how I see it. It would be nice to know who attacked the Blue Marble and why. Were they after Leng? Or someone else?

"Second, what are the biotics after? Information about Cerberus? Or something else? We need answers. Spend money. Do whatever needs doing. And let Jana know if you need some muscle."

Mott nodded. "Yes, sir."

"Good," the Illusive Man said. "Viewing window off."

Motes of light swirled, twinkled, and disappeared. Jana was waiting. "Any further orders?"

The Illusive Man's chair whirred as he turned to look out through the viewport. "Yes. Assign someone to watch Mott."

Jana nodded. "Yes, sir." Her heels clicked away.

The Illusive Man blew smoke at the glittering space station that hung suspended in front of him. It was obscured for a moment—but once it reappeared Omega looked just the same.

On Omega

Kahlee was frustrated. She and her companions had been looking for Nick and Gillian for days without success. That was understandable given the everyday realities on Omega. But she was surprised by the fact that Aria T'Loak hadn't been able to find them either.

Still, all they could do was keep looking, so as Anderson took his morning shower Kahlee sat down in front of the room's terminal. Extranet access was expensive on Omega and the additional fee levied by the hotel made it even more so. But so long as there was a chance, no matter how negligible, that Nick or Gillian would send her a message, Kahlee felt compelled to check on a regular basis.

There was a tiny bit of lag time, then her in-box appeared, and began to populate. There were at least half a dozen messages from Nick's parents all marked "Urgent," plus all of the usual dreck, most of which could be ignored. But nothing from either one of the missing teenagers.

Then, before Gillian could go any further, the words SECURITY ALERT, popped up on the screen followed by, "Your account has been accessed by an unauthorized person or device. For a list of potentially compromised files click here."

As the list opened Kahlee was expecting to see evidence of a financial hack. An attack on her bank accounts for example. But that wasn't the case. Only one folder had been accessed. And that was the one titled "Grayson."

Kahlee heard movement and turned to see Anderson emerge from the bathroom. He had one towel wrapped around his waist and was drying his hair with a second. "David . . . Come look. Someone hacked my computer and copied all of the Grayson files."

Anderson swore and looked over Kahlee's shoulder as she showed him the security alert. "That shouldn't have been possible," he said darkly. "I pay one of the top security companies a lot of money to prevent things like that."

"Remember all of the bugs they found in the apartment?" Kahlee inquired. "The outfit you use is no match for organizations like Cerberus because they can buy the very best talent."

"So you think it was Cerberus?"

"No," Kahlee replied. "That doesn't make sense. The Illusive Man knows everything there is to know about Grayson."

"Aria T'Loak," Anderson said. "It has to be her. She wanted the information enough to trade Gillian for it. Maybe she said to hell with the deal and went for it."

Kahlee had turned to face him by then. "So she double-crossed us?"

Anderson shrugged. "We should have known. She's a crime lord after all. Once you confirmed that you had the information, and told her where it was, she couldn't resist."

"Okay," Kahlee agreed. "But what does she want?"

"Let's get some breakfast," Anderson suggested. "Then we'll go over the Grayson stuff again. Maybe we'll be able to figure out what T'Loak is after."

"And if we can't?"

"We'll go see her," Anderson replied. "And ask her to come clean."

Kahlee frowned. "You think that will work?"

Anderson grinned. "No, but as far as I know we don't have anything better to do."

In spite of hours spent poring over the Grayson files Kahlee, Anderson, and Hendel hadn't been able to figure out why T'Loak was so interested in them. So once dinner was over, and with nothing to lose, they went to the Afterlife club. It was busy as usual, and shortly after Kahlee and her companions were seated, an asari waitress arrived to take their orders. Once the process was complete Kahlee gave the waitress a five-credit chip. "Do me a favor, would you? Let Aria T'Loak know that Kahlee Sanders, David Anderson, and Hendel Mitra are here. And ask if we could have five minutes of her time."

The server smiled, made the chip disappear, and left. Ten minutes passed before the waitress returned with the drinks *and* a message. "Aria can see you in half an hour. A staff member will come down to get you. The drinks are on the house."

Kahlee tipped the server again and settled back to enjoy her drink. Anderson and Hendel were busy ogling the asari dancers, the music was good, and if it hadn't been for the task at hand she would have been able to enjoy herself.

A good forty-five minutes passed before Tann Immo appeared at their table, reintroduced himself, and led the humans up to the second floor. But before the party could join T'Loak in her private booth they were ordered to surrender their weapons. "What's the deal?" Anderson wanted to know, as he gave his pistol to a krogan. "Last time we were allowed to keep the hardware."

Immo's face was inscrutable as always. "That was then," he said levelly. "This is now."

Anderson and Kahlee exchanged glances. If they needed proof that T'Loak was responsible for hacking Kahlee's computer there it was. The asari knew they knew, or assumed they did, and wasn't taking any chances. Hendel bristled at being asked to surrender both his shotgun and sidearm but did so at Kahlee's urging.

T'Loak looked beautiful as always, although there was something stiff about her expression, as if she was expecting trouble. "Please sit down," the asari said. "Welcome back."

Having introduced Hendel, Kahlee got right to the point. "There haven't been any developments regarding Gillian Grayson I take it."

T'Loak's eyebrows rose slightly. "No. I would have sent word if there were. It's as if she vanished into thin air. Perhaps she left Omega without being noticed."

Was T'Loak serious? Or was her comment an attempt at misdirection? All Kahlee could do was forge ahead. "Someone hacked my computer and copied the Grayson files."

T'Loak's expression was unchanged. "That's too bad. It sounds like you need a security upgrade."

Kahlee pressed harder. "Did you order your people to hack my computer?"

The crime lord shook her head. "No, of course not. Why would I do that?"

"Because you don't have Gillian, and you wanted the information," Anderson put in.

T'Loak shrugged. "You have my answer. Is there anything else?"

"Yes!" Hendel hissed, as he leaned forward. "Your bodyguards took my weapons, but I'm a biotic. Tell Kahlee what she wants to know or pay the price."

The stunner seemed to materialize in T'Loak's hand. She fired, Hendel jerked spasmodically, and slumped against Anderson who struggled to prop him up. "Your friend is an idiot," Aria said contemptuously. "Get him out of here." The audience was over.

The new day dawned the same way thousands had before it. Hendel was still suffering from the residual effects of being stunned so Kahlee and Anderson had breakfast without him. Then, having failed to extract any useful information from T'Loak, they went to see Harvey Nix. "It's a long shot," Anderson admitted as they left the hotel, "but maybe *he* knows what T'Loak is up to."

Having arrived at Nix's cramped office they were forced to wait as the reporter completed an interview with a large flat-faced elcor. Once that transaction was complete, and the quadruped left, Nix came forward to greet them. Light glinted off his eye-lens as he shook hands, and judging from his friendly demeanor, he was hoping for another consulting fee. "Miss Sanders . . . Admiral Anderson. This is an unexpected pleasure. What can I do for you?"

"We're looking for some information about T'Loak," Anderson replied. "The problem is that we don't know what to ask. So, if you're willing, we would appreciate a briefing. We'll pay the same fee as before."

"Yes, of course," Nix said eagerly. "Please sit down. Can you provide a time frame? T'Loak is hundreds of years old. And my knowledge is limited to the last five years."

"Let's start with the last year," Kahlee suggested. "Skip the minutiae and give us the highlights. We're looking for major activities, problems, that sort of thing."

"I'll do my best," Nix promised. "Realizing that T'Loak goes to considerable lengths to ensure her privacy." What followed was an interesting if somewhat speculative account of T'Loak's business dealings, a rumored love affair, and a trip to Thessia.

Kahlee interrupted at that point. "Aria went to Thessia? What for?"

"There's no way to know for sure," Nix responded. "Some people suggest that it was a long-delayed vacation and nothing more. Others claim that she went home to bury her daughter."

Anderson sat up straight. "Aria had a daughter?"

"Yes," Nix replied, "although very few people were aware of it. T'Loak did her best to keep the relationship secret both to ensure her daughter's privacy and to protect her from kidnappers. But sadly, in spite of those precautions, Liselle was murdered."

Kahlee felt her heart start to beat a little faster. "Murdered by whom?"

Nix shrugged. "I don't know. But according to the rumors the person who did it was human. And he worked for T'Loak."

Kahlee looked at Anderson. "Grayson worked for T'Loak. *And* Cerberus."

"That's true," Anderson said, "but he's dead. And she knows that. So what's she up to?"

"Grayson didn't do it," Kahlee said. "Or that's what T'Loak believes. And she's looking for the person who did."

Nix looked from Kahlee to Anderson and back. The zoom lens whirred softly. "If that's true the murderer is dead. Or soon will be."

Kahlee thought about that and knew it was true. But who was the killer? And where was he hiding? She was determined to find out.

Kai Leng was laying on his back staring at the ceiling. Tool marks could be seen where something or somebody had burrowed into the solid rock. A single glow strip dangled from a metal hook and twisted back and forth in response to the flow of air from the small hole connected to a ventilation shaft.

Other than the light, the bucket that had been placed in a corner, and the narrow bed, there was no furniture in the room. Nothing that could be transformed into a weapon, used as a pick, or otherwise turned against his captors. And Leng knew why. Cory Kim had been a prisoner—and knew everything there was to know about prisons.

* * *

He'd been a marine lieutenant back then. A member of the Alliance military who had been rated N6. Meaning that he was an elite special forces operative. And it was that training that got him in trouble, or saved his life, depending on how one chose to look at it.

Leng, Kim, and a couple of their buddies had been in a bar on the Citadel that fateful evening doing what off-duty marines do. Which is to drink, hit on members of the opposite sex, and tell war stories. And that was what Leng was doing, telling a story about a raid on what he referred to as "some lizards" when a huge krogan emerged from the gloom. His voice had a throaty quality and the anger in his amber-colored eyes was clear to see. "Tell me something, human . . . What is a 'lizard'?"

Leng, who generally referred to all nonhumans as "freaks," and was of the opinion that the Alliance should go its own way rather than surrender any of its autonomy to the other races, had been somewhat intoxicated. Not that it would have made much difference if he'd been sober. "Lizards are big ugly freaks that can't reproduce because the turians neutered them. And a good thing too—since they were spreading like lice. Why do you ask?"

The krogan was silent for a second as if unable to believe his ears. Then he produced a roar of outrage and attacked. Leng was ready. He ducked as a massive fist passed through the spot where his head had been and delivered a blow to the krogan's midriff. It was like punching concrete. Given the difference in size the contest was bound to be one of strength versus speed and agility. Neither one of combatants was carrying a gun, but the krogan wasted no time in snatching up a bar stool, which he held like a club.

That prompted Leng to pull the double-edged commando knife from the sheath strapped to the inside surface of his left forearm and look for openings. They were circling each other by that time, as their supporters shouted words of encouragement, and bets were placed on the outcome. "Only cowards run," the krogan growled. "Stand and fight."

As tipsy as he was, Leng wasn't stupid enough to fall for that. Because if he went toe-to-toe with the monster the contest would be over in a matter of seconds. Such thoughts were going through Leng's mind when one of the bystanders tripped him. A freak perhaps, or a human with money on the krogan, not that it made much difference.

Leng fell. And as he did the krogan rushed forward with the bar stool held high. It crashed down onto the spot where Leng had been seconds before and shattered into a dozen pieces. And it was then, as the krogan began to straighten up, that Leng slashed a leg.

The laceration wasn't very deep, but produced a grunt of pain, and a flow of blood. That was the first step in a process that Leng's instructors called "the death of a thousand cuts." Their name for the strategy that could be used to cripple a more powerful opponent.

But the krogan wasn't stupid. Far from it. Suddenly, as Leng danced around looking for a line of attack, the lizard threw himself forward and rolled across the floor. It happened so quickly that Leng's feet flew out from under him and he came crashing down.

The krogan was waiting. He pinned Leng down and powerful fingers wrapped themselves around the human's throat. As they tightened Leng brought the blade in time after time. The point went deep, but the krogan was determined, and Leng knew he was about to black out when a biotic blow struck both of them at the same time. Kim had weighed in.

The impact caused the krogan to loosen his grip and that was all Leng required. The knife entered the back of the krogan's neck, severed his spine, and killed him. The big body jerked convulsively and went limp.

A mixed chorus of cheers and groans was heard as Leng's friends moved in to drag the lizard off of him. They were helping him to his feet as a squad of C-Sec officers flooded the bar. Leng was arrested, as were his friends, all of whom were handed over to the Alliance for disciplinary action.

Leng didn't take the situation seriously at first. Yes, he knew there would be consequences, but figured he could live with a negative fitness report or a loss of pay.

So it came as a shock when the Alliance court-martialed Leng, broke him down to private, and sentenced him to twenty years on Misery. And, unlike the others who got off with little more than a written reprimand, Kim went with him. Because she was a biotic, witnesses had seen her raise her hands, and one of them had been hit by the resulting "throw."

Kim's sentence was five years for aiding and abetting. All because the people in charge of the Alliance wanted to appease the freaks.

* * *

Leng heard metal rattle and sat up as Kim entered. She was carrying a tray loaded with food and was accompanied by two well-armed biotics. That was when the realization hit him. There was only one way to escape from *this* prison, and that was with the help of his old friend Cory Kim.

"Ah," Leng said lightly, "dinner has arrived. Or is it breakfast?"

"It's food," Kim said curtly. "Which is all you need to know. Bon appetit."

There was a clang as the door closed and Leng was left alone again. He went to collect the food. It was cold and nearly tasteless. Still, he needed to consume some calories, and proceeded to do so with machine-like efficiency. In the meantime his brain continued to churn. The Biotic Underground had gone to considerable lengths to take him prisoner. Why? What did they hope to accomplish?

The Illusive Man would be looking for him. Or would he? "All of us are expendable. But Cerberus must survive." That's what the Illusive Man said. So maybe he'd been written off and left to whatever his fate might be. Especially since he had not only failed to complete his mission but allowed himself to be compromised.

The relationship with Kim went back more than ten years, to the brutal prison on Misery, where every day was a battle to stay alive. There were no cells, no kitchen facility, and no guards. Not inside the thirty-foot-tall electrified fence anyway. No, all of the "tools," as the prisoners referred to them, were *outside*. All cozy in their fifty-foot-high observation towers where they could watch the prisoners kill each other off without getting their high-gloss Class-A combat boots dirty.

Because Hell's Half Acre, the name given to it by the inmates, was a "self-governing" facility run by the prisoners themselves. All of whom were human. That meant the stronger inmates were in charge, the weak were forced to join gangs in order to survive, and so-called tribes were in a state of perpetual warfare.

Given his training Leng might have been able to seize control of a tribe and thereby carve out a place for himself as a leader in the prison's power structure. He had chosen not to. Partly to avoid all of the dangers attendant on such a position, but partly because he had no interest in running things, and preferred to stay in the background.

And Kim had chosen to pursue the same strategy. So by sticking together they had been able to secure positions in a tribe called The Blades. It controlled a significant chunk of the much-contested shantytown where most of the prisoners lived as well as a large garden that had to be defended night and day lest the other tribes raid or destroy it.

And that was what they were doing, living together and trying to stay alive, when Leng heard a knock and went to open the door of the hut that Kim and he shared. The man standing in the opening was older rather than younger. Long straggly hair framed a heavily lined face. He was dressed in a homemade cape, bits and pieces of castoff military uniforms, and was wearing a pair of hand-carved clogs on his grimy feet. His staff was about six feet long and functioned as both a weapon and a means of support—since a great deal of Hell's Half Acre was muddy at that time of year. A wisp of vapor drifted away from the visitor's mouth as he spoke. "Are you Kai Leng?"

"Yeah."

"My name is Foster. Mick Foster. I'd like to talk to you."

Leng was suspicious. And for good reason. He was surrounded by criminals. "About what?"

Foster smiled. His teeth were yellow. "About Cerberus. May I come in? It's cold out here."

Leng hesitated for a moment. He had heard about Cerberus. It had once been the code name for a black ops group that had been part of the Systems Alliance but had since gone rogue. According to the rumors the shadowy figure in charge of Cerberus was determined to make sure that humans weren't pushed aside or overwhelmed by the freaks. Leng stood to one side and gestured for Foster to enter. "Watch your head. The roof is kinda low."

"Ah, but it keeps the rain off," Foster said as he stepped down onto packed dirt.

Kim, who had been sitting next to the fire repairing a hoe, looked up. "The name's Foster," the man said as he reintroduced himself. "You must be Cory Kim."

Kim looked surprised. "Do we know each other?"

"Nope," Foster said. "Not yet. Mind if I sit down?"

"Go ahead," Leng replied, and pointed to the handcrafted chair where he'd been sitting a minute earlier.

"Ah, that feels good," Foster said, as he settled into the chair and held a pair of filthy hands out toward the crackling fire. "Home sweet home, eh?"

"Not exactly," Kim said as she placed the hoe on the floor. "No offense, but what do you want?"

"And none taken," Foster assured her. "Oh, wait a minute, I have something for each of you . . . Gifts from Cerberus." And with that Foster reached under his ratty cape, felt around, and brought out a pair of flick knives. Razor-sharp stainless-steel weapons equipped with five-inch blades. Each knife was worth a fortune inside Hell's Half Acre and Leng liked the weight of it. But rather than tuck it away he looked Foster in the eye. "There are no gifts. Not in this place. What do you want?"

"*You*," Foster said simply. "Both of you. I'm a recruiter. For Cerberus."

Kim frowned. "A recruiter? *Here?*"

"Where better? For our purposes at least. There are others such as yourselves. People who were thrown into prison for crimes against things you would expect to see in a zoo."

Leng looked at the knife and back to Foster. "How did you get these things in here?"

Foster chuckled. "Some of the tools are Cerberus sympathizers. The rest can be bought. Not cheaply mind you, but bought nevertheless. And that brings us back to you two. If you agree to work for Cerberus we will buy your freedom. You could be off Misery in a matter of days."

Kim wasn't sure. "Let's say we agree . . . What would we be asked to do?"

"The same sort of things you did as a member of the Alliance Marine Corps. Except that every mission you participate in will be dedicated to strengthening and protecting the human race. The freaks can look out for themselves."

"I like it," Leng said. "I'm in."

Kim paused for a moment and nodded. "Me too."

Kai Leng was removed from Hell's Half Acre in order to receive special medical treatment three days later. Shortly thereafter Cory Kim was assigned to a work detail outside the fence and never returned. Cerberus was two people stronger.

THIRTEEN

SOMEWHERE IN THE CRESCENT NEBULA

The Illusive Man had returned to his home. If the Spartan office on a remote mining world could be described as such. There were a lot of things to work on including a new guerrilla marketing campaign aimed at Alliance-held worlds, the construction of a new space station, and the need to monitor the steady stream of reports from his field agents. And that was what he was doing when Jana entered. "Sorry to interrupt, sir . . . But there's a message that you'll want to see."

The Illusive Man looked up. "From whom?"

"The Biotic Underground. They have Leng . . . And they want money."

The Illusive Man nodded. "Of course they do. But how did they know where to send the message?"

"They didn't. The message went to half a dozen of our front organizations all of which passed it along."

"Understood." There was a momentary flare of light as the Illusive Man lit a cigarette and touched a button. A computer-generated image appeared, shattered, and came back together again. Though human in appearance the avatar had an androgynous quality. "Greetings," the messenger said. "I represent the Biotic Underground. We are holding one of your top operatives. A human named Kai Leng."

At that point the video dissolved to a shot of Leng sitting on a cot in what looked like a cave. The camera was located above him looking down. He seemed to be unaware of it but there was a strong possibility that Leng was ignoring it. The avatar reappeared. "As you can see Leng is unharmed, and he will remain that way, assuming you follow my instructions."

The Illusive Man said, "Pause," and turned to Jana. "Were we able to trace this message?"

"It originated on Omega but that's all the information we have."

The Illusive Man flicked the ash off his cigarette and said, "Play."

The holo continued. "We want ten million credits," the avatar said, "to be paid in the form of Beryllium slugs on Omega. The payment will be delivered by the Illusive Man, and *only* the Illusive Man, so as to ensure that all of our conditions are met.

"We realize that the Illusive Man may be, and probably is, somewhere other than on Omega. With that in mind we will give him three standard days to arrive here. Once he's in position you will send a message to the contact number that will appear at the end of this holo. Final arrangements will be agreed on at that time. Or, if you would prefer to save the ten million credits, let us know. We'll shoot Leng and leave his body where your operatives can find it."

The avatar disappeared at that point and a string of numbers appeared. They seemed to waver as if viewed from underwater. "We have the number," Jana said grimly.

"So now we know," the Illusive Man said, as he stubbed the cigarette out. "They want money."

"Maybe. It could be a trap."

"True," the Illusive Man agreed. "Although an attempt to get money would be consistent with the attack on T'Loak's bank. They're building a war chest."

"There does seem to be a pattern," Jana agreed.

"So what would *you* do?" the Illusive Man inquired. "Pay the ransom? Or let them kill Leng?"

Such questions were intended to test Jana, and force her to consider complex issues, since she was being groomed to take on more responsibility in the future. Her features hardened slightly. "All of us are expendable."

The Illusive Man nodded approvingly. "That's true . . . And Leng is no exception. He *is* valuable, however. I wouldn't pay thirty for him, or twenty for that matter, but *ten*? Given all that he has accomplished, and may accomplish in the future, ten is a reasonable price."

Jana stood her ground. "What you say makes sense in many respects. But doesn't this situation call Leng's competence into question? He was taken prisoner by a third-rate group of biotic whackos."

The Illusive Man smiled. "You're tough, Jana. I like that. But consider this . . . Leng has no way to know if we'll pay the ransom or not. So he's sitting in that cave cursing his own stupidity. And if we pay he'll be grateful and determined to avoid making the same mistake again. Loyalty is a very valuable thing."

The Illusive Man watched Jana's eyes as she took it in. "Yes, sir. I see your point."

"Good. Here's what I want you to do . . . Send the biotics a message indicating that we'll pay five million and not a credit more. The biotics won't agree, not if they're after money, but they will be suspicious unless we haggle. And we need to buy time. Mott's on the ground trying to gather more information. Who knows? Maybe she'll get lucky."

Jana nodded. "I'll take care of it."

"And Jana . . ."

"Yes?"

"Tell the bastards that if they harm Leng I will turn all of my attention to eradicating their organization."

Jana smiled. She'd been a military officer before joining Cerberus and an echo of that could be heard in her reply. "Sir, yes, sir."

On Omega

T'Loak felt a grim sense of anticipation as she slipped into a doorway next to a pair of her merce-naries and eyed the gigantic crawler that loomed on the other side of a lopsided square. Ever since the at-tack on her bank the Omega's population had been waiting for some sort of reprisal. But there hadn't been any. The result was a great deal of speculation. Was the Pirate Queen getting soft? Were the Skulls on the rise? Such questions were being posed in every bar, club, and cafe on Omega.

And T'Loak knew it. But the Biotic Underground had evacuated the hotel where they had been staying and moved into new quarters somewhere. T'Loak felt confident that her operatives would find them soon. That left the Grim Skulls, who had chosen to remain in their graffiti-decorated crawler. A steel box that made a respectable fort and could serve as a coffin as well. And now, after considerable preparation, she was ready to strike.

Immo had been opposed to T'Loak taking part in what promised to be a very active firefight. But she insisted on being present in order to inspire her people—and to make the extent of her strength absolutely clear to everyone on Omega. A strategy calculated to prevent attacks on her holdings in the future.

The last couple of hours had been spent moving a hundred of her mercenaries into positions around the crawler. The idea was to get close, but not *too* close, lest the Skulls realize that an attack was in the offing.

Now, as the final seconds ticked away, T'Loak heard Immo speak through the plug in her right ear. "Standby . . . Ten seconds from now. Nine, eight, seven, six, five, four, three, two, one."

Nothing happened. T'Loak frowned, and was about to question Immo, when a muffled thump was heard and the ground shook under her feet. There was a momentary pause followed by a truly spectacular secondary explosion as the armory located deep inside the crawler went up and jets of fire and smoke shot out through doors, hatches, and other openings. The destruction had been caused by a specially modified subsurface torpedo launched from more than a kilometer away. After burrowing around a number of underground obstructions, the weapon had blown a hole in the crawler's belly, thereby striking the Skulls from the one place they weren't expecting it. And that was from below.

What happened next was delightfully predictable. T'Loak figured that dozens of Grim Skulls had been killed during the explosions. But there were a lot of compartments inside the crawler, so it was safe to assume that a significant number of the mercenaries had survived.

And that proved to be the case as at least a dozen Skulls dashed out through the main hatch. T'Loak's forces were waiting and cut them down with ruthless efficiency. That put a stop to the escape attempt. T'Loak opened her mike. "Let's go in and get the rest of them."

The mercs who had been assigned to act as T'Loak's bodyguards were ranked to either side of the asari as she left the relative safety of the doorway and began to zigzag across the open area in front of the crawler. Seconds later she jumped a body and joined the rest of the troops who were rushing the massive machine.

A trio of Skulls appeared in the main hatch, all firing automatic weapons, and one of T'Loak's operatives was snatched off her feet. But the return fire swept the entrance clean so that the attackers could step over the dead bodies and enter the crawler. Thick smoke made it difficult to see. "Spread out," T'Loak ordered over the radio. "Search every compartment. Kill all of them except for Tactus. I want him alive."

There were rooms on both sides of the dimly lit main corridor, each of which had to be checked and cleared. The first space T'Loak entered was empty, and judging from the look of it, had been used as a ready room. As she backed into the hall T'Loak heard

the rattle of an automatic weapon on her left and
turned to see a merc stagger as he took a burst of
projectiles in the back. Then there was a flash of light
and a loud bang as one of his buddies tossed a grenade into the compartment and the firing stopped.

And so it went as the invaders fought their way
deeper into the machine. T'Loak allowed others to
take the lead, but did her share of the fighting as they
climbed an access ladder up to the second deck,
and the living quarters there. That was when Immo
emerged from the swirling smoke. She nodded.
"How're we doing?"

"Well, so far."

"And Tactus?"

"No sign of him yet. We came across the woman
you interviewed at the bank though. She's in the sickbay along with two others. I wasn't sure how to handle that so I put a guard outside the door."

"Show me."

So Immo led T'Loak a few feet down the corridor
to the point where a merc was standing outside a
hatch. The word "SICKBAY" had been scrawled onto
the metal next to the opening. The guard stood aside
so that T'Loak could enter. The medical facility was
small but well-equipped. There were four beds against
the far bulkhead, two of which were in use. A turian
who was hooked up to a respirator and appeared to
be unconscious occupied one of them. And a human,
who T'Loak recognized as Shella, was propped up on
the other. A pillow supported her right knee. "So,"
T'Loak said, "we meet again."

Shella was scared. T'Loak could see it in her eyes.
But the human was determined to maintain her com-

posure and nodded in response. "There was no point in trying to run."

"No, there wasn't."

"So what happens now?"

Shella feared the worst. T'Loak could see it in her eyes. "I believe you told me the truth about what happened to my daughter. So I will keep my word. Immo will make arrangements to have you transferred to an appropriate medical facility."

Shella looked both surprised and relieved. "Thank you."

"You're welcome." And with that T'Loak left the room. Tactus was still on the loose. But as her troops pushed the Skulls deeper and deeper into the crawler's belly it wasn't long before the turian was cornered. Having been summoned to the scene T'Loak found herself in a poorly lit corridor. An intermittent buzzing sound could be heard as a batarian stepped in to brief her. "We believe that Tactus and two of his men are trapped in a compartment at the other end of the passageway. A couple of grenades would finish them off but we were told to take Tactus alive."

"That's correct," T'Loak said. "Standby for further orders." Having cupped her hands in front of her mouth, T'Loak shouted down the corridor. "Tactus . . . It's T'Loak. Can you hear me?"

"Yeah," came the reply. "I can hear you."

"Good. There's no way out of here except *my* way. So if you want to live, put the weapons down, and come out with your hands behind your head."

There was a moment of silence. "Okay. Don't shoot. We're coming out."

T'Loak turned to the batarian. "Put some additional light on the other end of the corridor. It would be a mistake to trust the bastard."

A handheld spot snapped into existence, wandered across the overhead, and focused on the partially opened hatch just in time for Tactus to emerge. His hands were behind his neck, and as he came forward, two additional Skulls appeared to stand next to him. T'Loak raised a pistol and fired twice. Heads jerked and the men fell. Tactus looked alarmed. "You promised!" he said accusingly.

"I promised to spare *you*," T'Loak replied. "And I will. Hold your position."

Immo had arrived by then and T'Loak turned to speak with him. "I want chains on Tactus. Lots of them. Then, once he's ready, parade him through the streets. It won't take long for the news to get around. Understood?"

Immo nodded. "Understood."

"And find whatever is left of my money. I want it back."

And so it was that the once proud Tactus was marched through the streets to the Afterlife club, where he was placed in a cage for everyone to stare at and make fun of. Word of the turian's humiliation spread quickly and the message was clear: Anyone who chose to attack the Pirate Queen would pay a steep price indeed. Normality, such as it was on Omega, had been restored.

The Blue Marble restaurant was a mess. The front window had been shattered and there were hundreds of pockmarks where projectiles had flattened themselves against the concrete facade. And as Mara Mott watched from the other side of the street workmen were already in the process of making repairs under the supervision of a portly human. The owner? Yes, Mott thought so and crossed the busy street to speak with him. "Hello . . . Are you the proprietor by any chance?"

As the man turned to face her Mott saw that he had a unibrow, a bulbous nose, and a five o'clock shadow. "Who wants to know?" he inquired belligerently.

"My name is Hoby," Mott lied. "Karol Hoby and I'm interested in what occurred here."

The man frowned. "Why?"

"I have a client," Mott replied. "A person who wants to know and is willing to pay. Assuming you're the owner that is."

A gleam of what might have been avarice appeared in the man's eyes. "My name is Garza and I'm the chef. The manager was killed in the fighting. Come . . . My kitchen is intact. We will have tea and talk. This location is far too public."

Mott knew Garza was correct. If she was watching others might be as well. So she followed the cook past the workmen and into the Blue Marble's interior. It was empty of people, and judging from all the damage, the interior was going to require work as well.

But true to the chef's word the kitchen had been spared. And there, against the back wall, was a small table where the restaurant's employees could take a break. Garza put water on to boil before sitting opposite her. "How much will you pay?"

"That depends on what you know," Mott replied. "If you can tell me who organized the attack, and why they did so, I'll pay you five hundred credits."

"A thousand."

"Six hundred. And that's final. Remember, this is found money. I doubt anyone else cares who launched the attack."

Garza looked cautious. "Yes and no. I can think of one person who might care . . . An individual who would be very upset were I to talk about them."

"I promise I won't tell."

"You drive a hard bargain citizen Hoby . . . If that's your name. Six hundred it is. Would you like cream and sugar with your tea?"

"Yes, please."

Having served his guest Garza sat down. Their eyes met. "There was a man. He came into the restaurant, sat down, and ordered Mexican food."

"Describe him."

Garza did so and Mott felt her pulse quicken. Because the description fit Leng to a T. "Okay. He sat down. Then what?"

"A salarian came to the back entrance," Garza said, as he jerked a thumb at the door behind him. "He told me that an attack was about to take place and said we could warn our customers."

"Except for the man who was eating Mexican food?"

"Exactly. I told the manager and he passed the word."

Mott frowned. "Why would the attackers warn you? It doesn't make sense."

Garza eyed her over the rim of his cup. "The manager ran the Blue Marble, but he didn't own it."

Mott felt a rising sense of excitement. "Who does?"

"Aria T'Loak."

"So she attacked her own restaurant?"

"Yes."

"Why?"

Garza shrugged. "She wanted to kill the man I described earlier. It didn't work though. A lot of people wound up dead but the man she was after escaped."

There were more questions and more answers. But none of them explained why T'Loak wanted Leng dead. So Mott paid Garza, left the restaurant, and resumed her investigation. It didn't take long to find out about the attack on the Grim Skulls and the way Tactus had been dragged through the streets.

Was there some sort of connection between the attack on the Skulls and T'Loak's attempt to murder Leng? Mott couldn't see one but knew that Jana and the Illusive Man would expect her to follow up on every possible lead.

With that in mind Mott went looking for people who had firsthand knowledge of the attack on Grim Skull headquarters, only to discover that most of the mercs were dead. And T'Loak's personnel weren't talking. But her legwork did succeed in turning up one possible lead. And that was a Skull who had not only been spared by T'Loak but taken to a hospital by the Pirate Queen's personnel. The obvious question being why T'Loak would kill all of the Skulls with the single exceptions of their leader and a lowly foot soldier?

So Mott set off for the so-called Chop House, the much storied medical facility where Omega's poor were cared for, but everyone else sought to avoid. The front of the plain two-story structure was decorated with a faded sign that read OMEGA GENERAL

HOSPITAL, and some poorly patched combat damage. As Mott approached a narrow, six-wheeled "meat wagon" was pulling away.

The patient who had been left behind was on a gurney, and judging from the bloody bandages on his chest, had been shot. Mott followed as a couple of orderlies pushed the cart into the hospital. They continued on, heading toward the brightly lit emergency room off to the left, but Mott paused in the lobby. It was a madhouse. At least twenty people where waiting to be seen, and a long line led up to the reception desk, which was staffed by a single harried-looking asari. A constant babble of conversation filled the air. It was punctuated by terse announcements and the incessant wail of a sick child. The overall impression was one of chaos, misery, and hopelessness.

So rather than join the line that led to the reception desk Mott strolled past it and made for the set of double doors that led to the first-floor wards. Once inside there were very few staff members. That meant patients had to rely on family members and friends for the majority of their care. And with so many people coming and going Mott was free to go wherever she chose.

Mott hadn't been able to obtain a picture of the woman named Shella but she knew the Grim Skull was human and female. So she could ignore human males, turians, batarians, and all the rest. But after making her way through the wards, and eyeballing every patient not hidden behind ratty-looking curtains, Mott had seen only three possibles. All of whom denied being Shella-Shella and didn't match the description the operative had.

So she rode a blood-splattered elevator up to the second floor where Mott continued her search. Conditions were similar to those on the floor below. Some of the patients directed wistful looks her way, clearly hoping that she was a doctor come to examine them, while others frowned resentfully.

But when success came it wasn't what she expected. The woman coming her way was dressed in street clothes and, if it hadn't been for the crutches she was using, would have been able to pass Mott without attracting attention. But the Cerberus operative knew that the person she was looking for had been shot in the knee, and moved to block the way. "Excuse me . . . Is your name Shella?"

The woman had extremely short hair and pinched features. "Who's asking?"

"My name is Hoby. I'd like to ask you some questions."

"About what?"

"The Grim Skulls, the attack on the crawler, and why you were spared."

"I have nothing to say. Please get out of the way."

Mott remained where she was. "There are better medical facilities on Omega."

"And they cost money."

"Answer my questions and you'll be able to afford one."

Shella was silent for a moment. "I need an operation. They can't perform it here and I wouldn't want them to."

"How much?"

"Ten thousand."

"Done."

Shella's eyebrows rose. "I should have demanded fifteen."

Mott smiled. "Something is better than nothing."

"Give me half up front and I'll tell you everything I know."

"I'll give you a thousand up front," Mott said. "And I'll get you out of here."

Shella paused but only for a second. "It's a deal."

"Shall we get your belongings?"

"What belongings? I'm wearing them."

Half an hour later the women were seated across from each other in a comfortable restaurant with Shella's leg propped up on a chair. The food in the Chop House had been awful so Shella took the opportunity to order a hearty meal. Immediately after their drinks arrived Mott began to ask questions. "You were a Grim Skull. And T'Loak killed all of the Grim Skulls except for you and Tactus. Why were you spared?"

Shella took a sip of caf. "Remind me. Who are you working for?"

"A person who can afford to pay you ten thousand credits," Mott replied. "Please answer the question."

Shella shrugged. "Okay . . . Have it your way. The Skulls teamed up with a group called the Biotic Underground in order rob a bank owned by T'Loak. And the plan worked. Except that I was shot in the knee and left behind.

"T'Loak was going to have me killed. But I had information regarding her daughter's death. So I offered to tell her what happened in exchange for my life. And she agreed."

Mott felt a rising sense of excitement. "The knowledge you referred to. How did you come by it?"

There was a long pause—as if Shella was considering her options. Then she spoke. "I used to be a freelancer. And at one point I worked for a very secretive group. An organization called Cerberus."

The answer was so unexpected that Mott knew there was a look of surprise on her face. "Cerberus? The human advocacy group?"

Shella produced a snort of derision. "That's how *they* describe it. But Cerberus does a lot more than promote human rights. They carry out all sorts of operations against people and organizations they perceive to be a threat."

"So where does T'Loak's daughter come in?"

"She doesn't. Not directly. But she was romantically involved with a man named Paul Grayson. And, for reasons I'm not entirely sure of, Cerberus was out to get him. So the operative in charge assembled a team and we broke into Grayson's apartment."

Mott's chest felt tight. "And his name was?"

"He went by Manning on Omega. But I doubt that was his real name."

Mott battled to keep a straight face. She knew Manning's real name and it was Leng. She was close. Very close. A few more questions and she would know why T'Loak was after Leng. "So, you broke in. Then what?"

Shella looked away before bringing her eyes back into contact with Mott's. "Grayson got away, but someone put a tranq dart into T'Loak's daughter, and she was laying there. Manning slit her throat."

Mott frowned. "Why?"

Shella shrugged. "I don't know. Maybe he had orders to kill her. Or maybe he was in the mood."

"So you told T'Loak and she let you go."

"Yes. Twice."

Mott thought about what she'd been told. Leng had killed T'Loak's daughter. No wonder the Pirate Queen was out to get him. "You're a lucky lady."

"Am I? I don't feel lucky."

"Maybe an additional nine thousand credits will make you feel better," Mott said. "Then, after that operation, you might want to leave Omega. It's a very dangerous place to live."

Keys rattled, the door opened, and Leng was ready. Once a day he was allowed to leave his cell and accompany Cory Kim down the spiraling pathway to the floor of the cavern. Sometimes they walked back and forth across it and on other occasions they walked in circles. Leng wasn't wearing restraints nor was there a need for them since Kim or any of the other biotics could slam his ass anytime they chose to.

But that didn't mean Leng couldn't escape. All he needed was some help. And Kim could supply it. That was the plan anyway as they arrived on the main floor and began to walk back and forth. It was the only time during the day when Leng could talk to Kim without being monitored by the pickups in his cell. That made every second precious. "So tell me something," he began. "Are there times when you miss Hell's Half Acre?"

Kim looked sideways at him. "You must be kidding."

Leng smiled crookedly. "Not the prison. That was horrible. I meant you and I."

Kim eyed the ground ahead. "Maybe. Sometimes. But was it real? We were trying to survive. So it made sense to team up."

"That's true," Leng said as they were forced to turn, and start back. "But there was more to it than that."

"Really? I never felt sure."

"You left me. Not the other way around."

"No," Kim said. "I left Cerberus. There's a difference. Or there used to be anyway."

"I owe Cerberus," Leng replied. "We both do. If it wasn't for Cerberus we'd be in Hell's Half Acre. Or dead."

"Cerberus is using you," Kim replied. "You don't seem to care but I did. There are limits to what one should do for a cause. Even a good one."

"So you joined the Biotic Underground. And now you're in the kidnapping business."

"I tried all sorts of things after I left Cerberus. The Biotic Underground being the latest. And we're not in the kidnapping business. We need money, that's all . . . Biotics are naturally superior. We're more intelligent thanks to the way our brains are put together, more resilient because of the dangers we have to overcome *before* we're born, so when we're in charge things will improve."

"For *who*?" Leng demanded. "For you? For humanity? Or for your leaders?"

"For everyone," Kim said stubbornly. "For *all* races."

Leng shrugged. "Maybe that's the problem, hon . . .

Maybe we should have been focused on ourselves. We had something special—and seeing you reminds me of that."

Kim smiled as they arrived at the other side of the cavern and made the turn. "Are you trying to sweet-talk me, Kai? If so, it won't work."

"No," Leng lied. "I'm thinking about my life, that's all. Thinking about what is—and what could have been."

There was a long moment of silence as they walked side by side. Kim was the first to speak. "Get over it Kai. What's gone is gone."

The words were harsh, but Leng thought he could detect a wistful tone in her voice. He wasn't free. Not by a long shot. But the first step had been taken.

FOURTEEN

ON OMEGA

The conference room consisted of a cavern located just off the main floor. And while Mythra Zon took her seat at the table the conversation stopped. Zon smiled as she looked from face to face. "Most of us are here for a change. That's good because we have plenty to talk about starting with T'Loak's efforts to locate us. Arrius? What can you tell us?"

Arrius Sallus was in charge of security. An important responsibility to begin with and one made even more so by the fact that the Pirate Queen was eager to find the organization and destroy it. "Well," Sallus responded, "T'Loak is offering a reward of five thousand credits to anyone who can provide her with information regarding our location."

Ocosta Lem frowned. "That's a real concern. Someone is bound to notice our movements and turn us in."

"True," Sallus replied. "Which is why I paid more than two dozen street people to submit bogus sightings. T'Loak's operatives will have to check on each one and that will take time."

"Well done," Zon said. "The last thing I want to do is wind up in a cage right next to Tactus. I think we all know what's going to happen to him once T'Loak has made her point."

"Tactus is an idiot," Rasna Vas Kathar put in sourly. "He should have prepared his people for a counterattack. Instead he just sat there counting T'Loak's money and drinking beer."

"But he was a useful idiot," Sallus countered. "Thanks to his stupidity T'Loak focused all of her attention on him. And we gained more time."

"That's true," Zon allowed. "But the clock is ticking. We'll have to pull out and do it soon. And when I say 'pull out' I mean leave Omega for a safer location. Who knows? Once we destroy Cerberus it might be time to tackle the Citadel."

"*If* we destroy Cerberus," Kathar put in doubtfully. "I've been thinking about the plan and I'm starting to have some doubts. If T'Loak can chase us off Omega, what makes us think we can destroy Cerberus?"

"Maybe we'll fail," Zon responded. "But it's worth a try. The plan Gillian put forward is so audacious it might work. Where *is* Gillian anyway? I thought she was going to join us."

Kathar chose his words carefully. The truth was that he didn't trust Gillian, although he wasn't sure why. Plus, he feared that her rising star might eclipse his own. "That was my hope," he lied. "But with T'Loak on the hunt I thought it would be best to put both Gillian and Nick on the front entrance."

Sallus frowned, opened his mouth as if about to object, and closed it again.

"Okay," Zon responded, "but I think the plan is sound. We have Leng, and judging from the Illusive Man's initial response, Cerberus wants him back. So all we have to do is get the Illusive Man to deliver the ransom and then kill him."

Zon made it sound simple. But Kathar wasn't buying it. Not for a moment. He couldn't say that however. "Yes, well, how are negotiations going?"

Ocosta Lem was in charge of the process and the salarian cleared his throat. "The Illusive Man refused our initial demand—and offered five million instead."

"That's to be expected," Zon said mildly. "The most important thing is bring the Illusive Man to Omega."

"Yes," Lem acknowledged. "Although it would behoove us to keep the amount as high as possible in hopes that we'll be able to kill the Illusive Man *and* keep the money."

Sallus grinned. "I like the way you think."

"So we countered at seven five," Lem said. "And we're waiting for a response."

"The Illusive Man will go for it," Zon predicted. "He wants Leng back."

"Speaking of Leng," Kathar said, "was it wise to place Kim in charge of monitoring him? They have a prior relationship you know."

"Yes, I'm aware of that," Sallus said pointedly. "Cory and I spoke about it. She assures me that they were acquaintances. Nothing more."

Kathar could tell that Sallus was still annoyed regarding his decision to put Gillian and Nick on guard duty. So rather than aggravate Sallus further he chose to back down. "Good. There's nothing to worry about then."

Zon was aware of the tension between her subordinates and sought to placate them. "There are dangers. But we know what they are . . . And we're prepared to deal with them. Thank you, everyone. This meeting is adjourned."

Anderson was dreaming. It was a nice dream, or would have been except for the klaxon that was bleating. Then a hand touched his arm and he awoke. "David," Kahlee said. "David . . . Pick up the handset. It could be important."

The comm was located on his side of the bed so Anderson fumbled for the receiver and brought it to his ear. Maybe Gillian was calling. Or someone who knew where Gillian was. "This is David Anderson."

There was a pause followed by a brief burst of static. "Admiral Anderson? Dor Hana here."

Anderson struggled to sit up. Hana! He felt a sudden wave of guilt. He was being paid to gather information about whoever had absconded with Paul Grayson's body and possible connections to the Reapers. But he'd spent all of his time looking for Gillian and Nick. He cleared his throat. "Good evening, sir. Or good morning as the case may be."

"I hope I didn't wake you," Hana said. "But I had a moment, and thought this would be an excellent time to check in. How is the investigation going? Have you been able to gather any information regarding the Reapers?"

Alarm bells went off in Anderson's head. But why? As the representative of a Council member Hana had every right to inquire about Anderson's progress. And, more than that, Anderson *wanted* the Council to take an active interest in the Reapers. But he couldn't shake the vague suspicions that haunted the back of his mind. Not that it mattered because he had nothing to report. "I'm sorry, sir . . . But no. I keep running into dead ends."

"I'm sorry to hear that," Hana replied. "But it's a difficult task and like all difficult tasks it's going to take time."

Was Hana being nice? Or was he relieved to hear that Anderson hadn't learned anything? It was impossible to tell. "Yes, sir. I can report that we have made some progress where Gillian Grayson and Nick Donahue are concerned and hope to locate them soon."

"Good," Hana said. "Keep me informed." The call came to an end a few seconds later.

"What was that about?" Kahlee wanted to know.

"That," Anderson said, "is a very good question. I wish I knew the answer."

Hendel was tired. And for good reason. The Biotic Amp and Supply Laboratory was open around the clock. So, having assigned himself the task of monitoring it, it was necessary to go without sleep for as long as he could. The theory was simple. Being a biotic himself, Hendel knew that amps require occasional maintenance. And since everyone agreed that the BA&S lab was the best on Omega, every biotic who could afford to go there would at some point. And that included Gillian Grayson and Nick Donahue. The problem being *when*. It might be days, weeks, or even months before one of the youngsters made an appearance. But Hendel had nothing better to do and, according to his reasoning, some effort was better than none.

"The hide," as he thought of it, consisted of a badly damaged delivery vehicle located across the street from the lab. It had been home to one of the city's beggars before Hendel threw him out and moved in. Then, after making appropriate arrangements with certain locals, he settled in. That was when? A day and a half earlier? Something like that. Although it could have been more given the way he smelled.

Gradually, bit by bit, the light level outside the truck increased slightly, signaling the start of a new artificial day. There hadn't been much foot traffic in or out of the lab during the night, but things were starting to pick up as members of the day shift arrived. Hendel had been watching long enough to recognize many of the employees and give them nicknames like "Stick Figure," "Four Eyes," and "Fatso." The problem was keeping his eyes open as he stared through the spotting scope that was set up in the back of the van's cargo compartment.

So Hendel welcomed the knocks that signaled the arrival of some much needed caf and his breakfast. He placed a hand on his pistol, said "Come," and watched as one of two back doors swung open. The street urchin's name was Cora and he was paying her to buy what he thought of as his rations and deliver them at regular intervals. Cora had lots of tangled hair, dark skin, and luminous brown eyes. "Do you like pancakes?" the little girl inquired, as she pushed a steaming carton into the truck. "I like pancakes."

"Then we'll share," Hendel said kindly. "Please close the door behind you."

Once Cora was inside, and the morning's feast was spread out on the floor, Hendel had no choice but to turn away from the scope in order to eat. Cora was hungry, and she was a chatterbox as well, which meant that she had a tendency to talk with her mouth full.

But that was okay with Hendel, since he had very little to say, especially to a seven-year-old street ur-chin. So he drank caf and listened patiently as Cora stuffed food into her mouth and told him all about her plans to grow up and be just like Aria T'Loak.

In between bites of food Hendel peered through the scope as people came and went. He was finishing his half of the sausage-filled pancakes when a large truck pulled up in front of the lab and stopped. Hendel swore as the driver got out, made his way to the back, and began to unload boxes. Due to the way the vehi-cle was positioned Hendel couldn't see the front of the building. And that meant people could come and go unobserved.

Fortunately it wasn't long before one of the lab's employees came out to collect the boxes, which freed the truck driver to move on. And it was then, as the vehicle pulled away, that Nick Donahue appeared. He'd been inside the building. For how long wasn't clear. A red jacket was draped over his shoulders, but was open in front, and Hendel could see the white bandages that ran diagonally across his chest.

The youngster looked taller than Hendel remem-bered him, and he was armed with two pistols. And there, at his side, was a pleasant-looking young woman with brown hair. And judging from the way she clung to him they were more than friends. Nick, the formerly awkward teenager, with a girlfriend? It was hard to believe.

The girl said something into Nick's ear and Hendel saw him nod. Then they turned away. Hendel knew he had only seconds in which to exit the wreck and catch up with them before the twosome disappeared into the surrounding maze. He left the scope where it was, grabbed the shotgun, and gave fifty credits to Cora. "Thanks, hon, and here's a piece of advice. Don't model yourself on Aria T'Loak. She isn't very nice." Then he threw the back door open and hit the pavement.

There were people on the street by then. Lots of them. And some looked annoyed as Hendel plowed through the crowd and shouldered pedestrians out of the way. Then, about ten seconds later he spotted the couple, strolling arm in arm up the street.

Hendel wanted to dash forward, grab Nick, and shake some sense into him. But that would be a mistake and he knew it. Nick might spill his guts regarding Gillian and the Biotic Underground and he might not. So the smart thing to do was to follow the boy home and decide what to do at that point. But, having completed whatever errand had taken them to the lab, it soon became clear that Nick and his girlfriend were in no hurry. They walked a long way, and wandered in and out of a dozen shops, before eventually hailing a pedicab.

That forced Hendel to jog for a while, worried lest they look back and spot him, before hiring a conveyance of his own. It was a cart hitched to a rough-looking turian. "See that cab?" Hendel demanded. "Follow it. But stay back."

If the ruffian between the traces was surprised by the order he gave no sign of it as he pulled Hendel through a maze of interconnecting streets. The ride continued for a good ten minutes before Hendel rounded a curve and saw the couple standing on a corner. Their cab was pulling away and had clearly been paid off.

"Keep going," Hendel instructed. "Pass them, turn into the next side street, and stop."

As Hendel passed the twosome he saw that Nick was taking a long careful look around as if to spot any sort of tail. The teenager's eyes swept across the cart and the man he had seen every day for years. But he failed to see past the beard, the scruffy clothing, and the situation. Nick didn't *expect* to see Hendel on Omega so he didn't.

Two minutes later Hendel was off the cart, on the street, and walking well back of the couple as they entered a narrow lane. A steep hill rose to the left of it and there was a shantytown on the right. It was lined by one- and two-story structures. Scruffy-looking people sat in front of many of them, eyeing passersby the way predators do, looking for any sign of weakness.

The debris-littered street turned gradually, so even though Hendel wanted to maintain eye contact, he was forced to hang back or risk being spotted. And that was how they lost him.

As Hendel rounded a curve he looked ahead fully expecting to see the couple in front of him. But they had disappeared. There was a door, however. A steel door that was set into the hillside and was partially open to allow a sleek gyrocycle to exit. The mechanically stabilized vehicle roared loudly and generated a cloud of dust as it sped away. A couple of guards, both of whom were wearing armor, stood watching as the gate closed. Were Nick and his companion inside? Yes, Hendel felt certain that they were, especially since the only other possibility was the shantytown off to the right.

Hendel was careful not to look around, or even glance at the guards, as he walked past. It would be a mistake to show how interested he was. But Hendel could think about the discovery and he did. *You may be wearing two guns,* the ex-security officer thought to himself, *and you may have a girlfriend. But you're still a pimply faced troublemaker and your ass is mine. Have a nice day, Nick. I'll be back.*

Kahlee and Anderson had been on Omega long enough to develop habits—one of which was to eat lunch at an upscale restaurant called Michele's. And that's where they were, comparing notes on a largely frustrating morning, when Hendel came barging in. He looked like a homeless person and was armed with a shotgun. So the restaurant's security people hurried to intercept him. Hendel was complaining loudly, and threatening the batarians with bodily harm, when Anderson arrived. "It's okay," he said soothingly. "In spite of all appearances to the contrary he's with us. Hendel, please stop threatening people. It makes the situation worse."

It took some talking and ten credits each to convince the guards that they should return to their posts.

Then, with a hand on Hendel's shoulder, Anderson escorted the biotic over to the table where Kahlee was waiting. "Good grief," she said disapprovingly. "Where have you been? We were worried about you. And you look terrible."

"He smells even worse," Anderson said, as the two men took their seats.

"Good morning to you too," Hendel said grumpily. "I was about five kilometers from here, sitting in the back of a wrecked truck, watching a place called the Biotic Amp and Supply Lab."

Kahlee frowned. "Why?"

"Because biotics go there."

Kahlee's eyes grew wider. "That was smart. Very smart. Did it work?"

"Yes," Hendel said smugly. "It did. Nick Donahue showed up this morning with a girl on his arm."

Anderson leaned forward. "And?"

"And they led me to what could be the Biotic Underground's headquarters."

"That's huge," Kahlee said. "What are we waiting for? Let's go there."

"Not so fast," Hendel said. "The place is bound to be full of Level Three biotics all armed to the teeth. We wouldn't stand a chance. Plus, if it's there it's behind a steel door inside a hill made out of solid rock."

"Hendel's right," Anderson said gloomily. "We would need a small army to tackle a place like that."

Kahlee broke the ensuing silence. "Right . . . So let's ask someone who has a small army if we can borrow it."

Anderson's eyebrows rose. "Aria T'Loak?"

Kahlee smiled. "Of course. Who else?"

* * *

Kai Leng lay on his back, staring at the rocky ceiling and feeling sorry for himself. Where the hell was Cerberus? Surely the organization could have located the cavern by then. Assuming they wanted to. But the decision to invest the necessary time and effort would have to be made by the Illusive Man himself. Leng thought to himself, *I put in more than ten years for Cerberus and they leave me to rot.*

Leng's thoughts were interrupted as an old-fashioned key rattled in the lock and the door to his cell swung open. "Rise and shine," Kim said as she stepped inside. "It's time for your walk."

"Just like a dog."

"Yeah, pretty much. Now get off your butt. You have all day but I don't."

So Leng swung his feet over the side of the bed and onto the floor. Then came the task of pulling his boots on. Once they were secured he slipped the toothbrush into one of them and stood. Kim jerked her head toward the open door. "You know the drill. Get going."

Leng walked past her, through the doorway, and out into the brighter illumination of the main cavern. As he looked down onto the area below he saw very little activity. There wasn't much going on insofar as he could tell.

Gravel crunched under Leng's boots as he followed the path down and out onto the floor. "Okay," Kim said, "start walking."

Leng obeyed. And it felt good to stretch his legs. They followed their shadows across to the far side of the cavern where they were forced to turn back. "So," Kim said, as she broke the silence. "Are you ready?"

"Ready for what?"

"Ready to escape. Look straight ahead. See the door? That's the only way out. Gillian Grayson is on duty and the second guard is taking a bio break. She's a lot more powerful than I am but I'll take her by surprise. There's a biometric scanner but I can open it.

"Then we'll run through the tunnel. That leads to a second door which you can open by hitting the slap switch. Two guards are stationed outside and I should be able to deal with both. But if something goes wrong jump in with both feet.

"From there we'll run straight across the street into the shantytown on the other side. People will follow us, but the place is like a maze, so with any luck at all we'll be able to lose them. Got it?"

Leng looked at her. He'd seen that expression before. Back in Hell's Half Acre. Kim had been in love with him then and still was in spite of words to the contrary. "So, you think I'm worth saving?"

Kim smiled. "Maybe . . . But it doesn't matter what I think. The Illusive Man wants to get you out of here. And he's willing to blow off all the work it took to place an agent in the Biotic Underground."

Leng's eyebrows rose. "So, you're still part of Cerberus?"

"Of course."

"Thank you."

Kim made a face. "You can thank me if we survive. Get ready . . . *Now!*"

Gillian was standing next to the first door looking at her omni-tool when Kim sent a biotic shockwave straight at her. The dark energy plucked Gillian off her feet and threw her against the wall. Then, before she could recover, Kim was there to pistol-whip her.

Leng felt helpless as he waited for Kim to step in front of the retinal scanner. It seemed to take forever before the green light came on and Kim hit the switch. As the door rumbled up out of the way Leng heard a distant shout and knew they had been spotted. The alarm was followed by a burst of gunfire as what sounded like a host of angry bees buzzed past his head. "Come on!" Kim shouted. "Follow me."

Leng followed the biotic as she ran to the next door and slapped a switch. The second door rumbled open to reveal a couple of street guards. They looked surprised. Kim slammed one of them and Leng took care of the second with a right cross. His fist connected with the man's jaw, the biotic went down, and his submachine gun fell free. Leng scooped it up and followed Kim as she led him across the street. A horn blared as a car came to a screeching halt. Leng dodged around the front of it as one of the guards shouted something unintelligible and gave chase.

As Leng and Kim entered the shantytown, and pounded down a narrow garbage-strewn lane, residents looked on in dull-eyed surprise. A mongrel gave chase. It was next to Kim, trying to nip at her legs, when she shot it with her pistol. The body tumbled end over end and hit a pile of trash.

Leng's leg had begun to ache by then. The gunshot wound suffered aboard the Grissom Academy space station was nearly healed. But every time he was forced to run it set the recovery process back. Still, there was no choice, so all Leng could do was grit his teeth and put up with the pain.

"This way!" Kim shouted, and led him into what amounted to an alley. That was when Leng heard a loud bang, saw a geyser of soil leap up near one of Kim's heels, and realized that one of the local residents had taken a shot at her. Because of the dog? Or for sport? There was no way to be sure as they dodged in between a couple of shacks and paused to rest.

But it soon became apparent there wouldn't be any time to rest as shouts were heard and some of their pursuers arrived on the scene. It was impossible to know how many without peeking around the corner and inviting a head shot. "We know you're in there!" a male voice said. "Put your weapons down and come out with your hands clasped behind your head."

Leng was surprised. He glanced at Kim. "They want to take us alive. *Why?*"

"They want to take *you* alive," she answered. "The Underground's leaders told the Illusive Man that he could have you back for ten million credits. He countered at five—and as of a day ago they were trying to get seven five."

Leng experienced a momentary surge of pleasure. Silly though it might be it felt good to know that the Illusive Man wanted him back. "First the bank job, now this . . . What are the biotics planning to do with all that money?"

"It isn't about money," Kim answered.

"This is your last chance," the male voice shouted. "Come out *now.*"

"Not about money?" Leng inquired, as he checked to make sure that the submachine gun was fully functional. "Well, if it isn't about money, what *is* it about?"

"The Illusive Man," Kim replied. "They want to lure him in, kill him, and destroy Cerberus. It was Gillian Grayson's idea."

Leng was still in the process of absorbing that news when he heard a clang as something landed on the metal roof of the structure to his right. That was followed by a rattling sound. He grabbed hold of Kim and jerked her back. *"Grenade!"*

It was a grenade. A flash-bang to be precise, and it went off in midair. Light strobed the passageway and the accompanying concussion shook flimsy walls on both sides of them. The purpose of the attack was to stun the fugitives so the biotics could turn the corner of the building and take them down. Only Leng had anticipated that strategy and been able to close his eyes in time.

Now, as he opened up on them he saw the first attacker step into the passageway. But rather than fire the assault rifle slung over his shoulder the man raised both hands as if to launch a biotic attack. That was a mistake, as the would-be attacker learned when a well-aimed burst of projectiles struck his armor. Sparks flew as the projectiles ate their way through the protective suit. But the *real* damage was inflicted by Kim who "threw" the man backward. He was still in the process of falling when she touched Leng's arm. "Let's go!"

As Kim ran down the garbage-strewn path between two shacks Leng followed. His goal was to escape rather than inflict casualties on the Biotic Underground. Because now that he knew what was going on Leng had to warn the Illusive Man.

But it wouldn't be easy. A shotgun blast narrowly missed Leng as he splashed through a rivulet of sewage and passed by an open window. It seemed that at least one local resident was unhappy about the battle taking place outside his home. Maybe he would shoot at the biotics too. Leng hoped so.

At that point Leng spotted a street up ahead and felt a surge of hope. If they could cross it, and plunge even deeper into the maze of shacks, perhaps it would be possible to shake their pursuers. It seemed that Kim was thinking the same thing as she ran into the pothole-cratered byway.

Leng was limping by then, his speed was half what it had been previously, and every time his foot landed it sent a jolt of pain up his leg. So Kim was already on the far side, waiting for him, when the roar of a powerful engine was heard.

Leng looked right, saw that a gyrocycle was coming straight toward him, and felt an invisible fist hammer his chest as the two-wheeled vehicle flashed past. There were two riders—a driver and a passenger. The latter having launched the attack.

Leng hit the ground hard, and laying on his back struggling to breathe when Kim arrived to help him up. Meanwhile, half a block away, the gyrocycle was halfway through a U-turn. Leng put paid to that plan by firing a long burst from the submachine gun.

The range was long, but luck went his way for a change, and a slug smashed the driver's visor. He toppled onto the ground, which left the passenger to scoot forward and take the controls. But being unable to steer *and* attack she sped away.

That was good, but far from the victory they

needed as a second engine was heard, signaling another attack. "We've got to find some cover," Kim
said. "Or better yet, a place to hide. You won't get far
with that leg."

Leng knew Kim was right as she helped him hobble
into the space between two dilapidated shacks. A
baby was crying somewhere nearby, a dog was bark-
ing, and the engine noise was louder. A local armed
with a shotgun appeared up ahead and Kim shot him
three times. With no armor to protect him he went
down as if poleaxed.

But no sooner had that threat been neutralized
than another materialized. Leng heard the screech of
brakes, followed by the sound of an over-revved engine, and turned to see another gyrocycle coming
straight at him. He was bringing the submachine gun
to bear when Kim pushed past him and sent a shockwave surging through the narrow passageway. The
tightly focused ball of energy struck the driver, who
lost control and crashed into a wall. Even the built-in
gyro stabilizer couldn't keep the vehicle upright and it
fell over, trapping both riders under its weight.

Leng turned back in the direction they had been
going and attempted to run. But there was no place to
go. *Three* biotics were standing shoulder to shoulder
blocking the passageway. The one in the center was
Mythra Zon, and judging from her expression, she
was pissed. Her hands were raised and Leng knew she
could kill him. "There is no point in further violence,"
Zon said. "Give up. You won't be harmed."

Leng knew that Zon was right. He couldn't escape.
What he could do was borrow Kim's pistol and shoot
himself in the head. That would end the plot to suck

the Illusive Man into a trap. Or would it? No, the biotics would simply pretend that he was alive, thereby making his act of self-sacrifice meaningless.

But there was someone else to consider. "What about Kim? What will happen to her?"

"She will be taken alive. But we have to maintain discipline. I imagine it's the same inside Cerberus."

Leng remembered McCann and the hard-fought battle in the men's room. He looked at Kim. Her face was expressionless, but he could see the fear in her eyes. He turned back toward Von. "So what does 'discipline' mean in this case?"

"There will be a trial," Zon replied. "Kim's peers will decide her fate."

That wasn't much, but it was something. At least the biotics weren't going to execute Kim on the spot. Maybe something good would happen before the trial took place. "Okay," Leng said wearily, and placed the submachine gun on the ground. He turned to Kim. "I'm sorry, hon. Whatever you do, don't tell them you work for Cerberus."

She shrugged. "My mother told me not to date soldiers. I should have listened." Kim thumbed the safety on and let the pistol fall.

"Good," Zon said. "Very good." The slam came without warning. One moment Leng was standing there. The next he was in the air. Then came the impact. Pain lanced up his leg, arrived in his brain, and exploded. That was followed by a long fall into nothingness. And a cessation of pain. The escape attempt was over.

FIFTEEN

ON OMEGA

It was dark and well into the evening when Aria T'Loak and her entourage arrived at the Afterlife club. Her bodyguards got out of the heavily armored limo first, and having consulted with the security guards stationed in front of the building, returned to open the door.

T'Loak got out, ignored the usual handful of on-lookers who'd been waiting to get a look at her, and swept in through the front door. A red carpet led straight to the cage located at the center of the lobby. Sy Tactus was there waiting for her. And he was a sight to see. His expression could best be described as a snarl, and he was standing with both hands on the vertical bars. "Good evening . . . Bitch."

T'Loak smiled serenely. "Nice try, Tactus, but I'm not ready to kill you just yet. Still, it is something to look forward to, isn't it?" And with that she walked away.

Tactus produced a mournful howl loud enough to be heard on the dance floor. But T'Loak didn't look back as she made her way up to her second-floor office. As always there was a lot of work waiting to be done. Everything from the need to hire a new exotic dancer to how to bribe a government official on Camala and get away with it. But T'Loak enjoyed such challenges and took pride in her ability to come up with solutions. So she was happily lost in her work when Immo entered the enclosure. "You have a call."

T'Loak looked up from her terminal. "Who is it?"

"The Illusive Man."

"Really? Well, that's interesting. Activate the privacy barrier. I'll take it."

The privacy barrier was a semiopaque electronically generated curtain that "dropped" into place on command—thereby sealing T'Loak and her guests off from the rest of the nightclub. But in this case she chose to take the call alone.

The lights dimmed slightly, the air seemed to boil as the image took shape, and the Illusive Man appeared. T'Loak had interacted with him on numerous occasions in the past and with one exception he looked the same. During past calls the Illusive Man had always been seated in front of an eye-catching backdrop. A sun perhaps, or a planetscape, but not this time. The background had a gray neutral appearance, as if he was in transit on a spaceship, or located in a place that he didn't want to reveal. He nodded politely. "Aria T'Loak. It's always a pleasure. You don't look a day over two hundred."

T'Loak smiled. "I'll bet you say that to all the girls."

"Only to members of your race. To do otherwise would be dangerous."

T'Loak chuckled. "So, what can I do for you?"

"I lost something and I want it back."

"I see. What sort of item are we talking about?"

"A man. One of my operatives. He was abducted."

T'Loak felt her pulse start to quicken. The conversation was getting interesting. *Very* interesting. "And he's on Omega?"

"Yes. That's why I called you."

"Of course," T'Loak said. As if that was the most natural thing in the world—which it was. "What can you tell me about him?"

"His name is Kai Leng," the Illusive Man said, as his lighter flared. "This is what he looks like. An organization called the Biotic Underground has him."

A three-dimensional image appeared in place of the Illusive Man and began to rotate slowly. And T'Loak felt something cold trickle into her bloodstream. The man with slightly Asiatic features was a perfect match for the human that Shella had described to her. Which was to say the man who murdered Liselle in cold blood.

Not only that, but if the Illusive Man was correct, Leng was being held by the Biotic Underground! One of the two organizations responsible for robbing her bank, and the one she hadn't been able to get a lead on until the day before, when Kahlee Sanders and David Anderson had stopped by. They knew where the biotics were hiding and hoped to rescue a couple of Sanders's ex-students. A silly impulse really, since both teenagers were on Omega by choice, but a blessing nevertheless.

But it was critical to keep that fact to herself, because while the Illusive Man wanted to rescue Kai Leng, she was determined to kill him. "Capture and store," T'Loak said, knowing the image of Leng would go into her files.

The Illusive Man reappeared. He was smoking and the ember on his cigarette glowed like a malevolent red eye as he took a deep drag. "I know where he is but I'm shorthanded and could use some help breaking him out. Can you help me?"

"Yes, I will. But it will cost you."

The Illusive Man smiled thinly. "Of course it will. How much?"

T'Loak took a moment to consider. It was important to set the fee high enough to make the Illusive Man wince, but not so high as to chase him away. She was looking forward to killing the Illusive Man's operative *and* making some money at the same time. "Two million."

The Illusive Man exhaled and the plume of smoke eddied as a current of air hit it. "Leng is valuable to me . . . But not *that* valuable. One million."

"One five."

"Okay, one five. *If* you move quickly. I'm stalling but the biotics are pushing hard, and I'm running out of time."

"Why don't you simply pay the ransom?"

The Illusive Man tapped some ash off the end of his cigarette. "Do you trust the Biotic Underground?"

"No."

"Neither do I."

T'Loak nodded. "I will launch a rescue attempt within the next two cycles."

"Aren't you going to ask where he is?"

T'Loak smiled. "I already know."

* * *

Things had gone terribly wrong—and Gillian had no idea how to put them right. One moment she'd been standing next to the inner gate, consulting her omni-tool, and the next she'd been flying through the air. No bones had been broken during the collision with the cavern wall, but Gillian had been knocked unconscious, and left behind when Zon and the rest of them took off to recapture Kim and Leng.

The whole episode had been humiliating, and to the extent that it lessened Gillian's status within the group, it could have repercussions as well. What if the group decided to kill Leng? Thereby eliminating the bait intended to draw the Illusive Man in? She would be a failure . . . And the possibility of that filled Gillian with angst.

Such were the teenager's thoughts and emotions as all of the biotics not required for guard duty assembled under the dome on the cavern's main floor. They sat on mismatched throw rugs arranged in a U-shaped formation all looking in to where Leng and Kim sat strapped to a pair of sturdy chairs. Both were doing their best to look expressionless but Leng was slightly better at it. Mythra Zon made the opening statement.

"This is a sad day. We are biotics. That means we are inherently superior to other beings regardless of race. But we have free will. So we can make bad choices. And that is what Cory Kim did when she made the decision to place her personal desires before the needs of our organization."

Kim looked defiant. "Let's get something straight . . . It's true that I had feelings for Kai at one time. But that isn't why I helped him escape."

Von looked surprised. "No? Why then?"

"Because I work for Cerberus too. We're everywhere, freak . . . Keep that in mind."

Leng groaned. "Are you out of your mind? Why did you . . ."

Leng wasn't allowed to finish. His body jerked convulsively as Sallus applied a shock baton to the back of his neck. His unconscious body slumped against the straps that held him in place. Kim kept her eyes up but bit her lower lip. Little dots of perspiration were visible on her forehead. Zon frowned. "That was a good question. Why would you tell us that?"

"Because I'm proud of it," Kim answered stiffly. "And you're going to kill me anyway."

Zon nodded. "You're a spy, and unlike Leng, we don't need you."

Leng had recovered consciousness by then. He opened his mouth as if about to speak and closed it again as Sallus held the shock baton up for him to look at. There was nothing the Cerberus operative could do.

Zon's eyes roamed the crowd and came to rest on Gillian. "The decision has been made. What we need is an executioner. And because Cory Kim attacked Gillian Grayson that privilege falls to her. Come forward, Gillian, and take your revenge."

Gillian felt sick to her stomach. She didn't want to serve as executioner and knew that, in spite of what Zon said, she was being punished for the moment of inattention that allowed Leng to escape. So as Gillian stood, and made her way forward, a battle was raging inside of her. What if she refused to kill Kim? *Then they will imprison you, or kill you,* the voice inside her head replied. *And you won't get the chance to avenge your father's murder.*

So the price for revenge is revenge, Gillian responded.

Yes, the voice answered. *In this case it is. Think about your father. Think about what the Illusive Man did to him. And will do to others if he is allowed to live. It's too bad about Kim. But she chose her fate. Just as you must choose yours.*

There was approval in Zon's eyes as Gillian arrived in front of her and accepted a large pistol. "Shoot her in the head," Zon instructed. "And take her place on the council."

Gillian felt a sense of satisfaction knowing that once on the council she would be in the ideal position to make sure that the plan to kill the Illusive Man was carried out. But as Gillian raised the heavy pistol, and the rest of the biotics looked on, Kim launched a last-ditch effort to save herself. But she was strapped in and unable to focus her biotic powers properly. The result was a weak and ineffectual "reave" that did little more than give Gillian a reason to pull the trigger.

There was a loud *BOOM* as Kim's head disintegrated. Bits of flesh and bone peppered the biotics seated in the front row. The resulting blood mist spread out to envelope Leng in a pink halo as the sound of the gunshot echoed back and forth between the cavern walls, and the chair to which Kim was strapped hit the floor. Justice had been served.

Leng closed his eyes and fought to control his emotions. He had orders to kill Gillian. But now it was personal, and what had been a duty was going to give him pleasure. The only question was when and how.

Mott was nervous, and for good reason. This was going to be her second one-on-one conversation with the Illusive Man. And she didn't want to make any mistakes. So as the video swirled and locked up she was very conscious of how she was seated, the way her hands were positioned, and the fact that a nervous twitch had taken control of her right foot.

The Illusive Man nodded. "It's good to see you again. We have a great deal to discuss."

The head of Cerberus had a magnetic quality that was still palpable even though he was light-years away. His glacier-blue eyes locked with hers. "I've been in contact with Aria T'Loak," he said. "She's going to provide us with some additional manpower."

Mott's eyebrows rose incrementally. "So she's willing to help? To participate in a raid?"

"*If* I pay her a large sum of money . . . Yes."

"That's very interesting," Mott replied. "But you might want to reconsider the deal with T'Loak."

The Illusive Man produced a cigarette but didn't light it. "Go on. I'm all ears."

"As you know the Grim Skulls teamed up with the Biotic Underground to rob T'Loak's private bank. Subsequent to the robbery she took her revenge by killing all of the Grim Skulls with the exception of their leader and a woman named Shella-Shella. I was able to speak with her and she has a very interesting story to tell. According to Shella she worked for a Cerberus operative at one time."

"So?"

"So, Shella told me that she reported to an operative named Manning who, according to the description she gave, is a dead ringer for Leng."

"That's interesting," the Illusive Man allowed,
"but so what? Leng has assumed dozens of identities
over the last ten years—and worked with hundreds of
different people."

Other individuals might have wilted under the Illusive Man's unblinking gaze, but not Mott. She was
on solid ground and knew it. "Yes, sir. Shella claims
that Leng was on Omega, tracking a man named Paul
Grayson, who was employed by T'Loak at the time.
In an attempt to capture his target Leng and his team
broke into Grayson's apartment. An asari was there
as well. They put a tranq dart into her and she went
down. Then, after taking a look around, Leng slit her
throat. Her name was Liselle . . . And she was T'Loak's
daughter."

The Illusive Man was silent for a moment. "You're
sure of this?"

"As certain as I can be without access to Leng's
personnel file."

The Illusive Man touched a button. "Jana, please
send Leng's P-one file to my terminal."

The reply was nearly instantaneous. "Yes, sir."

The Illusive Man's lighter flared, and by the time
the file appeared on his terminal, the head of Cerberus was taking smoke deep into his lungs. Mott
was too far away to read the text on the screen but
could tell that the Illusive Man was scrolling down
through what appeared to be a long document. The
better part of a minute passed before he said, "Ah,

here it is . . . Leng's report regarding the night in question. Bear with me while I skim it."

Mott continued to wait as the Illusive Man read the remainder of the report. Then, once he was finished, it vanished off the screen. "So," he said, as his eyes flicked her way. "Your information is correct. Leng's report mentions killing an asari female but doesn't provide a name."

Mott shrugged. "My guess is that he didn't know who she was. And thought it was necessary to eliminate witnesses. In any case, it looks like T'Loak thought Grayson was responsible for her daughter's murder until the bank robbery brought her into contact with Shella-Shella, who offered a firsthand account of what actually took place. At that point Leng became a marked man. T'Loak tried to kill him in the Blue Marble restaurant and failed. Then, before she could go after Leng again, the biotics captured him. So," Mott concluded, "if she helps Cerberus attack the biotics it will be for the purpose of killing Leng. Not rescuing him."

The Illusive Man sent a plume of gray cigarette smoke out to hover in front of him. His voice was calm. "All right . . . Unfortunately we can't stop T'Loak from going after Leng because she knows where he is. So we'll have to handle this in a different way. Here's what you need to do."

Mott listened carefully. And once the Illusive Man finished speaking she nodded her head. "Yes, sir. But I'm extremely worried about the timing."

The Illusive Man exhaled a stream of smoke. "Yes. So am I."

* * *

Gillian wanted to sleep but couldn't. Because every time she began to drift off Cory Kim was there to confront her. Time after time Gillian felt the pistol go off, saw the chunks of bone flying into the air, and listened to the echo that lasted forever. Then she awoke with a start, her heart beating wildly, her bedding soaked with sweat.

So, short of using drugs to sedate herself, the only thing Gillian could do was to exercise so hard that her body would be forced to surrender the moment she put her head down. That was why she was in the middle of the cavern, in the area reserved for biotic workouts, when Mythra Zon came to speak with her. Gillian was halfway through what she thought of as the dance at that point. The series of carefully choreographed movements were intended to strengthen her body and biotic abilities at the same time.

"That's very impressive," Zon said, as Gillian completed the sequence of movements she called the "falling leaf." "I wish all our members would work out as hard as you do. Perhaps you could give some lessons during the days ahead. Please join me . . . I have some news that you'll find interesting."

So Gillian used a towel to wipe the sweat off her face and followed Zon over to the side cavern where the leadership council held its meetings. None of the other members were present. "Please," Zon said, as she gestured to an empty chair. "Have a seat."

Gillian was more than a little curious by that time and listened carefully as Zon spoke. "There are two things I want to discuss with you regarding what the other biotics said. And they're closely related. First, I would like to welcome you to the leadership council on behalf of its members. We were very impressed by the way you handled the Cory Kim situation. It wasn't easy, we know that, but you put your responsibility to the group before whatever personal feelings you had for Cory. And that's the kind of commitment we're looking for."

That wasn't entirely true, since Gillian's primary motivation for playing the role of executioner was to avenge her father's death, but she saw no reason to mention that and didn't.

"I said I have news," Zon continued, "and I do. The Illusive Man agreed to our ransom request."

Gillian felt her heart start to beat a little bit faster. "That's wonderful . . . Have we got a time and a place?"

"Yes. The exchange will take place at a location chosen by Cerberus at oh nine hundred local tomorrow."

"They get to choose the location? Is that safe?"

"No, it isn't," Zon admitted. "But the Illusive Man isn't willing to show up in person otherwise. And that's critical if we want to kill him. Which we most assuredly do."

"Yes," Gillian said emphatically. "That will put an end to Cerberus."

"Precisely," Zon agreed. "What we need to do at this point is to make sure that we're ready for tomorrow. The ransom team will consist of me, you, Lem, and Sallus plus a dozen lesser talents. Kathar will remain here along with your friend Nick, and the balance of our warriors. We will abandon the cavern in the near future, but continue to use it for the next week or so, which means we have to protect it. Do you have any questions?"

Gillian had questions. Lots of them. But none Zon could answer. Not unless she could predict the future. "No. Thank you."

"All right then. We won't know the exact location of the handoff until one hour before it takes place. That makes it all the more important to assign key roles, create plans to cover all of the possible scenarios, and stage some run-throughs. So meet us out on the floor in half an hour. In addition to being a member of the council you are one of our most powerful biotics. We'll be counting on your strength."

Gillian felt a new sense of purpose and determination as she made her way up a ramp to her quarters. She would have her revenge. And in the wake of the Illusive Man's death she would have more as well. The future was hers.

On Omega

There were three things that the majority of the beings on Omega needed: air, food, and water. The first being more important than the others because without it the oxygen breathers would die very quickly. And that was why Hendel, Immo, and a batarian named Pa-dah were crawling through a duct that was labeled OMAS 462.3410.497 on the detailed schematic provided by T'Loak's staff. It had been created after her rise to power hundreds of years earlier and updated on a regular basis. Not because the Pirate Queen was looking for ways to be of service to her fellow citizens, but because she thought the information might come in handy someday, which it had.

Like all the infrastructure on Omega, the hundreds of kilometers of ventilation ducts that served the space station had evolved according to the ever-changing needs, whims, and technological capabilities of those who lived on it. Among other things, that meant there was no such thing as standard-sized ducts. Some were large enough to stand in. Others, like the one Hendel was traversing, were barely wider than his shoulders. And that was uncomfortable. Especially for a man who didn't like small spaces. But by concentrating on the task at hand, which was to scout out a route that would allow T'Loak's mercs to launch a surprise attack on the Biotic Underground, Hendel managed to keep his fear under control.

His headlamp flooded the first couple of meters ahead, and Hendel had a crink in his neck from looking up, as he elbowed his way forward. Whenever he arrived at an intersection it was necessary to pause and check the schematic on his omni-tool. Some of the side shafts were marked and others weren't. It wouldn't do Hendel any good, but the trip was being recorded via the cameras located over his ears, so that T'Loak's staff could add even more detail to the master schematic.

In addition to the tight quarters there were other obstacles. They included the desiccated bodies of dead rats, a dust-encrusted maintenance bot that had to be pushed ahead of him until it could be shunted into a side shaft, and a fan that had to be stopped and dismantled before the party could proceed.

Now, as Hendel came upon an intersection, it was

time to check the map yet again. According to the schematic the time had come to make a left turn. Hendel made use of a small cylinder of spray paint to sketch a luminescent arrow onto the interior surface of the duct. Later, when the combat team came through, the directional markings would enable them to move quickly.

"We're getting close," Immo said, from further back. "Or that's the way it looks on the schematic. I doubt the biotics went to the trouble to install sensors inside the ducts but you never know. Keep your eyes peeled."

Hendel's eyes *were* peeled and the last thing he needed was to have one of T'Loak's functionaries telling him what to do. But he managed to conceal his annoyance by answering with a grunt instead of words.

Having completed the tight left-hand turn, Hendel passed a side duct through which air was flowing from a heavy-duty fan, and hit a straightaway that led to a spot where some light could be seen. From below? Hendel hoped so as he elbowed his way forward and tumbled into a spacious metal box where four ducts of various shapes and sizes had been married together many years before.

Once inside the junction box Hendel was forced to make room for Immo and Pa-dah. Then it was time to look down through some dirty grillwork onto the cavern floor some thirty meters below. And that's where a couple dozen people could be seen, all gathered around a single individual, who was leading a group exercise. Hendel tried to identify Gillian and Nick but couldn't do so with any certainty. But they were there, he felt certain of it, and wished that the attack could take place immediately.

"Nice work," Immo said, as he peered down through the grate. "We'll go back, prep the team, and give these people a surprise they won't forget."

It was, Hendel decided, the one thing they could agree on.

The crematorium's mass converter was located at the center of a bowl-shaped depression where it was surrounded by forty-eight fluted columns. Like so many things on the ancient space station, the exact origins of the facility were uncertain. Some said the crematorium had been a temple once, and Mott thought that was possible, given the beauty of the place. Not that it mattered so long as it could serve the purpose she had in mind. And that was to use the facility as a venue for the coming handover.

So as a salarian funeral procession entered the amphitheater-like space and followed a gently sloping ramp down toward the glowing mass converter, Mott took a seat in the top row of the curving bench-style seats and settled in to watch. And to figure out where each one of the Illusive Man's assets should be placed. Other spectators were present as well, including beggars, food vendors, and the merely curious. A woman with a tray of religious medals approached Mott and the Cerberus agent waved her off.

The salarian death chant had a repetitive quality, and even though Mott couldn't understand the language, the sadness inherent in the words didn't require translation. Unfortunately, except for people like T'Loak, most of Omega's residents couldn't afford to ship dead bodies off-station. And there wasn't enough space for a cemetery. So most corpses were cremated. That included dozens of nameless victims who had fallen prey to the rampant crime on Omega. They were routinely taken to the morgue where they were held for two cycles. Then, if the bodies hadn't been claimed, they were "processed." A euphemism for an assembly-line-like process in which dozens of bodies were fed into the mass converter without so much as a cursory prayer.

But in this case it appeared that the salarian had probably died of natural causes and had enough money to pay for a more dignified departure. The coffin, which was borne on the shoulders of four males, was heavily embossed with hieroglyphics that looked a lot like circuitry. The pallbearers handled their burden with great dignity and made their way forward with a distinctive slide step.

What Mott liked about the site was the fact that it was fairly contained, the tightly spaced columns would make it impossible for a large number of adversaries to flood the amphitheater at once, and there were open lines of sight back and forth across the bowl-shaped interior. Plus, thanks to the fact that they would have to enter via the single entrance, the biotics could be channeled down the ramp.

Of course, that was when things would get interesting. The Cerberus operatives might be outnumbered and, with no Level 3 biotics of their own, vulnerable to "throws" and all the rest of it. So in order to level the playing field a bit, Mott planned to have a surprise ready. But would it work? Even with the advantages that the venue offered there were so many variables that even the most carefully conceived plan could easily go awry.

As Mott laid her plans the mourners formed a semicircle in front of the converter. The pillar of iridescent light shimmered brightly as if eager to consume anything fed into its coruscating maw. Once inside, the object would be transformed into energy, thereby completing the age-old rhythm of creation, destruction, and rebirth.

There was a platform at the end of the ramp and directly in front of the converter. The coffin had been placed on it. And as the chant grew louder, the salarian in charge of the ceremony touched a button, and one end of the flat surface fell. That sent the beautifully decorated coffin sliding into the column of fire. It vanished in a momentary flash of light. The funeral was over—and as the mourners left Mott did as well.

Nearly a full cycle had elapsed since the scouting mission had been completed and the attack on the cavern was under way. Except that Hendel thought of an "attack" as an all-out assault on an enemy-held position rather than a long-drawn-out slither through a maze of interconnecting ducts. Adding to his sense of dissatisfaction was the fact that while he was the one who had discovered where the biotics were hiding, and led the scouting party the day before, Pa-dah had been named to lead the six-person aerial team. But some role was better than no role, especially since his participation meant he would be one of the first people to enter the biotic stronghold.

Having been given no other choice Hendel was forced to accept his position as the people in front of him elbowed their way forward, air whispered past his ears, and his headlamp played across a pair of worn boot soles. The close quarters meant that none of the mercs could wear anything more than light armor—or carry any weapons other than light machine pistols. The exceptions being two of T'Loak's biotics who were supposed to protect the rest of them from the Level 3s they expected to encounter inside the cavern. Would Gillian and Nick be among them? Quite possibly. And if Gillian was there which person would he encounter? The naive teenager he was sworn to protect? Or the killer she had become? Each was equally possible.

In spite of the long crawl the aerial team made good time thanks to the updated schematic that Pa-dah could reference and the directional arrows Hen-del had spray-painted onto the ductwork. One after another they tumbled into the junction box, which was barely large enough to hold them. Then it was time for Pa-dah to give some last-minute instructions while two of the mercs prepared the drop lines. "Okay," the batarian said, "we'll do this the way we planned it. The objective is to hit the floor in one piece. Then we'll engage the guards and draw them away from the entrance.

"That may be all we can accomplish. But if things go especially well I will try to find Kai Leng and take him prisoner. Meanwhile Hendel will attempt to open the gate from the inside. Are there any questions? No? Then let's get going."

A plasma torch was used to carve a hole into the center of the grate, and when the metal disk smacked onto the floor many meters below it sent a cloud of dust into the air. A biotic looked up, saw the invaders sliding down the drop lines, and shouted a warning. A well-aimed burst from a merc cut him down. That was when the defenders began to fire upward—and used their biotic abilities as well.

As Hendel slid down the rope he saw a merc on line two ripped off the rope. She screamed as she fell toward the rock-hard surface below, hit with a sickening thud, and lay broken on the floor. A small cloud of dust marked her location.

But in spite of that most of the invaders were able to make it down untouched. That included Hendel, who saw two female biotics rushing toward him. He threw up his hands, willed a singularity into existence, and plucked the defenders off the ground. They were floating helplessly at that point, feet kicking, as he drew his pistol. One of the defenders was an asari. The other was human. Both wore armor without helmets. So Hendel put two rounds into each head. Their bodies went limp and he allowed them to fall.

Hendel was about to engage another biotic, the turian who seemed to be in charge, when a shockwave hit him from behind. The force of the blow threw him facedown. And when Hendel managed to roll over he found himself staring up at Nick Donahue and the business end of a large-caliber pistol. "Mr. Mitra!" Nick exclaimed. "What are you doing here? You killed Marisa!"

Fighting raged all around and Hendel was dimly aware of a ground-shaking *BOOM* as he propped himself up on his elbows. "Marisa? Was she your girlfriend?"

"Yes, damn you . . . We were going to get married."

"I'm sorry," Hendel said. "But you brought this on yourself. Remember what Kahlee and I taught you? Those who use their biotic powers to hurt people will pay. It's just a matter of time."

"You bastard," Nick said through gritted teeth. "You rotten bastard. First you kill Marisa and then you have the balls to claim that it's *my* fault. Goodbye, Mr. Mitra. You can preach to the people in hell."

"Where is Gillian," Hendel demanded. "Is she alive?"

He saw the spark, but didn't live long enough to hear the report, or feel the projectile smash into his forehead. Nor did Hendel see one of T'Loak's Level 3 adepts smash Nick to the ground. Their bodies lay two meters apart.

SIXTEEN

ON OMEGA

T'Loak was leaving very little to chance. Two guards, both stationed outside of the steel door, had been killed by snipers before they could give an alarm. Then a small army consisting of more than two hundred mercs had swept into the area, taken control of the adjacent shantytown, and sealed off the street that ran in front of the cavern. "No one goes in—and no one comes out." That was the order T'Loak had given to Immo.

Then, after receiving a radio message from Pa-dah, T'Loak's forces had blown the outer door. The dust was still swirling as a phalanx of mercs charged past a couple of vehicles into the tunnel beyond. Immo came next, followed by T'Loak, and the humans. Kahlee and Anderson were useless baggage insofar as the Pirate Queen was concerned. But she didn't mind them coming along unless they got in the way. And who knew? If she was lucky one or both of the meddlesome pair would be killed during the fighting. *Her* goal was to find Kai Leng. So as T'Loak led the way Kahlee and Anderson were right behind her with weapons at the ready.

The group was about halfway through the tunnel when another explosion was heard and the second gate collapsed inward. The mercs went in firing. One was hurled backward, his arms flailing, as a biotic threw him. Another shook spastically as a hail of projectiles chewed through his armor and pulped his vital organs.

T'Loak might have been hit as well but wasn't. She was safe inside the biotic barrier that one of her Level 3 adepts had created to protect her. As a result the only thing on the asari's mind as her entourage swept into the compound was the need to locate the man responsible for her daughter's death. "Find Leng," she ordered grimly, "and bring him to me."

By prior agreement Kahlee and Anderson were determined to ignore T'Loak and go looking for Nick and Gillian. As T'Loak's mercs passed through the second gate, and fanned out across the cavern's floor, they followed behind. Kahlee saw a body, feared that it might be Gillian's, and ran to check. But the moment that she knelt next to the bloodstained corpse she realized the woman was older. Kahlee was back on her feet when Anderson's voice flooded her helmet. He was on a little-used frequency, which the two of them had chosen for personal communications. "Kahlee . . . Over here."

The battle for control of the main floor was over by that time so T'Loak and her mercs were busy working their way up along the spiraling path. There were sporadic bursts of gunfire as the invaders paused to deal with biotics who had taken cover in side caves. So the danger was minimal as Kahlee made her way over to the point where Anderson was standing with hands on knees. "It's Hendel," he said. "And Nick."

Kahlee uttered an involuntary gasp as she looked at what remained of Hendel's face. He'd been shot at point-blank range. A pistol was laying not far from Nick's out-flung hand, and Anderson was in the process of removing a second weapon from one of the boy's holsters, as Kahlee dropped to one knee. She felt for a pulse. "I think he's alive. Nick? Can you hear me? It's Kahlee Sanders."

Anderson removed the canteen that was clipped to his belt and splashed some water onto the boy's face. Nick's eyelids fluttered and popped open. He stared upward for a moment, as if reluctant to believe what he was seeing, and blinked. "Miss Sanders? I should have known that if Mr. Mitra was here you would be too."

"How do you feel?"

"Bad . . . Real bad. But it doesn't matter. Mr. Mitra killed Marisa."

Kahlee remembered what Hendel had told her, about seeing Nick with a girl, and guessed the rest. "So you shot him?"

"Yeah . . . I was angry."

"I'm sorry to hear that Nick. Hendel was a fine man and he deserved better. Especially from a person he was trying to help."

Nick looked like he might cry.

"Where's Gillian? Was she involved in the fighting?"

Nick shook his head. "No. We have a prisoner. A

Cerberus agent named Leng. Gillian took him away just before the attack. The Illusive Man is going to pay millions of credits to get him back."

The mention of Leng and the Illusive Man triggered mental alarms for both Kahlee and Anderson. Their eyes met momentarily before returning to Nick. "Just *before* the attack?" Anderson demanded.

"Yes."

"Nick, where did they go? Where is the handover?"

"At the crematorium," Nick said. "Miss Sanders . . . My parents. Tell them . . ."

"Yes?"

Nick jerked spasmodically as a shot rang out. Both Kahlee and Anderson looked up to see Immo standing about a meter away with a pistol in his hand. More shots could be heard in the background as other biotics were put to death. The salarian nodded politely. "Aria T'Loak would like to speak with you."

"Why you rotten bastard," Kahlee said, as she came to her feet. "I should . . ."

But there was no need to say what she should do as the butt of Anderson's rifle made contact with the salarian's head. Immo crumpled to the ground.

"Come on!" Kahlee said. "If we hurry maybe we can make it."

"The handover could be over with by now," Anderson said, as they ran for the tunnel.

"True," Kahlee replied, "but we've got to try."

"Look!" Anderson exclaimed. "Gyrocycles. I saw them on the way in. Let's grab one."

"You can drive it?"

A much younger version of Anderson appeared when he smiled. "I can con a spaceship, can't I?"

Anderson had already swung a leg over the nearest machine, and thumbed the start switch, when a shout was heard. "Stop the humans! T'Loak wants to speak with them."

Kahlee climbed on behind Anderson as the engine roared to life, gravel flew, and some mercs were forced to scatter when Anderson drove straight at them. Then the couple were through the tunnel, out on the street, and speeding away. Projectiles were flying by then, but all of them went wide, as they entered the maze of twisting-turning streets.

Anderson had been on Omega long enough to navigate between major landmarks by that time, and he had a pretty good idea of where the crematorium was. The problem was heavy traffic. Fortunately the gyrocycle was very maneuverable, which meant he could weave in and out between carts, veer onto sidewalks, and bump his way down a long flight of stairs.

A tight left-hand turn was called for, but the gyro-stabilized bike took it with ease, and Anderson performed an unintentional wheelie as he cranked the throttle open. There was a thud as the front tire came down, a street vendor went diving for cover, and the two-wheeler hit a rare section of straightaway. "There it is!" Kahlee shouted into his right ear, as a grouping of columns appeared on the rise ahead.

Anderson released the throttle, applied the brakes, and pulled over next to a tiny shop that sold religious paraphernalia to mourners. Then they were off, running up the slope, hoping to arrive in time.

Gillian had been assigned to guard Leng and felt a rising sense of excitement as the group entered the crematorium. Leng went first. His hands were cuffed in front of him and the leg shackles made walking difficult. Gillian was immediately behind him followed by Von. Only three people. That was all the Illusive Man had been willing to agree to. They were protected by the biotic barrier Von had established, however, and that made Gillian feel safer.

As they passed between a pair of fluted columns a downward sloping ramp appeared. And there, standing in front of a three-meter-high pillar of flame, was a human male. The Illusive Man? *Yes!* He looked like the descriptions she'd heard. The protective shield shimmered, sounds were slightly muffled, and the scene took on a slightly surreal quality as Leng shuffled forward.

Leng felt like a rat in a trap. It was the worst situation he'd ever been in. But as he led the others down the ramp Leng spotted the Illusive Man. And there, on the platform next to him, two satchels could be seen. The ransom. And the key to his freedom.

He could hardly believe his eyes. All sorts of emotions welled up inside of him. The first was surprise. The Illusive Man was taking a huge risk by taking part in the handover. The second was gratitude. Because it would have been easy, appropriate even, for the Illusive Man to write him off. Yet there he was, standing all alone, waiting for the threesome to arrive. It was a sight Leng wouldn't forget.

They were halfway down the ramp and everything had gone flawlessly so far. But Gillian knew that could change in an instant. So she was looking for signs of treachery. But the Illusive Man was like a magnet that drew her gaze. The distance was closing and the seconds were ticking away. Zon would make the call, but not until they were close enough to grab the satchels that were sitting on the platform.

As the gap closed to little more than a few meters what felt like bands of steel began to close around Gillian's chest. Then, when Leng was still a good five meters away, the Illusive Man spoke. "Hello, Kai, it's good to see you. And the young lady as well."

"You killed my father," Gillian said coldly, as she gathered the energy necessary to kill the man in front of her.

"Your father was well on the way toward killing himself," the Illusive Man said, "but yes, I played a role. It was for a good cause, however. We learned a great deal from the experiments that were performed on your father. Enough to make an army of Graysons."

Gillian launched a reave. It should have ripped the Illusive Man's nervous system apart and killed him within a matter of seconds. It didn't. The Illusive Man smiled grimly. "That's what I thought . . . You and your kind can't be trusted. But the agreement stands. Take the ransom and leave Leng."

Gillian was both confused and angry. The Illusive Man should have been dead. But there he was talking to her! Zon said, "Gillian! Do what he says! Take the satchels!"

But Gillian didn't care about the satchels. So she unleashed a series of biotic attacks that sent a cloud of trash whirling through the air and caused one of the massive three-meter-tall statues that flanked the converter to fall sideways. There was a flash of light as the one-ton object was consumed and disappeared, but the Illusive Man remained untouched.

Gillian screamed her rage as she drew a pistol and fired. Hits could be seen *behind* the Illusive Man, as projectiles stuck the supports to either side of the converter, and threw sparks in all directions. That was when Gillian realized that the pellets were passing through the Illusive Man and shouted a warning. "He isn't real! It's a holo!"

Leng felt both disappointment and exultation. On the one hand the Illusive Man hadn't been willing to put his life on the line. On the other hand the head of Cerberus was going to extreme lengths to get him back. But what to do? Allow the biotics to take him away? Or fight? It was an easy decision.

Rather than connect his handcuffs to a waist chain the way they should have, the biotics had left his arms free. That was a mistake and Gillian paid for it as Leng brought his hands around. They were clenched, so as to form a bony club, and when it struck the side of Gillian's skull she went flying. Her body hit, rolled, and came to a stop.

Leng charged in. He was determined to follow up quickly and put the biotic out of action for good. But Gillian was quick. She sprang to her feet and delivered a blow of her own. It plucked Leng off the floor and slammed him down. The problem was obvious. She had a long-range weapon while he had none. So the key was to get in close where the girl's talents would be of limited value—and his strength would make the critical difference. But how? Leng allowed himself to go limp.

Gillian saw Leng hit the floor and remain there. The whole plan had gone terribly wrong. But one thing was clear. The Illusive Man clearly cared about Leng. So if she could recapture the assassin, and march out of the crematorium, she would have leverage over the Illusive Man.

It appeared as though Leng was either unconscious or dead. But what if it was a trick? Gillian drew her pistol and approached one step at a time. Her eyes were focused on Leng's face—and that was a mistake. A sudden kick knocked her feet out from under her, the handgun went flying, and Leng came back to life. He pounced on Gillian and his weight held her down.

But she wasn't about to give up. The head butt was one of many things learned from Hendel. She felt the contact, saw the look of surprise on Leng's face, and tried to knee him in the groin. But rather than knock the assassin unconscious the blow made him angry.

The weapon had been a toothbrush. But after countless hours of surreptitious sharpening the formerly innocent object had been transformed into a prison-style shank. The point went deep. Gillian jerked spasmodically, frowned, and stared up at Leng with an accusing look on her face. She tried to say something, but there was too much blood and all that came out was a gargling sound.

Leng struggled to his feet just in time to see Zon reach the top of the ramp and back out the door. The biotics were escaping.

Mott hurried forward to free his hands. The Illusive Man's likeness looked Leng in the eye. "Welcome back, Kai . . . And don't worry about your legs. Once the doctors are finished with you, you'll be better than you were before. *Much* better. I'll see you shortly."

The simulacrum disappeared, and with two heavily armed operatives to protect them, Mott and Leng left. The satchels, both of which were full of rocks, were left unclaimed.

As Kahlee and Anderson ran up the slope to the crematorium a white delivery van pulled away. There was no one to stop them as they entered the crematorium and paused at the top of the downward sloping ramp. At first glance it seemed as though the amphitheater was empty. But then Anderson spotted the body that was sprawled in front of the brightly glowing converter. "Look! It's Gillian."

Together they hurried down the ramp to the point where the body lay in a pool of quickly congealing blood. A quick check revealed that Anderson was right. The body was Gillian's, some sort of weapon was protruding from her neck, and her breathing was shallow.

"Don't pull it out," Anderson advised. "That could make things even worse."

Kahlee opened a medi-gel-impregnated battle dressing and wrapped it around the point where the weapon had gone in. But it was too little too late. That much was obvious as she leaned forward to look down into the teenager's face. "Gillian? It's Kahlee."

Gillian's voice was little more than a whisper. "Kahlee?"

"Yes. And David Anderson."

"We tried to kill the Illusive Man," the teenager said, as she gripped Kahlee's hand. "But it didn't work." Gillian coughed and blood dribbled down her chin.

"I'm sorry," Kahlee replied, by which she meant she was sorry about the choices Gillian had made, the people she had killed, and the fact that she was dying.

But Gillian was unaware of the subtleties involved. "It's okay . . . At least I tried. But there's something else . . . Something important."

Kahlee squeezed Gillian's hand. "Yes? What is it?"

Kahlee brought a hand up to the gold chain and the jewel that was attached to it. Both were covered in blood. "Data . . . From my father . . . Taken from Cerberus. Reapers. All about them. And . . ."

"Yes?"

"An army . . . The Illusive Man told me. My father was the first. They're building an army. An army of . . ."

"Of what?" Kahlee inquired.

But Gillian was silent. Kahlee felt the grip on her hand ease, saw the light disappear from the teenager's eyes, and bit her lower lip. "Damn, damn, damn."

"Yeah," Anderson said soberly. "What a waste."

On the Citadel

In the wake of the attack on the Biotic Underground, and the confrontation in the crematorium, Kahlee and Anderson had been forced to leave Omega in a hurry. Because Anderson's attack on Immo was equivalent to attacking the Pirate Queen herself, to hang around would have been suicidal.

Plus, once they were safely in space, and had the opportunity to open the jewel-like data storage device that Gillian had given them, they knew there was something more to do. And that was to deliver a second report to the Citadel Council.

Now, as the transparent elevator carried Kahlee and Anderson up toward the Council Chamber, she marveled at the beauty of the wide-open vista in front of her. The sun-drenched view made quite a contrast to the dark, poorly lit streets of Omega.

When the doors parted Anderson led Kahlee out into the hallway. Eight honor guards were on duty, just as they had been during the last visit, and the asari named Jai M'Lani was waiting for them at the other end of the corridor. She was wearing a different colored gown this time but was otherwise unchanged. "Good morning. It's good to see you again. The meeting just began and you are second on the agenda. As you know the stairs will take you up to Council level—the pathway on the right will take you into the waiting room. I will come and get you about ten minutes before your presentation."

They thanked M'Lani and made their way up the stairs and into the waiting room. It was empty except for three turians so the rest of the seats were vacant. And as they sat down Kahlee was reminded of Nick and the last time they had been there. If only she'd been aware of what he had planned to do. Maybe she would have been able to stop it—or maybe he would have joined the Biotic Underground anyway. And then there was Gillian. Poor Gillian. *This is for you,*

Kahlee thought to herself, as she took a seat next to Anderson. *Win or lose we're going to try.*

A turian could be seen on the big wall screen, and Kahlee got the impression that he was arguing against some sort of tariff, which according to him was completely unfair. B'Than thanked the turian, and was in the process of telling him that the Council would take the matter under advisement, when M'Lani came to get them.

The asari led them to a small waiting area behind the Petitioner's Stage. Then, once the turian left, it was their turn to walk out onto the platform. Even though Kahlee had been there before it still felt strange to look out across the gap to the Council members on the other side. The asari sat on the far left, flanked by the salarian, the turian, and the human. They were dwarfed by the five-meter-tall holographic likeness that hovered over their heads.

The asari spoke first. "Greetings Admiral Anderson and Miss Sanders. I'm told that you just returned from Omega. Welcome back. Who will speak first?"

"I will," Anderson replied. "The last time Miss Sanders and I appeared before you it was to show you Paul Grayson's body and what had been done to it. As you know, we're of the opinion that the Reapers are the only ones who could conceivably have the technology used to modify Grayson's body, even if Cerberus played a role.

"Since the last time we appeared before you additional information has come our way, and we would like to share it with you in hopes that the Council will take action against the Reapers."

The human Council member was clearly annoyed.

"With all due respect, Admiral, your fascination with the Reapers has all the hallmarks of a fixation. But if we have to walk this road again let's do so as efficiently as possible. Please proceed."

All sorts of information was stored on Gillian's data jewel. That included a very disturbing holo that Anderson and Kahlee hoped would shake the Council out of its complacency. The air at the center of the chamber shimmered, a picture took shape, and Grayson began to scream. His body was naked, he had been strapped to some sort of framework, and his skin had a grayish tint. Open incisions could be seen on his legs. And as he screamed, thin snakelike cables could be seen entering his body, apparently of their own volition.

As the camera zoomed out, people wearing lab coats could be seen. "No!" Grayson said, as his eyes flicked from face to face. "For the love of god stop them. I'll do anything . . . Anything you want. Don't let them do this to me."

But rather than stop the process the onlookers took notes as the cable things squirmed under the surface of Grayson's skin, dimly seen lights appeared under his epidermis, and the cords in his neck stood out. "Kill meeeee," Grayson whimpered. "*Please* kill me," but no one did.

"We've seen enough," the turian Council member put in crossly. "Kill the holo. All right, Admiral . . . What's the purpose of this display? Thanks to you the Council is already familiar with the way in which Grayson was abused. I fail to see how the holo sheds any light on the situation."

Anderson was angry and struggling to control it.

His jaw clenched and unclenched. "Have any of you ever seen anything similar? Or even heard of something like what they did to Grayson? I don't think so. Ask yourselves . . . Where did this technology come from? And where could it lead?"

"To Cerberus," the asari said reasonably. "*You* were part of the raid on the Cerberus space station where the experiments took place, as I recall, and saw firsthand what had been taking place there. Somehow, by a means unknown, Cerberus has acquired technology we aren't familiar with. But that doesn't mean the Reapers were involved."

Kahlee took a step forward and spoke for the first time. "When Gillian Grayson died she gave us the device on which that holo was stored and she said something that could be very important. She said that 'They're building an army.' Think about that. Think about what an army of Graysons could do."

"What *could* they do?" the turian demanded contemptuously.

"Grayson single-handedly took over a space station," Anderson reminded them.

"Which was lightly defended," the salarian observed. "Thank you both . . . But unless you have hard proof of a connection between Grayson and the Reapers, I suggest that we bring this discussion to a close."

Kahlee started to speak, realized that none of the Council members were willing to listen, and turned to Anderson. "He's right. This discussion is over. Let's go home."

On the planet Eden Prime

The sun filtered down through the trees to create pools of gold on the ground. The air was warm, colorful insects flitted from place to place, and birds could be heard calling to each other in the foliage above. It was called the Forest of Remembrance, and it was made up of thousands upon thousands of leafy trees, each planted to honor the memory of a person who had passed on. So having been unable to hold memorial services for Hendel, Nick, or Gillian on Omega, Kahlee and Anderson had traveled to Eden Prime.

There was plenty of room in the sun-splashed glade. So Anderson dug three holes. They were spaced so that the mature trees could not only grow tall and strong, but offer each other protection during the coming rainy season, when the winds would whip the forest into a frenzy of thrashing branches. Once Anderson was done Kahlee placed each sapling, covered its roots with rich black soil, and watered them in. "There," she said, as she stood. "They were troubled people, but each was trying to do something good, even if they went about it in self-destructive ways. I'll miss them."

Anderson nodded. "Well said. Come on . . . It's a two-mile walk back to the hotel."

The sun had just started to dip below Eden Prime's western horizon as Kahlee went out to join Anderson on the balcony. The hotel was located on the twenty-third floor of the pyramid-shaped "Amazon" arcology that was located near the center of a thousand square miles of virgin rain forest. There was nothing but an undulating carpet of green for as far as the eye could see. "It's beautiful," she said, as David put an arm around her shoulders. "Especially after Omega."

"So you're glad we came?"

"Very. We needed this."

"I agree. But there's still work to be done."

"You mean the 'army' that Gillian referred to?"

"Yes."

"Maybe Gillian was wrong."

"Mythra Zon might know, but she got away."

Kahlee nodded. "Maybe we can find her."

"But not tonight."

"No," Kahlee said, as the sun disappeared. "Not tonight."